MORE THAN MURDER

Robert Karp

—

Disclaimer

All characters appearing in this work are fictitious. Any resemblance to real persons, living or dead, is purely coincidental. Many places and institutions named in this book do exist. However there has been no attempt to accurately portray, describe, or define how they work, how they function, or their mission. This book is fiction.

ISBN 978-09980344-2-3

The moment of a murder is a terrible thing. No one… no, no one touched by such an event can just go on as usual. It hits hard and generates its own intensity. Before it's all over will the world of those involved, those who are still standing, ever be the same again? At the start it's murder, but it's always more than murder.

— **EARLY FALL, 2002** —

PART I – ON THE RUN

FRIDAY MORNING I

SOMETHING'S HAPPENING HERE/ *Buzzzzzzzzzzz. Buzzzzzzzzzzz. Buzzzz. Buzzzz.*

"Shit!... What the fuck?...What time is it?"

"Look at that. The clock. It's exactly six o'clock."

"So what is that supposed to mean? Who the…."

Buzzzzzzzzzzz. Buzzzzzzzzzz. Buzzzzzzzz.

"Henry! Answer it! Quickly…Before it wakes Thom up… Please!"

The room was still dark. He pushed the covers off and shuffled to the bedroom door and down the creaky wooden hallway floor to the intercom apparatus flanking the front door. It started to buzz again as he pushed the speaker button.

"Yeah, yeah, what's…."

"Henry, it's Dad. Please let me in."

Henry was mystified. What was his father doing in New York City at six in the morning during the week?

* * *

Henry, in a hole punctured, faded green UVM tee-shirt and plaid pajama bottoms, stood in the open doorway to the apartment when the elevator arrived discharging Ted Vallan. Ted walked slowly down the poorly lit hallway. He was unshaven and looked tired and tense. No one spoke as Henry stepped back, motioned Ted into the apartment, then followed him in.

Ted was wearing a light fleece jacket partially covering a white shirt embroidered with 'Burlington Medical Center Security' over the left chest pocket and dark blue khakis; his work clothes for his job in charge of hospital security. Henry was totally confused by every aspect of the man standing beside him.

"Dad, what is going on? Why are you in the City? And at this hour? Dressed for work?"

Before speaking Ted looked around, briefly noting the sound of stirring down the short corridor where the bedroom was. He was unable to hide his nervousness.

"I've been outside for a few hours."

The explanation for the buzzer going off at exactly six was now obvious to Henry. That was the way his father did things; reluctant to disturb until a decent hour even if something serious was going on.

"I felt I should get out of Vermont quickly and I didn't know where else to go. I won't be here long. I can't stay here."

Henry Vallan, the youngest in the family, was astonished at what he was hearing and his face showed it. His father had recently retired from practically running the Major Crime Investigation Unit of the Vermont State Police. The hospital job looked to be an easy way to supplement his generous pension and also be where Henry's mother, Dr. Liza Vallan, was working. What on earth would explain him suddenly showing up like this at his apartment on the Upper West Side?

They conversed in barely more than whispers though it was clear everyone in the apartment was now awake. Dressed in a hastily wrapped robe Doreen opened the bedroom door and walked out into the hallway. She gave the two men a quick glance then continued two more steps, opened another door, and walked in. She came back out in a matter of seconds, producing a small child, actually a large baby, attached to her shoulder. Despite how distracted he was Ted still managed a slight grimace, reacting to the idea his grandson was living in what appeared to Liza and him to be a closet.

"Dad, this is some surprise. Are you okay? Is there something wrong?"

There was a hint of annoyance in her voice. She realized how she sounded and tried to soften her words, recognizing her father-in-law wasn't likely to be standing in front of her looking like shit unless there was a serious problem. "Come on in and sit down. I'm gonna get some cereal for the baby. Then I'll make some coffee for all of us. Okay?"

Her tone was more pleasant but still reflected her concern and she wasn't happy with the scene. Her father-in-law looked old and disheveled and was fidgeting nervously; way out of character. His manner and appearance frightened her and she felt no inclination to lean into him with a hug or a kiss. Ted took no notice of Doreen's behavior. He was preoccupied and anxious.

He wasn't at all sure he had done the right thing getting out of Vermont without telling anyone. Despite the complete disaster he found himself in he marveled a worry kept popping into his head that Liza wouldn't find the car keys he carefully perched on the top shelf of his locker in the security office before he fled.

* * *

Henry, Doreen, and the carried child migrated to the tiny kitchen while Ted relieved himself in the bathroom. Even the baby said nothing as they moved around setting up a short notice breakfast. But the looks they gave each other were like piercing arrows as their eyes darted back and forth.

Henry began to get it that something terrible must have happened. His eyes communicated this to Doreen. They each started to react alertly and seriously to the possibility, actually likelihood, of something grim going on.

Ted looked only minimally better when he re-joined them. He had peed. Washing his face was the extent of his clean-up. He spoke up, immediately, as he came into the kitchen. He was very focused and all business. It was clear he had been thinking over what he wanted to talk about for some time. After he finished each sentence he paused, as though he needed to be sure he remembered to ask everything he wanted to know.

"Henry, I know your first book was kind of based on some stuff that really happened to me and Mom in the mid-seventies. But you insisted to us the next book, that takes place in the eighties, was completely made up, although you got some advice about the medical parts from Mom. That's all correct, right? Nothing in that story was based on anything that really happened in our lives. Right?"

His tone was earnest. He was hoping to confirm his thoughts.

Henry quickly understood his father expected him to give a response; presumably confirmation of what he had just said. But why on earth were they talking about his books at all right now? This was really crazy. His father was all on edge and looked like a wreck. What was going on? What had happened?

"Dad, I don't get this. Why are you asking about my books? You know that second one was all made up except for some suggestions Mom made, actually helped me with, about the medical stuff. The thing is fic…"

Ted interrupted.

"How much did you and Mom work on the book?"

What an odd question, Henry thought. He didn't know how to answer his father. What could he be looking for? Henry was increasingly unhappy with the whole situation: his father in his kitchen at this hour, appearing all shook up, and asking such odd questions. And it seemed maybe he was implying Henry and his mother had done something wrong or bad. Henry looked at Doreen and started to turn towards his father again.

The telephone began to ring.

"Don't answer that." Ted's voice was firm. It seemed he had been anticipating a call. He knew how he wanted it handled.

Henry was getting more upset by the minute. For the first time Doreen appeared frightened. Ted knew his command, and uttered in such an emphatic and authoritative way, would escalate the mystery and their confusion.

The three of them and the baby sat, motionless, at a tiny pink colored plastic laminate table, with a three inch stainless steel lower border, parked by a small window at the far end of the miniature kitchen. It was flanked by appliances that seemed too big for the room. Henry and Doreen stared at Ted while the phone continued to ring. Finally the answering machine kicked in.

It was heart breaking. Liza, clearly distraught, spoke slowly and deliberately to Henry indicating his father had disappeared.

"I'm surprised you're not home at this hour. I hope everything is okay with the three of you?" Then her tears were only to be imagined as she became more emotional. "I don't know what is going on; what is happening. Henry, please call me as soon as you hear this. I need to hear from you!"

Liza Vallan was the uncontested rock of the Vallan family. Cool-headed; organized; virtually unflappable. Henry and Doreen were more than jolted by her words and tone as they listened to her speak. Her voice was steady, as always, but not at all reflective of her usual sense of control. It broke Henry's heart to hear her express her upset and be unable to re-assure her his father was there.

Henry looked intently at his father while his mother was speaking.

Ted's face betrayed no emotion. After a short while Ted looked down at the table, just listening. When Liza was finished and the machine gave three short beeps Ted looked up at Henry.

"I guess I never should have come here. I'm sorry to bring you folks into this. Just didn't know where to go. I'm gonna go."

"Dad! What is happening? You're frightening us with whatever is going on. I guess it's obvious you're in some kind of trouble, but why wouldn't you speak to Mom and let her know you're here? At least you could've let me tell her you *were* here. Is there something going on between you and Mom?" Henry stood up and shook his head. "Dad, none of this makes any sense. Tell me what's going on so we can try to help you."

Ted stood also. He looked distant now. His eyes briefly fixed on Henry and then, surprisingly, on Doreen. Very earnestly he asked if they had any money they could give him.

Henry started to feel palpably ill; sick to his stomach. His father was on the run. He wasn't going to share anything or let him do more for him than give him money. One thing Henry and Doreen Vallan certainly had very little of was actual cash. What they had wasn't going to make much of a difference for a man on the run.

But Ted took it. And thanked them, sounding almost like a panhandler. Then it was obvious he was anxious to leave. Henry didn't want him to go but quickly gathered his father was determined and wasn't to be dissuaded.

Doreen stood, with the baby. He reached out to Ted. "Pawpaw."

Ted offered only a weak smile.

"Dad, what do you want me to do when Mom calls again or if anything related to you happens? I don't get it. And I don't think any of this sounds good. You're obviously in trouble and you won't even tell us what's going on. How will anyone find you?"

With that the obvious intention of his father to leave made any further talk moot. Ted moved to the foyer and walked the short distance to the apartment door. He turned to Henry, Doreen, and the baby.

"I know this all seems crazy and that's the way I feel about it too. Something really crazy has happened and it looks like I'm in big trouble. You need to stay out of it so nothing happens to you and the little guy. I have a lot to figure out."

Ted proceeded into the hallway and walked right to the stairwell, bypassing the elevator. He headed down the eight flights. Two or three minutes after Henry closed the apartment door the phone began to ring again.

* * *

He descended the stairwell in no particular hurry. But at the ground floor he rushed through the small lobby and turned left, east, after he exited the mid-block building. He then consciously kept his pace at a stroll. When he reached the intersection of Broadway and 97th street he turned the corner and stopped. A blue and white NYPD squad car came through the intersection and headed down the street he had just traversed.

Ted hugged close to the corner and followed the squad car with his eyes, which became wider as he watched it stop in front of Henry's building. A man in a suit got out of the passenger side and walked, casually, into the building. At that moment Ted made his first mistake this early morning. He decided to go north, uptown, instead of heading south, downtown, where he could be more anonymous.

* * *

Henry and Doreen were almost startled into paralysis by Ted's sudden visit. Henry decided he was not ready to pick up the phone when his mother called a second time. Her voice and words were gut-wrenching. They sat at the table with Henry looking down and Doreen looking at him while the baby played on the floor. The young Vallan family had responsibilities and things to do but they just sat there.

Buzzzzz, Buzzzzz.

"Thank goodness. He's decided to come back."

Henry shot up from his chair and went over to the intercom.

Intensely, *"Yes?"*

"Mr. Henry Vallan? This is Detective James Wiley, NYPD. You an author?"

"Yes, that's right."

"Mr. Vallan I need to come up and talk to you. Please let me in."

All of Henry's fears appeared to be rapidly coming true. His father was really in trouble. Something very serious had happened. Ted Vallan's life was that of an Eagle Scout who became a leader in the Vermont State Police. A detail oriented detective known for virtually always getting his man. Maybe a little too serious and a shade more conservative than the rest of the family, honesty and integrity were all he knew. He loved his job and he loved his family. The idea of his father in trouble with the law was incomprehensible. And yet there was a New York City cop on the way up to his apartment obviously planning to ask Henry if his father was there or if Henry knew where he was.

It would have been a surprise if Detective James Wiley, newly minted in his position working out of the 24th precinct, Upper Westside, didn't have immediate suspicions about the truth of Henry Vallan's responses to his questions. Henry was uncertain how he should act although he wasn't at all conflicted about the need to avoid offering any information about his father's presence in the City. But he was nervous and he suspected it showed.

Detective Wiley was invited into the small living room and offered a chair and then Henry sat also. Doreen and the baby stayed in the kitchen, where Doreen adeptly managed to remove any signs that three adults had been using it.

Henry was far too unsettled to make much of Detective Wiley's appearance much less his affect. In truth, despite only being in his present position for two months, the Detective came as close to looking and behaving like a stereotypical NYPD cop as anyone could imagine. Young, but with a bit of a paunch; a big moustache and an acne scarred face, and wearing an ill-fitting, baggy, dark suit. But mostly it was his manner. He came across as being skeptical of everything, even what *he* was saying; a been there, seen that before attitude. What appeared to be routine for the Detective was far from that for Henry.

If Henry had been comfortable enough with what was going on to be able to take time to try to assess the appearance of the man quizzing him he probably would have sensed a chronic unhappiness in the policeman. All in all Wiley was actually younger than the way he presented himself.

"Mista Vallan I don' know if you are aware that there is an alert out for your father, Ted Vallan, who I guess until recently was a captain in the Vermont State Police. He's wanted for questioning about a major crime in Vermont and I guess no one knows where he is. NYPD was contacted by Vermont authorities because a family member, you, lives in the City.

"So you seen or heard from your father in the last twenty-four hours, Mr. Vallan?" Wiley's obviously practiced manner and tone made his words seem like he was already a bit bored by a discussion that had barely begun. Maybe, Henry hoped, he would think Henry Vallan's tiny apartment was unlikely to harbor much of anything.

Henry tried to project a serious response. He was also intent on getting more information.

"No. No Detective Wiley. I haven't. And I don't understand what's going on. Is my father in trouble? Why…what do you mean a *major* crime? I don't understand."

Henry was more inclined to try to find out what his father was running from than bluffing about his recent visit. He hoped pursuing that tack would help hide his anxiety and difficulty responding to the Detective's queries.

The Detective appeared to take it all in stride and remained in control of the conversation. Henry's degree of discomfort was written all over his face.

"Mista Vallan, it's a criminal offense to aid, in any way, an individual with an outstanding arrest warrant; even if it's a family member. I'm sure you know that, right?" Very directly, "Did your father contact you in any way the last day or so?"

Henry determined it was best to stay the course and act mystified and upset.

"No, I told you I know nothing about any of this. What is my father being accused of?"

Wiley looked down at his hands. He contemplated his next sentence and with a slight shrug decided to go ahead with it.

"Best I know your father's whittling knife was found in the chest of a dead man; a patient at a hospital. Don' know anything more than that about it…Question is, what do you know about your father and where he is that might fit…"

"What! What are you saying?" Henry didn't have to try to act stunned. He truly was. His father involved in a murder? Unbelievable. "Whittling knife? I haven't seen him whittle anything in my lifetime."

This was bizarre. Ted Vallan had used a knife to save himself in New York City way back in 1976 and Henry chronicled that in his first book, written a few years before. That really happened. But Henry just made up that his father had used an old whittling knife. Henry knew nothing about the history of the knife. He never saw his father do anything like that with any knife.

"Detective none of this makes any sense."

Wiley was becoming more formal. "Well Mister Vallan, that's what I got in my notes." He reached to his side and pulled a small pad from an outside pocket of his suit and peered down at it. "Says here 'a whittling knife with a yellow handle was pulled from the decedent's chest.'" Detective Wiley wondered what kind of a game Henry Vallan was playing.

But Henry persisted.

"Detective, *I'm the one* who decided to write that my father's knife had been used as a whittling knife in the past. *I made that up!* There never was a real knife like that. I don't remember any color for the handle. None of this makes any sense."

Wiley felt a little unclear with what was going on now himself. He also was getting pissed with Henry Vallan's insistence this was somehow all a mistake and yet, at the same time, when asked about his father's whereabouts, he looked guilty as hell.

"Well then maybe you folks in your family should have gotten together to talk about this before 'cause the call I got from a Lieutenant Trooper Barry indicated family members, I assume that means your family, confirmed that said knife was your father's."

He paused and looked right at Henry. His frustration with what seemed to be nonsense he was getting from Henry was turning to anger.

"So what's the story here Vallan? Sounds like everybody's straight with what happened except you. You being square with me?"

At that moment, listening from the kitchen, Doreen decided she should try to see if she could break the building tension. She grabbed the baby and walked into the living room planning to pass through slowly and, hopefully, distract the cop. She paused as she passed between the two tense men.

Detective Wiley took the bait and looked up at the baby. His face softened and he showed genuine interest. He didn't get up or move.

"Hey there little guy. I got a little fella…"

The baby reached out an arm and said:

"Pawpaw."

****

FOOTNOTE — * **FOUR MONTHS EARLIER**

NO ONE GETS OLD. WE JUST KEEP GROWING UP/

For Captain Ted Vallan, a Chief Investigative officer of the Vermont State Police Major Crime Investigation Unit, it was time to retire… with a full pension. His wife, Liza, an internist, started late in medicine and had no interest in stopping for a while.

The passing years were kind to all the Vallans. They were healthy and looked it, maintaining pleasant appearances and good weights. Ted and Liza stayed active as runners and followed a healthy lifestyle. In their later fifties they knew no restrictions. Only Ted's flecks of gray at his temples belied the youthful appearance of his wiry frame. Early in life Ted learned to accept that he seemed to have been born with a fixed, impassive expression on his face which usually impacted his interactions with just about everybody. For a law enforcement officer maybe that was okay.

Liza heard about a new security position at the hospital in Burlington and Ted promised her he would think about it. The folks at the hospital were great. They were in no rush and encouraged Ted to take some time off to relax a little before coming to work with them. What could be bad?

Ted spoke with administrators and found out hospital security was no longer just walking the hospital corridors or monitoring a shift of security guards. No, they wanted Ted to help develop and work in the emerging field of protecting hospital information systems; something he knew virtually nothing about.

Everyone seemed very pleased and positive about having Ted do this work for the hospital…except Ted. His family, the present director of security, and important hospital administrators all suggested he was a natural fit for the job. After all, despite Ted's success and career long desire to work on violent crime, he was also renowned for his ability to untangle complex white collar crime cases. With some misgivings he took the position.

Early one gray and damp late spring morning he met with a cheerful, very young man wearing a plaid shirt with a knit tie and a name tag crowded with his name, Hiram Wouk, and 'Director, Information Technology, Burlington Medical Center Hospital.' They sat in a brightly lit windowless room intentionally kept most unseasonably cool. It was not until after pleasantries were exchanged and Hiram Wouk began to talk about computers and hospital information systems that Ted's worse fears were confirmed. Despite what others might think of his abilities Ted knew virtually nothing about computers. As a matter of fact, his discomfort with the computer was actually one of the determining factors in his deciding it was time to retire.

Sure, he knew how to use it for setting up a spreadsheet and he had learned to use the relatively new internet to do some police related searches. But he recognized his discomfort and frequent frustration when using a computer. So, despite what others might have assumed, he spent very little personal time at home with their PC, actually intentionally shying away from putting in the time to learn or become comfortable using it. During their initial meeting Hiram Wouk raised one of his bushy eyebrows when Ted mentioned, in casual discussion, he had virtually never looked at the personal email account Liza set up for him years before.

Gradually it became clear to him most of his new work would entail working with and monitoring security for hospital computer systems and programs. He was very disappointed. He kept it to himself but realized he had hoped the hospital job, indeed, would mean supervising and managing day to day safety enforcement in the physical hospital.

Ted Vallan wasn't sure he wanted to put the time and effort into learning about information technology. Retirement was a loaded word for him as it was for many, many others in his position. He had managed thirty years in the State Police and society now offered him almost his entire salary in retirement. But he was only in his late fifties. Certainly too young to spend the rest of his life doing volunteer work or hobbies. With his and Liza's incomes Ted didn't have anywhere near the kind of financial pressure his father felt when he was forced to retire at sixty-two. So need for money wasn't a major concern either. But there were strong reasons to spend some years at the hospital

Of course his wife, Liza, was there. Liza Vallan, with Ted's constant support for her and their family during medical school and her residency, was now a well-regarded internal medicine clinician and teacher. She worked in the hospital faculty practice which was housed in a structure attached to the hospital. To say she was successful was, to put it mildly, very true. Her clinical skills, empathy, and caring led her to be continually sought after as a primary care physician. That success meant long hours in the office and hospital and definitely impacted family life when their children were still at home.

Liza's career began when women were surprisingly rare in medicine. Now she was a valued mentor to many young women. She was well aware her struggle to achieve her goals had to have been shared by her family also and stressed that with trainees. Looking back neither Ted or Liza could imagine how they did it. But they did. Many things were different in those days. Not to mention how so many colleagues could not restrain themselves from quietly questioning how a doctor could be married to a state trooper. By now her career was probably the primary motivating factor in her life. That led to some strain at home. Both Liza and Ted hoped his work at the hospital would be good for their relationship.

And his daughter, Kathy, was a nurse educator at the hospital. She and her two little children lived only a few miles from the hospital. A good friend, Dr. Samir Balasubramanian, was the state's Chief Medical Examiner and he worked out of the hospital. Not surprisingly, Ted knew many people who worked in Burlington, Vermont's only hospital, which was, by far, the largest hospital in the state. His job in major crime investigation accounted for that.

Ted knew a lot of people in the area. In a small state like Vermont, where he put in many years leading virtually all the major crime investigations focused, in particular, in Chittenden County, where Burlington is located, he was a fixture and face of law enforcement. Generally he was well respected and often admired but it's likely he made some enemies also.

Vermont is a state with as many cows as people, and not too many of either. Burlington and the surrounding county make up a disproportionate percentage of the state's population. A visitor to Chittenden county and downtown Burlington would quickly recognize its suburban and semi-urban features. It was changing much faster than the rest of this traditionally rural state. One of the adages local boosters now liked to recite about the area stressed that a great reason for living in Chittenden County is because it's so close to Vermont.

Indeed the word 'bucolic' still remained easily applicable to most of the rest of Vermont. Not far from Burlington farms and mountains ruled the countryside. None of the many other small towns and cities seemed to be morphing into even true semi-urban settings. Well, maybe a very few; but only a few.

****

FRIDAY MORNING II

ON THE OUTSIDE...TRYING TO LOOK IN/   Exiting Henry Vallan's building Detective Wiley's visage reflected his awareness something wasn't right. In the patrol car he radioed his headquarters. He requested someone immediately track down Lieutenant Shawn Barry, an investigator in the Major Crime Investigation Unit of the Vermont State Police. Wiley had no idea how long it would take to hear from the Vermont Trooper so he told his uniformed driver to ride around the neighborhood.

The patrolman drove slowly, in something like enlarging city block rectangles approximating a growing circle. Wiley said they should look for a middle-aged white guy who might look nervous and like he wasn't comfortable in the City. Maybe someone who didn't seem to be part of the usual early morning rush.

After a long twenty minutes Shawn Barry was patched through.

"Detective Wiley, It's good to hear from you so soon. Do you have something?"

"I think so Lieutenant. Just left your man's son's apartment. Not square with me. The guy, his wife, and maybe even the baby all real nervous and scared. Didn't seem to know much about what happened but good chance the son has had some contact with his father."

Wiley's eyes kept scanning the passing neighborhood as he spoke. His face was impassive now, looking while re-thinking his interaction with Henry.

"Don't believe anyone else was in the apartment, Lieutenant…"

"Shawn, Detective, please Shawn. That's really some important news. We've had no good idea about where he might be until now." There was an eagerness in his tone that didn't feel exactly right to Wiley. "Any ideas about what can be done to find him if he really is in your city?"

Wiley stayed formal. "Lieutenant, for all I know he could have only talked with him on the phone. Something about the way my showing up seemed to rattle him so it's possible, maybe a good bet, he's in the City. But we don't know that, and you know, more than a coupla' million folks on just this island down here. Needle in a haystack right now if he's in the City."

Shawn Barry's next words were direct. His tone confused Wiley. He spoke as though he was explaining an order rather than wanting to continue a discussion.

"Wiley, this is a very big case up here and I aim to find out what role Ted Vallan plays in it as quickly as possible. Soon as the dead man was found that bastard ran like a road runner. So good bet he's guilty of homicide. In fact this case looks like a *slam dunk* and he needs to be in custody. If there's something else going on, though doesn't seem likely, I've got a responsibility to the guy who was my boss for a lotta years to bring him in before anything happens to him."

Wiley winced when the Trooper called the cop he used to work for a 'bastard.' Not likely buddies those guys.

"I'm going to have some pictures and prints faxed and emailed to your precinct so your people can get them out on the street with an APB for the Captain. And Wiley, let me give you my cell so you can pass it around and anyone can call me directly at any time. Got it?"

Detective Wiley, correctly, guessed Shawn Barry really didn't get it about the huge population crowded into the City. And he didn't like being ordered around by some hick from the sticks. He already had enough bosses.

* * *

The early morning fall chill had an impact on the pace of activity on the streets. It was still before eight. Ted leaned a little forward, into the wind, as he marched uptown. His coat was zipped and collar pulled firmly to his neck to seal out the cool breeze. He wasn't at all clear where he was headed and had no good idea where to go. Ted's mind was mostly far away from his immediate surroundings. His brain was stuck on one real issue and only that: why was it made to look like he had killed the man in the hospital?

The case from 1976 was so long ago and even Henry's book about it was more than several years old now. Why would Liza think that knife was his? The way she asked him made it clear to everyone that was what she thought. He had never seen the knife sitting in that man's chest before. And of all the people to turn up dead in that hospital why did it have to be that shithead, Dr. Harvey Becker? The last few weeks that jerk had been nothing but trouble for Ted.

It was small consolation Becker was a pain in the ass to other folks in the hospital too. As much trouble as that idiot was for Ted there was nothing between them that would begin to lead Ted to want to or actually kill that jerk. He was an annoying troublemaker making Ted's work that much more difficult. Liza said he had real personality issues; delusions of grandeur; almost paranoia. Ted had bet he was a shitty doctor but Liza wasn't so sure.

As he wandered uptown on Broadway he made sure he gauged his pace to approximate the speed of the crowd going in that direction. He would have lost track of his distance except for the chronologic numbering of the streets and his assumption every two city blocks were about a tenth of a mile. After about thirty minutes, maybe a little more, he finished seeing signs and activity suggesting to

him he was past Columbia University. The neighborhood began
to change, especially the color of the inhabitants. Ted knew about
Harlem, he just had no sure idea this was it.

Lingering on a corner, he purposely gravitated to a doorway away
from the sidewalk and street. It happened to be the entrance to
some kind of small food store and Ted thought he would be less
visible standing behind the few carts chained in front. He hoped
he could rest and think for a while. Concentrating all he could on
what was going on was fine but offered him no good solution for
where he was or should head in the City.

An inescapable thought kept bombarding his brain and reflected
how utterly alone and unsupported he felt. There might be no one,
not even his family, who would be able to help him now. The idea
of returning to Vermont and turning himself in just didn't make
good sense to him. He wondered why not? He had far more friends
than enemies on the force. Surely the force would work to unravel
this craziness. But what if that didn't happen? Ted Vallan was no
longer a member of the force.

There was a lot on his mind. He didn't feel as low as very early
that morning when he found himself loitering a few blocks from
Henry's place after walking and being awake all night. No, any idea
of surrendering to an uncertain fate only made him more anxious.
He fought a simple battle with himself over what to do because,
probably right from the beginning of all this, Ted felt there really
was only one solution for him. He had to solve his own case.

In his present state he was unable to challenge that thought. His
strong sense of what he had to do defied any likely possibility
of how on earth he could or would accomplish that. Ted didn't
consider his more than obvious limitations for finding a killer and
proving his own innocence while he was a hunted man. But Ted
was a crime investigator. One way or another he solved most of
what society handed him. How could he not consider himself the
one to get to the bottom of this case and, in accomplishing that,
clear himself?

Standing under an awning, behind the carts, he was lost in these thoughts and pleased to be ignored by those walking by or passing in and out of the store's entrance. Suddenly his eye caught sight of a slow moving NYPD patrol car proceeding into the intersection from a side street. Ted felt panic. He knew there were literally thousands of these squad cars in this city. but he immediately worried this was the one he had seen pull up to Henry's apartment building.

Recognizing it was very unlikely to be the same car did little to reassure him since his instant sense of panic reminded him he was still at loose ends and not yet, anyway, coping well with his miserable situation. The slow speed of the car made it suspicious to him. Beyond being able to observe there were two men in the car he had no reason to know it was the same patrol car.

Ted didn't move. He followed the vehicle with his eyes. For maybe the tenth time since he left Vermont he felt for his left pants pocket to make sure his cellphone wasn't there, eliminating any ability to track him electronically. He knew it was in the locker of one of his security guards; a man out on temporary disability for a few weeks. Ted had a master key and decided to toss the phone in there when he executed his sudden disappearance.

The police turned south onto Broadway.

"Nothin' here. Don' even really know who we're looking for. That's enough. Drive back to the station and we should pick up whatever shots of this guy they sent us. We can get them out on the street in his kid's neighborhood. If the guy was there and was smart enough not to hang around, to shoot crosstown or down, he's already long gone for us."

Ted watched the squad car drift into the distance. If the police went south he figured he should continue walking north. He had no idea what to do. Off he went, walking at a slower pace. He was tired.

* * *

Sirens must be a constant in a city like New York, Ted thought. From the time of his first unhappy visits to this metropolis, decades before, he always was impressed by the frequency and impressive noise of emergency vehicles here. They made up a significant component of the incessant din in the City. So terribly loud. Roads flanked by miles of tall buildings create canyons that amplify the sounds, further enhancing the decibels. Ted was amazed at the apparent tolerance so many New Yorkers developed to the almost continuous piercing and screeching sounds. Very few looked even briefly affected as a wailing vehicle came up and passed on. The sounds persisted day and night, desensitizing most, he assumed.

Ted also thought an emergency siren in the City frequently could be heard a surprisingly long time. Despite appearing to move rapidly, faster than other vehicles on the streets, city traffic congestion often acts as a governor accounting for emergency vehicles commonly proceeding at surprisingly slow speeds for a true emergency. Not to mention the frequency of emergency vehicles, sirens continuing, driving into traffic that is completely stopped. In Vermont, even on country roads, speeds during an emergency were usually much faster.

Ted was far from comfortable with all the sirens. From the honking, basso ship's horn sound of the big fire trucks to the less and less frequent traditional wail of ambulances. It was the staccato, irregular *WUP, WUP* of the patrol cars he keyed on today as he continued to slowly work his way uptown for no particular or good reason. The short bursts often blared fitfully as a squad car battled through traffic or as a sudden call to attention when arriving at the site of an incident.

An occasional blue and white patrol car, often notable for how beat up it looked, passed nearby. There were two or three uniformed police on the streets he walked also. He did not believe he was being followed. The day was passing and he realized his path had taken him to neighborhoods where he was one of very few white people. Standing out certainly was not his goal. Going inside somewhere for a few hours made sense but he worried his presence anywhere likely would be notable around there. Time to sit and think through his situation was what he needed to be doing but hadn't been possible yet.

Who knew if the neighborhoods further north would change to allow him to feel more anonymous? He couldn't exactly ask anyone that question. After making it up to 145th street he decided going any farther would probably only compound the mistake he had obviously already made. So he walked east a few long blocks and then started south on Frederick Douglas Boulevard, heading downtown. Ted was angry with himself, realizing he had made a bad decision. Why hadn't he recalled the crowds, especially tourists, were down below the sixties? That was a long way and he was tired. But there he would look like any other visitor wandering around and he could eat something and find a place to sit for a while without standing out.

****

**THE DAY BEFORE — THURSDAY AFTERNOON;
DAY OF THE MURDER**

STRAIGHT FORWARD OR COMPLICATED?/   They were standing alone or in small clusters of two or three in the partially lit hallway outside the Board room next to the hospital CEO's office. A security guard was on his way, coming to unlock the door so those waiting could enter. The guard arrived and with a needless flourish removed a large chain of keys from his belt and held them up in the air while he searched for the one he wanted.

The door open, those waiting in the hall walked through in single file. As they entered it was very unclear how much any one of them knew about the murder or the investigation. The disparate group included individuals probably with pieces of information only. It was doubtful anyone among them, other than the police, who were to arrive shortly, had knowledge of all that was known so far.

Everyone gathered there was glad to let Liza Vallan and her daughter, Kathy, enter first. They looked awful, especially Liza. Liza wasn't crying at that moment but was obviously tired and worn out. Her sad expression included clear reflection of long periods of tears.

Liza's face appeared hopeless while Kathy's projected pure anger.

Samir Balasubramanian was there along with Hiram Wouk and several nursing administrators, including Samantha Pulls, Director of Nursing. Looking completely exhausted, clinical night nurses and aides from the floor Harvey Becker was on walked in wearing scrubs. Dr. Sam Smith, Chief Medical Officer, Dr. Stanley Rabbitt, Chairman of Medicine, and Dr. Harry Bennett, the surgeon who was Becker's Attending Physician, were there. The security guards for the recent night and day shifts were also there along with two orderlies and a woman from housecleaning. Clyde Stevens, head of risk management, was the last to walk in; at least for a few more minutes. He rushed in, with a pile of poorly organized papers flapping under his arm, worried he was late. Lars Tennyson, head of the in-house legal staff for as long as anyone could remember, lingered in the hall, his gaze riveted on the door to the CEO's suite.

Inside the CEO's grouping of rooms State Police Major Crime Unit Investigator Lieutenant Shawn Barry and his deputy, Trooper Donald Dark, sat across from the hospital CEO and President, Mark Manion, a middle-aged man who looked like he was comfortable being in charge of everything. His jacket was off. He was clearly in crisis mode and unhappy.

"Lieutenant, Dr. Becker was a force to be reckoned with. A very difficult man. I can't say his death will be mourned by everyone. A true pain in the ass. He seemed to have a passion for making life more difficult for many of us here."

Actually, Dr. Harvey Becker really was considered a pain in the ass by most people. Becker was a large man, more tall than wide. He appeared top heavy as he often leaned into conversations to stress points he was making. And he was always talking. He seemed unable to restrict his need to offer his views on most any topic, be it in private with a patient or, and this is what he was most known for, haranguing on virtually any or all topics at medical staff or committee meetings. Best to think of as a libertarian, he consistently saw practically every issue as a grave intrusion on individual rights.

Most any discussion eventually led to allusions about the founding fathers or the importance of the issue for the future of the world. He and a few others were always in revolt about almost everything that seemed logical. He was born in the US but spoke with a lilt and made his words sound more British than American. His speech was stilted and his words took off in a flood of flowery and dramatic phrasing often suggesting an urgency more appropriate for stirring troops to attack at a battlement than a committee meeting. He was smart and good with words, happy to verbally duel with anyone in a public setting.

Becker relished the battle. He was indefatigable once he picked his side on an issue. When he was on his performances were often something to watch, no matter how nonsensical or paranoid his thoughts were. Speaking individually to a colleague he always tried to maintain an appropriate collegiality and his medical skills were considered satisfactory by most. His high opinion of himself kept him very comfortable with the excessive fees he charged his patients. At a time of a severe shortage in the area of physicians in his specialty his practice always seemed to have openings. Not really a surprise.

Harvey Becker was divorced and known to have had occasional relationships over the years. He had a small group of politically like-minded friends, all physicians, he socialized with. An older man, it became clear most of his colleagues and the hospital administrators he repeatedly challenged made a tacit, unspoken decision to ignore as much of his vitriol as possible and await his presumed pending retirement...someday

* * *

Several minutes later the door to the CEO's suite flew open and Mark Manion strode rapidly through it followed by Lieutenant Barry and Trooper Dark. The CEO looked worried. Lieutenant Barry, even as he walked briskly, appeared more relaxed than anyone else present for this hastily organized meeting. Trooper Dark never let his eyes leave Shawn Barry.

Lars Tennyson waited for a faint acknowledgement from CEO Manion and then followed the other three into the Board room. Clyde Stevens had stayed by the door and closed it after Tennyson was in. The room, used for Trustees meetings, was furnished with a long and wide beautifully finished natural oak table and twenty overstuffed maroon colored leather chairs, on casters. The walls were light wood paneled and the floor was a gray carpet with a thick plush nap. The setting was well appointed but would never be mistaken for anything opulent. An odor of stale coffee helped insure it didn't seem too fancy for a non-profit hospital.

A chair next to the CEO was left for Lieutenant Barry but he chose to stand, as did his deputy. Liza, Kathy, and Samir were at a far end. For a moment it was unclear who was going to initiate the session. Most of those there were hospital employees and assumed the CEO would be in charge. However no one had been explicit with any of them about why they were asked to be at this meeting. Liza and Kathy and probably a few others weren't at all sure they wanted to be there. The purpose of the gathering was never mentioned but the word was you better show.

In reality, all the CEO did was introduce Lieutenant Barry and then sit quietly. Lieutenant Barry continued with his serious but confident look and walked to the side of the huge table.

"Thank you Dr. Manion. Folks, the State Police needs your assistance. You all know a terrible tragedy happened in the hospital early this morning. A doctor who was a patient here was found to be the victim of a homicide. An investigation started immediately and the police have learned a significant amount about the circumstances of the death. I have details from the Medical Examiner's post-mortem exam that are very important and helpful and most of you in this room have given your initial statements to the police." Shawn Barry paused. He leaned forward resting his hands on the back of a vacant chair. "All helpful, but putting together an exact sequence or record of events has been challenging. I've asked all of you to be here this afternoon to give you an opportunity to listen to each other so the police can better time how and when this all happened.

"No one is being interrogated here. Just need, as a group, to try to go over a timeline of Dr. Becker's last day in the hospital and also what anyone saw of Ted Vallan during that time also."

Lieutenant Barry paused again but only for a few moments, and looked toward the far end of the table.

"Dr. Vallan, can you tell me exactly the times you saw Captain Vallan since five o'clock last night and then when you arrived at the hospital in a car together this morning?"

Liza Vallan looked up from her chair. She appeared to be in a daze but reacted to hearing her name. Before she even began to think about the Lieutenant's query, or begin considering to speak, Kathy spoke up.

"Shawn, just what the hell is going on here? My mother isn't about to sit through your attempt to fill in the blanks of your investigation in a place like this…We…"

Lieutenant Barry cut her off. "Kathy…I mean Ms. Conover, there are discrepancies in the timeline so it has to be better hammered out." He stopped to gaze around the room. He didn't appear particularly fazed by her interruption. "We've talked to everyone who's here but there are things that don't add up. This way, having all of the people we know of who had contact with Captain Vallan or Dr. Becker over the last twenty-four hours in the same room, I'm hoping hearing others' recollections will help to pin down the events of the last day or so."

"Shawn, you must be fucking crazy." The room was absolutely silent. Most heads were directed down as though a critter running under the long table had captured their attention. Kathy stood and her face morphed into red. Kathy Vallan was an attractive, energetic young woman. Her mid length wavy reddish-brown hair scooped down over her left forehead. The contrast of the hue of her face and white nursing uniform highlighted her intense anger and fury.

"That's *your* job, Shawn. This is just gonna make everyone's memories change. Why would you do something like this? Come on Mom, we're not staying for this. Makes no sense."

Lieutenant Barry placed his arms on his hips, akimbo, and just stared as the Vallans got up to leave. Then Dr. Balasubramanian moved forward in his chair and began to stand. With that the Lieutenant stiffened and, for the first time, started to look angry.

"Kathy, we know you worked a per diem shift in the hospital from eleven to seven last night. I'm sure you're tired but…"

Kathy raised her arm and flashed a *stop*. She was fuming. Shawn looked away from her, maybe hoping she didn't really exist, and tried to focus on the ME.

"Dr. Sam, you're the Medical Examiner. Your comments are very important in helping to clarify a possible sequence of events…You must…"

"Lieutenant, with all due respect, my information cannot be made public in this way. You have my preliminary findings. I can't legally comment in a room like this. I would think you know…"

Stanley Rabbitt spoke from his seat.

"Lieutenant Barry you've asked so many of us to be here. Now I'm wondering if I should or can even say anything publicly in a meeting like this, either." Speaking up was not a problem for him. He was a chairman and chairs are used to talking whenever they please. "I'm wondering if something like this, everyone giving their own recollections informally, in public, is the right thing to do. Maybe Lars could say something about all this?"

Lieutenant Barry wanted to speak, but most in the room knew or knew of Lars Tennyson and turned to look towards him.

Old Lars had an expression on his face that suggested he might not be up to saying anything. Sitting next to the CEO it was that man's protection he felt responsible for. So he leaned forward in his chair giving the appearance he was quickly considering the situation and discussion so far. Liza, Kathy, and Samir were close to the door by now. Tennyson coughed and then spoke.

"No…no, I guess that's right. Makes sense. I mean I can't see how any information from a meeting like this could do more than actually taint whatever any of these people might say under oath…I guess." He spoke without conviction, underlining how little thought he had given to this meeting before.

Lieutenant Barry and his deputy reverted to bland expressions. A closer look at Barry showed his ears were slowly turning red. He felt he was being belittled and he was mad. He knew this plan to improve his understanding of at least the timeline of the case was falling apart.

CEO Manion was furious. No other interpretations of his expression or the motions of his body were possible. He realized he had been had by the Lieutenant but his greater anger was directed at old Tennyson, sitting next to him, who never offered this simple advice before. Tennyson's days as counsel were numbered.

Clyde Stevens stood up, but before he could say anything Manion cleared his throat and started to speak. "Lieutenant I think I need to tell our hospital employees that it is not wise for them to answer your questions in public this way. I think there has been some miss-understanding and this meeting should end…Now."

Lieutenant Barry truly believed what he was after would not have, in any way, compromised his investigation. He hoped to jar some memories so inconsistencies he had heard might be straightened out and the events of the last twenty-four hours more accurately placed. He now also understood the meeting might not have been such a good idea.

* * *

It wasn't the first time that day he recognized something in this case was throwing him off. Already he was aware he wasn't thinking or acting as smoothly as he should. By now it was obvious it was the specter of his old boss and that man's likely involvement in the homicide. Barry wasn't doing things and making connections like he thought he should and routinely did; something so different from his usual ability to develop and work a case.

After all the others got up and walked out Shawn Barry sat down. His deputy sat also, two chairs away. Trooper Dark knew not to say a word. Shawn Barry fell deep in thought. As he sat there looking at nothing in particular he reckoned it was time he accepted what was almost eating him up. This homicide seemed to have clear features; nothing complicated. Barry's problem was he wasn't sure if he wanted Ted Vallan to be guilty or innocent.

* * *

No, none of this was going as well as he thought it should and Barry knew it. Early on everything he learned made him think it would all keep falling in place. He had the weapon and he had a motive. The suspect ran off before anyone, even his own wife, could talk with him. Sure seemed guilty. That might be fine for a start. Now he had an odd feeling the rapid trajectory he projected for completing the investigation was turning to shit. His efforts to sew things up quickly only seemed to get people mad at him.

What to make of Ted's wife?...And 'Samir Ball-a-suburbian... whatever the fuck his name is', the Medical Examiner? Was he intentionally trying to complicate this case? And of course Ted Vallan, the Lieutenant's old boss, being the suspect was mind-blowing. Extraordinary. Shawn started out priding himself he would act no differently on the case than any other capital case. Even in this short time any reason that led him to think that was possible was already falling apart. For a few hours he wasn't completely sure why. Now he accepted he was struggling.

Almost the last four or five years his time on the force working under Ted was never what he hoped. That short time with Kathy got everyone upset. Shawn still thought he took all the heat for it and it wasn't that simple. Shawn Barry's progress in the VSP continued, but he was angry and felt his career was forever stunted; working under a cloud with a man who he assumed despised him for that mistake.

It wasn't all bad. Recently, now running his own show, he felt better about his job and himself. Shawn was comfortable as an administrator even if solving cases never came easy. Like his old boss he recognized staying fit improved a policeman's image. Approaching middle age he still had a full head of blond hair, with an unruly tuft in front, and his well-defined facial features suggested a serious, bright individual.

There was so much to do. Barry worked his own mind also. He needed to push away his feelings about Ted Vallan and his family. This was truly completely his own case now. No solicited or unsolicited advice even possible on this one from the retired Trooper who used to be his boss. Vallan recommended him as his replacement but Shawn wasn't satisfied with the way he did it. It was like he made it clear Shawn wasn't anything like he was as a major case investigator.

Finding Ted Vallan was one priority he could devote his energy toward without upsetting anyone. Guilty or innocent, Vallan had no business being on the loose. There was more than enough reason for him to be in custody.

* * *

After the debacle in the hospital conference room late that day Shawn determined he would first turn all his attention to finding Ted. He called the NYPD in the evening. He finally was connected with a detective in the precinct where Henry Vallan lived. He would not have been surprised if the detective he spoke with had called him out on how he could be so sure Ted, a fellow cop, was his man. That was, actually, the third time that day he found his words and expressions sounding like Ted was surely guilty.

Early that morning when the homicide was discovered Shawn Barry went right to the hospital and stayed all day. In early afternoon he interrupted his talk with two nurses when Dr. Balasubramanian called and said he was ready to discuss Harvey Becker's post with him. It was a simple matter of walking down a few flights to the sub-basement where the Medical Examiner's office and the morgue were located.

Shawn and Dr. Sam, as he requested to be called, were well acquainted from many years of professional contact. But, to Shawn, Samir and Ted were friends who often worked in a way that left Shawn feeling he was relegated to a secondary or lesser role when both were around. On his own with Samir he did somewhat better. For Shawn Dr. Sam would always be linked to his relationship with Ted and, even this last year, Shawn remained generally insecure around Dr. Sam.

The staff in the morgue were on edge, possibly unhappy or at least upset a trooper was stationed at the sole prosecting room entrance. What was the point? Unlikely anyone would want to steal or kill a dead man. As the day wore on word among the staff was Lieutenant Barry had concerns about some of the evidence or tampering. None of that sat well with the staff.

Barry blew through the basement stairway door and walked rapidly to the morgue, which was around a corner from the ME office complex. He was anxious about many things, including the confirmation of cause of death but also the manner in which Dr. Sam would relate to him. Nodding to the trooper at the doorway he received no indication from him of any problems in the morgue.

Walking to the area of the two prosecting tables he found Samir standing around Becker's body with one of the dieners, or pathology assistants. The whole day had been difficult for Shawn. He was nervous and found himself blurting out:

"Hey Doc, big a mess as this is I guess at least cause of death is kinda straight forward, eh?"

"Hello Lieutenant." The ME's back was to Shawn. "You are correct, Dr. Becker appears to have died from the effects of being stabbed in his chest. His heart was barely pierced by the blade. The more major trauma, and likely most immediate reason he died, came from the knife tearing his aorta and main pulmonary artery, causing bleeding, although tamponade from the cardiac wound may have been a contributing cause."

Samir's tone was firm but bland. It should have been easy for Shawn to sense the condescension in his voice. But he didn't. He took the Doc's words as an affable response to a logical statement. He felt some of his tension fade.

Now Barry was comfortable with Dr. Sam's manner. So he decided to keep talking and recognized he felt a need, right away, to directly implicate Vallan in front of a friend of Ted's.

"Ted Vallan's knife, ya' know. Got that from his wife, Liza, and already found out this knife has a history of being his for many years. Know that from that book about the Captain his son wrote a bunch of years ago. Really something, huh?"

"No prints I heard." Samir still had his back to Shawn, although he seemed to be looking at Becker's body more than doing anything to it.

"Yeah, but really Doc, not a surprise. The Captain was a dedicated professional. He would never slip up on something like that." Since Sam didn't turn around Shawn started to walk to the end of the stainless steel table Becker was resting on. Shawn continued to talk and Samir looked over at him.

"Don' know if you know but I guess the Captain and this Dr. Becker were involved in a big row that was spilling over the last coupla' weeks. A bunch of hospital staff knew about them battling. Need to find out more. Some reason this Becker went bat-shit crazy at the Captain and told a few people what he was going to do. Said he was gonna destroy Capn's reputation and his job. But no one seems to know much about details of their fight. Not sure anyone knows …except the Captain now. And he's gone. And Becker's dead, after being in the hospital for some kind of what they call 'elective' surgery."

Samir walked a few steps from the table and turned from Shawn to look again at the body.

"Yes Lieutenant, Dr. Becker was in the hospital for prostate surgery. Have you read the chart?" He only paused for a moment and continued, not waiting for a reply. "He should have been up and around and out of the hospital by about yesterday, at the latest. And yet he was still barely getting out of bed, only with assistance, and there's not much in the record about his slow recovery and delayed course.

"In fact, I see the last two days he was on oxygen and no one was really sure why he needed it."

Shawn was unable to resist a slight wrinkle of his face, projecting an expression of 'so what?' The Doc was found dead with Ted's yellow knife sticking out of his chest. Wasn't that the story here? Any medical problems or complications weren't going to change that main finding and fact. Why was the Doc even talking about anything else.

"You know Ted and I always did something in many situations in our professional lives that was very similar. And you know this. At a crime scene or at an autopsy we each always took a moment to step back from what looked obvious in front of us and try to consider other explanations or possibilities for the findings. It's important.

"Lieutenant, did you know about the oxygen tubing at the bedside that was tangled, or possibly occluded, so not sure oxygen could pass through it? Trooper Jansen told me about it."

Shawn was also briefed about that finding earlier. He knew about that and the IV tubing that was clotted. But, in the setting of a man dead from a knife in his heart, he assumed none of that was of any consequence. He nodded to Samir.

"Well I went back to the record and it shows a continuing drop in the levels of Dr. Becker's blood oxygen saturation beginning three days ago. Indeed, yesterday he was sent for a lung scan, looking for a pulmonary embolus, that's blood clots in the lungs. Came back negative. So no one seemed to know why that was going on. And then his oxygen tubing was found almost in a knot this morning so he wasn't getting much, or maybe any, oxygen at least around the time he died, which was sometime between four and six a.m."

Dr. Sam walked over to a bench at a wall perpendicular to an end of the prosecting table and sat down. Shawn wasn't sure what he should do. He was beginning to feel uncomfortable again. He stayed standing.

"In the thorax I looked carefully at his lungs. We often find small and, occasionally, not so small pulmonary emboli that, for some reason, are missed on the scans. There was nothing significant there beyond usual post-mortem changes. Lieutenant, I looked in places where Becker's oxygenation could have been affected but there's no obvious explanation so far."

Shawn was not especially impressed with Dr. Sam's apparent focus on this. Whether the pathologist was vexed by a small question that had come up or not, the dead man on the table was found with a knife in his chest which, Shawn was just told, had penetrated his heart and caused him to bleed to death. There were plenty of loose ends but he had a suspect and finding Ted Vallan remained a most important immediate goal right now.

From Barry's perspective there was no reason to make this business any more complicated. Whatever the Doc was a little hung up on seemed far from important just then. He felt a need to respond but his words were tainted with a hint of sarcasm.

"Deep chest wound penetrating the heart. What else would I need to be looking for? Even if he wasn't doing too well doubt he stabbed himself. A suicide?" He took a few steps away and paused to hear out the Doctor. He wanted Dr. Sam to get that he had heard enough. He would move on with his investigation.

There was no change in Samir's facial expression. He followed the Lieutenant with his eyes and his face remained purposely flat. Shawn Barry apparently still didn't pick up on it.

"Well there's the tox stuff and the micro still to be looked at. That will take some time. If possible, I hope some more answers are out there. But you may be right; may be nothing else serious besides catastrophic trauma to his great vessels and heart. Far from closing this case yet, though, and I will notify you when I'm done.

"You know Captain Vallan was a friend of mind. Dr. Becker behaved like an ass but I respected him also. It's difficult for me to figure out any of this."

Climbing the stairs back up to the third floor Shawn blotted out everything on his mind except imagining Ted Vallan stealthily walking into Becker's darkened, private room and plunging his knife into the man's chest. Shawn Barry was determined to keep his focus on finding Ted Vallan. Problem was, beyond possibly heading to New York City where his son lived, he had no idea where he might be.

****

FRIDAY AFTERNOON

LOST IN THE CITY/   On balance, Ted thought being lost in this City wasn't good. He might be hard to find there but knowing so little about his location was making him increasingly anxious… about everything. Never in the hours he was walking did he feel able in any organized or even reflective way to begin to approach his overarching dilemma: the homicide he was going to be accused of. That's what he needed to be concentrating on. And soon. What was being in New York City going to do for him besides providing a place to hide…and for how long?

Would he be in Harlem, or was it Spanish Harlem now, forever? How big could it be? When he started east the streets were actually filled with more dark skinned people. Some were looking at him. He was very out of place and felt he stood out glaringly even though there were a few other white faces. But he was sure he was being looked at.

How much more walking could he do? Sore feet and hunger were becoming more acute than his fatigue. He was going south, towards downtown, on Frederick Douglas Boulevard. Central Park was in his mind. He could sit there, in a quiet spot, and rest. In the one hundred thirties there was a vendor with a cart selling soft pretzels. Ted, standing in a doorway across the street, watched him for a few minutes. He had to get something. A pretzel certainly fit his tight budget. So he walked, slowly, to a light and crossed over.

At first it seemed the transaction was going to take place silently. Ted pointed and nodded his interest in a pretzel and the vendor set about fishing one out of his warmer, salting it and slipping it into a small white bag. The vendor was a big, chubby black man, probably in his sixties, dressed in layers of old military garb and fingertip free mittens. His beard was difficult for Ted to figure out. There were scattered tufts of curly gray hair along with patches of just smooth skin. Nappy gray hair exploded from the sides of his small knit watch cap. Before money changed hands he spoke up:

"Papaya?" was all he said, in a strong voice.

Ted wasn't sure what that meant. The puzzled look on his face was sort of acknowledged by the vendor.

In a rapid, staccato delivery. "You want papaya? I got papaya. Got no more mango."

Ted assumed the man was asking about some fruit or a drink. He was very thirsty.

"Ye…yes." He spoke hesitantly and softly. Maybe this man would think he was a visitor (well, of course) and didn't speak much English. The vendor wanted more.

"Got no mango. Got papaya. You want papaya? Got papaya."

Ted made sure his nod satisfied the man who then removed a cool glass bottle from a compartment in the cart.

Ted needed to sit. He doubted this man was interested in much conversation. Hoping to maintain his notion he was performing a successful ruse as a foreigner he shrugged his shoulders and looked, questioningly, at the vendor.

"Park?"

The vendor gave no obvious acknowledgement but raised his right arm and pointed to the west. Ted nodded thanks and walked off with his pretzel and drink. He assumed he was on his way to Central Park, which he thought might be close by.

Of course Central Park's northern border didn't begin until 110th street. But Manhattan has many parks, just none anywhere close to the size of Central Park.

By the time he was half-way along the block greenery was visible a short distance ahead. The street he was on ended. Across from that a park appeared to stretch at least a few blocks north and south of his location. At a light he crossed the street and headed for a cluster of green painted benches facing into the park.

With his back to the busy street and about thirty feet into the greenery, he sat down; collapsed into the bench is a more accurate description. Ted was exhausted. He had been essentially completely awake innumerable hours, barely eaten anything, and he was lost. Daylight was just beginning to fade. At that moment he was too tired to even think about planning anything.

A few bites of the pretzel tasted good. He wondered if he should have bought two. He placed the pretzel back in its white paper bag, put it on his lap, and reached to his side for his drink. He twisted the top off the bottle and took a long pull.

It was exquisite. It looked like milk but the taste was sweeter; almost a creamy, smooth texture with an unusual fruity taste he didn't recognize. It was sugary. Ted thought this was exactly the meal he needed at that moment. He paced his intake and, for the first time in many hours, felt his body begin to relax. Ted drank some more. Very refreshing. Then he carefully twisted the cap back on, treating the container like it was a rare, valuable substance. He reached over to his left side and tucked the bottle next to him on the bench. He felt he was finally catching his breath and sighed, almost audibly. He extended his arms over the top of the back of the bench and flayed his legs out in front of him.

"Jez-us, man, wha ta fuck you doin' here?"

A surprisingly large, young black male plopped down next to him, brushing his left arm. Ted instinctively reached with his right arm and snatched the papaya bottle before it would be trapped by the girth of this man. The kid was fat and big and looked nervous as hell.

Immediately on guard Ted looked at him, trying to maintain a neutral expression on his face.

"She-it, this ain't right. You lightin' up the street. What you doing here? Shit this is bad. You know that. Fuckers ain't gonna like this… At all! Man! No cop here man."

The kid wasn't the only one who was confused. How could he know Ted was a cop? Was a cop, Ted meant, meaning had been a cop. That made no sense. He quickly figured out this kid thought he was still a cop. But why? They had never seen each other before; ever.

Being the only white face in a sea of color should have made a connection easier but Ted was worn out and on edge. Slow to react. He wasn't sure what to say to the kid. The guy was sweating and squirming on his part of the bench. Really nervous.

"I…I don't know what you're talking about. I'm…"

From behind Ted a large arm on his right grabbed and pulled his right arm starting to lift him up from his side of the bench. The glass papaya juice bottle went flying and smashed on the sidewalk ten feet away.

* * *

Pulled to his feet Ted realized he was also being pulled away from the bench. A large black man with a pock-marked and scarred face with a mean, angry scowl wanted to shove Ted's body farther into the park and to the ground. The man said nothing and neither did Ted. It was natural for Ted to fear for his life and resist. It never crossed his mind to speak out. Who knew what would happen next?

He worked to maintain his balance and try to stand his ground. It was all so sudden. Fighting just to remain erect his eye caught a glimpse of a second man moving around the left side of the bench. He was small and thin. His face had a nasty expression too but also a frightening hint of a smirk.

The fat man sitting on the bench was in terror; like he was staring at a ghost. He started to try to get up, but with his girth it was obvious that would not be an easy or rapid maneuver for him. The small man and fat man yelled at each other but Ted had no idea what they were saying. Without pausing a second more the small man produced a silver knife with a five inch blade. He seemed to smile as he rushed it forward plunging it in the young man's massive right thigh as he tried to stand. The young man crumpled back to the bench, perhaps passed out. The small man bent down to pull his knife free of the body. With it in his hand again he moved to prop the kid up, presumably planning another, better located, stick.

Ted continued to struggle with the silent force beside him on his right. He managed to stabilize his stance and started to pull free of his assailant. He was momentarily untouched when he saw the small man display the knife and ready it to stab again. Suddenly, as he was about to be grabbed again, Ted lurched to his left to get a hand on the small man. That maneuver caused the man on his right, who had leaned in to re-exert his grasp on Ted, to lose his balance and fall to the ground.

Ted pushed the small man, disturbing his balance also but just for a second. That man's face was all business now and he only gave Ted a quick glance. He was furious. But the small man turned back to the fat kid. Ted knew then he was not the target of this assault.

As the man wound up again to drive the knife into the motionless, fat kid Ted lunged for his hand and, surprisingly easily, grabbed the knife from him. The small man swung around and hit Ted in the chest with his other hand. Ted fell backwards, away from the bench. The diminutive man was yelling and on him like a cat jumping from the ground.

The ensuing struggle was alarmingly brief. Ted, knife in his hand, tried to get up off the ground, pushing the man off of him. He succeeded and the result was the small man falling back onto the bench and also passing out, a five inch blade stuck in his groin.

Both people on the bench were unconscious or barely conscious. They might have been mistaken for two men who had overdosed except they were bleeding. The really tough and nasty big guy was standing again but appeared frozen. His mouth was hanging open. Ted also worked quickly to get back on his feet, anticipating further violence. They shared an instant of angry stares. There was no question in Ted's mind the man was thinking his options over. Ted figured they had him pegged as a cop. He felt weak and wondered if he was going to pass out. He wasn't the one they were after. After all this carnage, though, would the man attack him?

No, he wouldn't. The man surveyed the gathering crowd on the sidewalk at the street. He looked one last time at the two on the bench and ran off into the greenery of the park. He never looked back at Ted again.

Ted was angry and confused. He had no idea what to do. All his professional career, actually all his adult life, he knew exactly what to do in the aftermath of a scene like this. But this was different. The small group of bystanders, all black and brown faces, were angry and looked at him like he was a cop. He was sure of it.

First aid? Tourniquet the wounds? Use his belt for the kid's thigh wound?

WUP, WUP!

The siren instantly diverted his thoughts. How could any cops show up at a crime scene so rapidly, he thought? Were the sirens for this assault? Yes, he quickly decided. He was in a monster city. There were cops everywhere. He saw flashing lights coming down the street.

Ted wanted to greet the cops and tell them what happened. It was a natural response for a law officer. But he knew that could be fatal for him. But…maybe not. For just a second he considered if, with all the deepening mess and loneliness and isolation, he should use this contact with the police to, in effect, turn himself in. Maybe working through the legal system was a better way to respond to his disaster. He certainly wasn't going anywhere safe or making any progress toward proving his innocence now. Nothing good had come of running away. He belonged in Vermont, defending himself.

As the crowd size increased, walking stiffly, Ted disappeared into the park. He pulled his collar up and re-zipped his coat. Too much remained unexplained. He wasn't sure who he could trust anymore. Maybe he wasn't able to concentrate on his situation yet but he was still free to hope there was time for him to work his own case. As discouraging and disheartening as the thought was, he only had confidence in himself to get out of the crime he was sure he was being accused of in his absence.

* * *

Hiding in New York City wasn't going well at all. As he walked he tried to use some of the adrenalin that had just been provoked to get more serious and directed about his dilemma. One thing he decided was staying in New York sure was proving unlikely to be helpful at all. Contacting Henry again was no longer an option anyway.

Ted was so upset, yet pleased to sense a chance for even a brief improvement in his ability to focus on the main problem of his life. For a short period that helped allow him to quickly blot out from his thoughts the harrowing experience and danger he survived only minutes before. It was so sudden and brief he mostly considered himself no more than a bystander. He never speculated about how his presence may have instigated it. Hours later, after finally thinking about developing a rudimentary plan for moving his own investigation forward, he realized more immediate trouble from that incident was very likely.

The fate of the five inch knife was uncertain. Ted tried hard to remember what most likely happened to it after it plunged into that man's gut as he jumped on top of Ted while they were struggling. Did the man, or anyone else, grab it or try to pull it out? A wave of nausea and weakness came over him as he wondered if he had to accept the greater likelihood, when the police arrived, that knife was still impaled in that man, the handle covered with Ted's prints.

Probably. Ted had to get out of the City.

****

FRIDAY EVENING I

ON THE TRAIL OF A SERIAL KILLER?/   "Lieutenant Barry? Is that you?"

"I'm here Detective Wiley. Have you got some information for me?"

"I'm not too sure what to make of what I have Lieutenant. But it certainly seems you should hear about it."

Shawn Barry offered something like a grunt on his end of the phone. Wiley wasn't sure what to make of that, either. He decided to just go ahead and tell the Lieutenant his news.

"Well, late this afternoon, at Saint Nicholas Park in Harlem on the Upper West Side, there was a scuffle between four men that led to two stabbings. One of the men is in critical condition. From bystanders we know there were four men fighting but only the two who were stabbed were still at the scene when our people arrived.

"Neither of the guys stabbed are talking, at all. They each got sheets, one is well known as big trouble in the neighborhood…"

As he listened to the Detective recount his story Shawn Barry was confused. From their brief contacts he suspected he could read this cop well enough to assume there was something coming in this story that would have value for his case. But it sure was taking a long time for Wiley to get to his point.

Barry's words came out flat. "Wiley, where are you going with this?"

Not one of their few conversations were satisfactory to either of them. They conversed as professionals but never hit it off on any level. On this call Wiley thought Barry's tone and manner on the phone was condescending, reflecting Barry's dissatisfaction with the way Wiley responded to him the evening before. Wiley sensed Barry's unjustified or needless show of contempt or, at the very least, impatience. He decided to brush it off, continue on, and give the idiot the information he recently obtained.

"We pulled a knife out of one of the vics. No good reason why but prints on the knife match your man's."

Barry gave an audible gasp.

"Statements from working the crowd often not too helpful in that neighborhood and the people around during that fight not much use. Poor agreement about the two who were gone by the time patrol car showed up. Stabbed men not talking. So maybe one or two in the crowd said one of the runners was white. We now think turns out that proly was correct."

Wiley's tone and volume were ratcheted up. Now he sounded like the unhappy one. He could only imagine how Shawn Barry was reacting to his report.

"Lieutenant, what the hell was your boy doing in a knife fight in Harlem? Some things you not telling me? Would think your guy wouldn't have wandered into trouble like that. Too smart. What was he doing? What's the real story why he's down here? In Harlem. Drugs got something to do wit' what happened up there?"

There was silence on the other end of the line. Shawn had no idea why Ted Vallan would be in a knife fight anywhere in New York City. He figured Ted was desperate to avoid capture and, like this jerk Wiley just said, would absolutely have tried to avoid trouble of any kind… But, wait a minute.

This homicide case was odd, in many ways. Could there be an angle that did involve drugs or something like that? Was Ted in New York chasing after something? Was he injured in the fight? Shawn felt he had to try to use this crazy information he was hearing. Maybe nothing was as it seemed and maybe there was strange stuff going on in Vermont he hadn't uncovered…yet? Shawn assumed Ted went to the City because his son lived there and hoped he might be able to help him in some way.

"Lieutenant? You still there?…What the fuck is going on? You said your guy might show up at his son's place. You never really did say why he was gonna do that."

"Detective…I don't get this." He and Wiley were increasingly unable to tolerate each other, even at this level. It was unclear why. Then Shawn, pissed to be on the defensive in a case that just seemed to be getting more complicated by the minute, managed a more formal timbre to his voice.

"Wiley, this investigation is in its very early stages. We're still gathering as much information as we can. I have seen nothing to suggest anything about drugs but there are avenues we are exploring that could…you never know…turn up some other things."

"Lieutenant, don't bullshit me with any press release crap. Your boy was in a knife fight and fled the scene. That's strange stuff.

"Listen, I'm gonna go back to his kid an lean on him…a little harder this time. We gonna be getting your Captain's face out on the street very soon. When you're ready to spill a better story you let me know. In the meantime I need that guy for a fight that may turn into a homicide. Got it?"

'This fucker must be a really nasty guy, not only a jerk' Shawn thought. 'Yesterday, I guess he didn't like the way I was pushing Vallan as my perp. And now he's decided I'm not giving him the facts. Well fuck him!'

"Yeah Wiley, why don't you find the Captain before he winds up dead in your city. Practically ran a major criminal investigation division for the State Police in Vermont since before you were thinking you might wanna be a cop. Wherever this investigation goes NYPD ain't gonna look too good if there's no city wide effort to find this man. You might wanna talk to some of your higher-ups and let them know a VIP cop, in trouble with everybody, is apparently running around in your city. And maybe, just maybe, your take on all this isn't the only story. Keep me informed, will ya?"

Well, Wiley 'got it' too. Barry was right. This Vallan had been a big shot and no matter what the story was he was on the loose, probably still in the City, it seemed. Causing trouble or in trouble, or who the fuck knew what he was doing. He wouldn't admit it to Barry but he was going to bump this situation up the line, immediately. He planned to stay involved, if he was permitted, and wanted to get to Vallan's kid as soon as possible to go over all of it again, and press the kid this time.

What Detective Wiley didn't know and couldn't really have known is Lieutenant Barry actually knew Henry Vallan more than just casually. He had been around for years while Henry grew up. If Wiley had been aware of this it would have added to his concerns and mistrust of Shawn Barry since Shawn Barry had no intention of contacting Henry himself to ask him anything.

****

FRIDAY EVENING II

LIVING ON THE STREETS IS A LOSING GAME FOR A WANTED MAN/   Being hunted, or at least knowing he was a fugitive, was a unique experience for Ted Vallan. In calmer times, or when he was the hunter, it would have surprised him fear of apprehension could be usurped by exhaustion, sleep deprivation, or hunger. But that's what was happening to him. He was filthy. Sweat and grime were overtaking him. Peeing behind a building was easy enough but his transition into a bum was a progressive nightmare. How could he be falling apart like this so quickly?

Everything he thought this city would offer him was a challenge now. So much had gone wrong in such a short time. If only he could find some quiet, some food, and, mostly, rest. How much longer before every police officer in the City heard about him and was looking for him? He had started downtown from somewhere in the one-forties. The effort of walking almost a hundred blocks to get there was finishing him.

Soon, like many on the run, Ted assumed he stood out from the crowd; an easy mark for any cop or authority looking for an outlier. Even with the sidewalks increasingly filled with people as he approached the upper fifties he could not relax at all. He saw some homeless people, alone or in groups, right on the sidewalk alongside a building. They were beginning to prepare their gear for the night. A bizarre scene for him. It was getting colder and people were walking around them while these folks were busy adjusting blankets or sleeping bags on the cement.

As he walked his eyes kept being drawn to the people settling in to sleep on a busy sidewalk. Slowly Ted realized he felt some envy for them. They were truly anonymous and were approaching sleep; something he was increasingly desperate for. Continuing to head farther downtown he consciously kept his pace controlled, trying to match the crowd's on the street.

* * *

Barely more than one day before, which seemed a very long time ago, he felt sure getting to New York City was the smartest move he could make. He ran out immediately, before he understood everything that had happened. Finding Becker dead was not the complete shock to Ted it might be to others. Ted kicked himself for keeping his investigation completely to himself. When Becker started after him publicly he should have shared his preliminary findings with someone; maybe the Burlington PD, or even the force.

It's just he didn't fully understand how the hospital systems worked yet and any potential for the hospital computers to facilitate crime. He still wasn't completely sure what he found was as big a deal as he thought it might be. He had been over and over all these thoughts a hundred times in the last two days. By now it rattled his brain, a tonic low level rumble of confusion and regret.

The moment of his implication was a constant replay also. Just as he and Liza arrived in the morning he was paged to go to that room. Liza followed him to the urgent call he received. The room was filled with staff. Her face was blown up in his brain. Every few minutes it obscured everything else. That look on her face.

Did she enter at exactly the same moment or just after him? The knife with a bright yellow handle was immediately visible protruding above Becker's still chest.

"Oh Ted." Drawn out slowly, like an admonishment. "That's your knife, isn't it?" Plainly loud enough for all to hear.

The look on her face. More than shock. Sorrow? Disappointment? Disgust? 'Ohhh Ted, that's your knife, isn't it?' What the fuck was that supposed to mean? Her words publicly exclaiming his guilt came out sounding like something that dripped or oozed from her, all but indicting him. Like 'Now look what you've done!' Ted had never seen that knife before. What was going on?

Then everything went crazy. All the running around. Codes had been called. Masses of people in the room and hallway. The images were torture to Ted. But with the constant repetition in his brain they eventually lost some of their bite and terror, despite continuing to consume his thoughts.

And then Liza left the room. What?

The last time he saw Liza was when he left the dead man's room and walked down one floor to go to his office to find notes that might be significant now. Walking swiftly around a corner he saw Liza, maybe twenty, thirty yards away. She was leaning with her back against a wall, facing a man in a white coat whose head was no more than two or three inches from hers, preventing Ted from telling if he knew him. He thought she looked relaxed! 'What the fuck!' Did she look over his way and then turn back and continue talking with that man? Was Ted imagining all that? He no longer knew.

At his office he was in a sweat. He had no idea what was going on.

'*THAT'S YOUR KNIFE, ISN'T IT?*' kept exploding in his brain. What was Liza doing? He packed up what he could, left his car keys and headed downtown, on foot, into Burlington. Maybe not his best move of the day, he now knew.

Over thirty six hours Liza's blown-up visage during that moment became an increasingly sinister recurring image; almost baiting or laughing at him as he wandered New York. And yet she seemed so upset on her call to Henry. Whatever was going on he still leaned toward not regretting his rapid flight from Burlington and Vermont.

Fatigue and loneliness only served to re-enforce any germ of thoughts about some sort of conspiracy. He had been set up. But by who? And why?

****

FRIDAY NIGHT I

NIGHT IN THE CITY/   A definite improvement in anonymity, even with how light it seemed from all the bright neon lights of the West Side in the forties. A slice of pizza and another bottle of papaya juice, enjoyed leaning against a wall with others eating also. This time eating engendered no excitement; just satisfaction. Ted had no answer for his apparent continuing bad luck. 'What was up with those black guys?' He was mistaken for someone else. But why? 'Those guys were willing to kill that kid. Must have assumed the kid was singing to me. Kill him? A rough place. Willing to kill the kid in front of me but still not try to kill me. I got in the middle.'

'Shit!' He wondered if either one had died. He hoped not. But that encounter sure fucked him. He had no reason to think that knife wouldn't have his prints. Ever since he saw that cop go into Henry's building he was sure his picture and prints had made their way to Manhattan. Best to get out of the City before the story of a knife-wielding ex-state trooper made its way to this city's cops, and maybe the media. Some story, he thought: 'Ex-trooper being sought for two knife attacks…in two states…in two days… And with two different knives. Shit!'

With sustenance he was able to push away his sense of loneliness and desperation for a short time. Anger boiled up about the way life was playing him. Had he been too good? Being straight in his career and in life had worked in his favor, he thought. At retirement he felt he had done what he wanted in life, proud of his family and what he achieved professionally. His tendency to be modest and so easy to feel guilt was a reflection of the basic puritan ethic of the way he was raised. Ted knew that because of chiding from his wife and kids, chronically preying on his Boy Scout attitudes and conservative tendencies. Had he been dumb enough to assume he would continue to live happily ever after?

Now where was he? In deeper trouble and shit than ever before in his life. Could he even trust his own wife anymore? Ted remembered that worry from almost a year before. In his latest book Henry had documented a period of tension in Ted's relationship with Liza. It was unspoken but there was a suggestion Liza might be having some sort of an affair. After reading the book Ted didn't have the courage to bring any of that up with Liza. He planned to ask Henry about his inference the next time he saw him.

The idea ate away at Ted for weeks until he saw Henry again. It was shortly after the baby was born and he and Liza were in the City for a few days to see the baby and help out. Doreen and Liza took the baby for a walk in the carriage that was one of the gifts they brought. As soon as the ladies were in the elevator Henry asked Ted what was up; why he seemed nervous?

Ted tried to blow off that reaction and started talking about how exciting all this was. Less than five minutes later he decided it was then or not for another long time.

"Henry, your latest book. One of the things that gets me confused about some of the stuff in your books is how much comes out of your mind and what parts you think really happened. You know what I mean?"

Henry's face was blank; non-committal.

"Yeah, I guess so. I mean, you know, some of it, mostly in the first book, came from what you and Mom told and showed me. I guess there's things in this book that happened too. But that's because I grew up in our home. You know Dad so much of one family's life can be similar to other's. So writing things about personal actions and interactions can sometimes seem familiar to many of us. So I'm not sure what parts you're talking about but I can't say it's not possible that it seemed to you there were things that happened that you remember happening in our family. After all, Dad, that's my memory bank."

Henry was not thrilled with his answer, which had become long-winded and may not have captured the essence of what he was trying to say.

"So some of our family may be in that book, but not because I intentionally planned it."

Ted wasn't satisfied.

"Are you sure?"

Henry thought that was a strange question.

"Well Dad, just what parts are you thinking about?"

Ted halted. He just couldn't speak the words to his son that expressed his worry; or jealousy.

"Oh, who knows. I just was wondering." He paused, then spoke again. "Did you talk with Mom about the mother in the book? Her life? She's a doctor also, you know?"

Didn't help. Henry was trying but he didn't understand what his father was after. And perhaps Henry was a little reluctant to admit to himself how much he used his family in his character constructions for his novels.

"Sure, Mom and I talked about the character who was a mother and a doctor. Mostly, though, she helped me with the medical stuff I needed to know."

If Henry had an idea of what Ted was getting at he didn't let on or wasn't going to go there with his father then. Many months later, in the same apartment, only hours before, Ted had asked pretty much the same question. The setting was considerably different now because Ted was running to save his life. Henry, of course, was very upset but never seemed to respond to Ted's query any more directly this time. Tonight Ted felt a rush of weakness and renewed upset, tacitly accepting the likelihood Henry had taken his story from some actual part of Liza and Ted's life.

****

FRIDAY NIGHT II

I'M LEAVING...ON A BUS/   At the Port Authority, on
Fortieth Street, the city was buzzing and alive close to nine. Even
as he walked inside he wasn't exactly sure where he was going to
go. He was clear in his mind he had to get out of the City, but he
had no idea where he should head. Other than assuming if he went
north perhaps there would be a better chance he could sometime
figure a way to work his own case, he realized his very limited
finances would have the greatest impact on where he went.

Ted was pleased with the Friday evening crowds. He stayed to a side
near a corner where he could look at the large, lighted board listing
departures. Albany; Boston; down the list to Plattsburgh. Looked
like lots of buses leaving through the evening. Many choices. He
went to the Greyhound and Adirondack Trailways counters to pick
up fare schedules.

The costs made his decision easier. Albany was sixteen dollars,
a helluva lot cheaper than his trip down or anywhere else. Ted
had been there before for a meeting. He assumed it qualified as a
reasonably sized city where he could remain anonymous. And it was
in the right direction.

There was a 12:01 a.m. bus. Probably would be empty and quiet
so he could think and sleep. Before he bought a ticket and settled

in an out of the way waiting spot he decided he had to clean up. He was never much of a body odor person, but his hair and beard were a mess; certain to attract attention. Only $36.42 left; a major, possibly his most critical, immediate problem. He refused to worry about that right then. Since he had time he left the terminal for a drug store he had noted close by. Their 'Men's Travel Kit' went for $6.99, plus tax, much more than he hoped to spend for what looked like cheap junk.

There was no option, he felt. He bought it and went back to the terminal and shaved in a public restroom as out of the way as he could find. One or two policemen wandering the floor; none in the men's room. Ted felt better after the shave. He relaxed a bit. Never do two things in quick succession. Wait an hour and get a ticket.

* * *

'Shit! Shit! Shit!'

Now Ted knew what the ticket agent meant when he said 'you're it' as he pushed the ticket at him. He must have gotten the last ticket. Even almost an hour before it was to leave there was a large crowd milling around the gate. Last bus to Albany, New York for the night; 12:01 a.m.

Mostly young people, quite up and awake. Ted's hope of leaning into the window and sleeping for most of the trip was very uncertain now. He had envisioned a silent, dark bus bouncing its way north. He hoped the trip would take all night. Now his only goal was to try to secure a window seat.

With some effort he determined it was Friday night. Kids from schools going home for the weekend? Maybe worse; one large group who would party all night long? He hoped not. He resolved to sit, again, off to the side of the waiting area but remain vigilant for the first call for departure. He would time his arrival at the gate so he was just after the first few on line. Ted was desperate for a window seat so he could be assured of a chance to sleep.

Sitting and waiting was difficult. He doubted anything specific would have been circulated about him to rank and file law enforcement yet. 'Damn!' He should have had a book or a newspaper in front of him to look occupied. Instead he stretched his legs out and looked down at his feet. Soon he was barely awake.

His mind buzzed with frustration about what on earth he might, could, do to save himself. Tonight he would sleep on the bus. What about the next night or the next? Money? He was about to have almost none. What could he do?

The background music rose and bits caught his ear. Up tempo Muzak. The Beatles with strings. The lyrics were automatic in his brain.

HELP!...

I never needed anybody's help in any way...

...Now my independence seems to vanish....

...Help me if you can I'm feeling down and I do appreciate your being 'round...

Won't you please, please Help me?

Could he trust anyone? Who? If everyone was convinced he had killed someone what would anyone do for him?

Those thoughts jarred him awake. 'Trust'? What a miserable thought; there was no one he could trust. Even Henry could no longer be contacted for fear what might happen to him if he tried to get involved. '*HELP!*'

Ted pushed that awful thought away. What was he going to do when he got to Albany? Stay at the terminal until the city started to wake up? Bus and train terminals offered a modicum of security to transients. If open always heated in winter and there were toilets. But they were patrolled and cops could get pretty nosy with transients. The identification Ted had on him might be better thrown in the garbage than keeping it on him. Using his credit card would be like having a GPS device on his ankle. Same for an ATM, although Ted had never used one and wasn't sure if his card could be used for that anyway.

The reality was the NYPD had developed surprisingly good ability at surveillance in large public transportation settings. Both profiling for people of concern and quickly disseminating identification mechanisms like descriptions and even photos of wanted individuals were notably advanced. In addition to work directly in the terminal and crowds there was extensive and growing video monitoring. More and more of that was being done now and the monitoring was fed into only a few central locations with highly trained staff. All forces were able to maintain close, immediate, contact at the terminals and other sites with mobile devices.

Ted was not aware of the extent or the capabilities of urban police surveillance and did not think he was being watched or, more importantly, even looked for yet. He assumed that would all change by early the next morning.

Before he reached for his wallet to consider trying to shred his driver's license, a Port Authority cop started walking in his direction. Wasn't looking at Ted but was about to walk right in front of him. Ted didn't move. The cop passed by on his way to the men's room. Ted remained fixed to his position, periodically glancing, with his eyes only, across the large terminal at the door where the line would form to go to the bus.

* * *

Desperate times call for desperate actions. Without money he was forced to spend much more time and effort trying to sustain his basic survival. Living on the street was a losing game. It was only a matter of time until he would have a run in with law enforcement. The odds of continuing much longer like this were miserable. Ted knew less about Albany than he did about New York City. Given all his immediate challenges, being closer to home might only be of marginal benefit, if any.

Ted spent his whole career as a trooper. He knew the cons on the street. Like jumping out from a corner, slamming a hand hard and loud near the rear of a cornering car, and screaming while going to the ground. That was often good for twenty to a hundred dollars depending on how good the acting was and the affluence of the mark. There were others. The problem with most of them was the high incidence of police involvement.

Ted was aware pawn shops offered another avenue to get cash. If he believed his life depended on avoiding capture and incarceration then why wouldn't he do anything he could to maintain his flight? His watch was valuable but as a retirement gift it was clearly inscribed in recognition of his career and status in the Vermont State Police. Unlikely to work. What else did he possess? All through his marriage he wore a simple gold wedding band. Probably more symbolically valuable than worth much money.

If Liza and Ted's marriage had failed and Liza was no longer committed to Ted then what purpose was served by keeping his ring? Well it probably wasn't going to get him much money anyway and he knew that. Even that train of thought though led to thinking about Liza and actions she seemed to be taking. Terribly upsetting to Ted; again and again. He silently vowed he would never do anything with that ring. Ever.

A wave of emotion overcame Ted. He leaned back and felt tears welling up in his eyes. He began to shake, ever so slightly. So much trouble; so many bad things; so suddenly his whole life in jeopardy. Sleep deprived; hungry; seemingly without options. Alone.

That was the worst of all, of course. He couldn't rely on those he loved and respected, mostly Liza, his wife. If he thought about even trying to contact her or anyone who might, in any way, help or support him, that person would instantly become a criminal also.

He told himself he must hang on. Not give up.

* * *

Only infrequently since his exodus from Vermont did Ted think about his former deputy, Shawn Barry. Ted presumed Shawn would be conducting the investigation into Becker's apparent murder and Ted's disappearance. Unless Captain Jim Steffens, in charge of major crime for the entire state, decided to run it. Ted figured Steffens might leave Shawn in charge but keep a constant hand in; probably following up at least daily.

He would have been surprised to know the way Captain Steffens had charged Barry to run the investigation. Both Steffens and Colonel Blair, the Director of the Vermont State Police, were in agreement on that course. Those officers told Lieutenant Barry to manage the investigation no differently than other major crime case. If Ted knew that he would have been more unhappy and uncertain about his situation.

Ted had very mixed feelings about Shawn Barry. As Shawn's mentor and boss for many years they knew each other well. They shared many cases and quite possibly had each saved the other's life in the course of their professional efforts. Professionally Ted had little to dislike or challenge about Shawn's abilities and the skills he developed working with Ted. But Ted felt, and he knew Shawn was aware of it, Shawn never achieved the level of skill Ted had in criminology. Over time he probably became a superior administrator to Ted but, in the force, honors and admiration were always reflective of success at case, not desk, work.

Years before, Shawn was married, with one kid and Kathy was engaged. They had a brief affair. Ted held Shawn responsible although he also felt a degree of estrangement from Kathy which had continued ever since. Shawn's marriage fell apart but Kathy reconciled with her fiancé. She now had two kids and, to all appearances, a happy marriage. She and Shawn barely ever acknowledged each other after that.

Ted never felt completely good about Shawn again. Working together was a strain for both of them. But Shawn was capable and Ted worked hard not to let his personal feelings interfere with how the force ran. Not a lot of people knew about their affair. Kathy hated Shawn now, but she also was unhappy with Ted's apparent inability to forgive her and move on.

Kathy was furious her father kept Shawn Barry on the force. She blamed Shawn, the older, married man, for everything that happened. She couldn't believe her father could see it any differently. But Ted thought long and hard about what to do. He was not the kind of person to want to seek advice from his peers or superiors about such a situation.

Ted's actions were true to his personality and history. In his VSP position he felt he had to be endlessly fair to everybody. He told himself he didn't think he really had any choice but to maintain Shawn on the force and not ding his career for what appeared to be the actions of two consenting adults. Liza appeared upset but refused to tell Ted what she thought he should do. He had tried to consider what he would do if he had no personal involvement in what happened. Over time he had to admit it didn't work out well.

Even after all this time Ted was reasonably sure Shawn would likely jump at a chance to ruin him. If given the opportunity he doubted Shawn would hesitate to tear at Ted's respect and legacy on the force. How he would respond and act in the investigation of Becker's death was unclear but, with himself as the obvious prime suspect, Ted doubted Shawn would be inclined to look hard elsewhere.

It appeared someone or some people had set him up. Exactly how or why he didn't think he knew. It was Becker who started publicly threatening Ted, with no apparent provocation, around the same time Ted uncovered inklings of criminal activity at the hospital. Was there a link to Becker and what Ted found? Probably. How would Shawn ever find out any of this? If he did find a way to get information to Shawn what would Shawn do with it? He could ignore it and let him take the fall when he finally is caught. Ted decided it was quite possible Shawn could do something like that.

No, Shawn probably wasn't even a wild card in Ted's future. Ted couldn't rely on Shawn to follow any hints or trails he set up for him. What if he managed to get his knowledge to someone who could force Shawn's hand on further investigation? Naturally his first thought was to think of Liza. That launched another sequence of depression and heartache that diverted his thinking for a time. But a seed was planted. Was there anyone he could risk contacting somehow?

****

FRIDAY OVERNIGHT

ALL THROUGH THE NIGHT/   A pale yellow light started to flash above the closed door with the gate number Ted was monitoring. Immediately a large number of people sitting close to the door began to stir but so did others more dispersed around this far corner of the huge terminal waiting area. The bus would, indeed, be full. Ted was ready. He aimed to be among the fifth to tenth on the line so he stood as soon as the light flashed and slowly traversed the thirty yards or so to the gate. Others were congregating but, initially, there was no clear line. He stood close and as soon as three people made a move and appeared to fall in to establish one he joined as the fourth. His quick action and the pounding of his heart reminded Ted how nervous he was. That upset him.

He had made it only this far in just short of forty eight hours so he questioned whether he should continue on. Reflection while sitting on the bench and now getting on line placed his situation and progress as dismal. Yet enough had gone so terribly wrong in New York he thought maybe catching some kind of a break was in his future. Flight had exhausted him and his mind remained consumed by anger, confusion, and fear. No way he could begin to plan or consider options for his plight.

Well, not really. His mind was clear enough he realized nothing good or useful had been accomplished so far and probably the only reasonable thing to do would be to turn himself in. There had to be people who would help him and work with him to figure all this out. Time spent eluding capture seemed like a waste. He was only further incriminating himself by his actions; digging it deeper. Standing on line a brief wave of surrender hit him. What was the use?

Without Liza's support he felt desolate. All he knew was it sure appeared he had been set-up and actions like Liza's behavior must have been part of all that. Who knew who else or what else? If Liza was part of a set-up everything could be even worse for him in custody. Forced to face and daily live with her actions and her sacrificing him, for some reason, might be unbearable. Terrible images frozen in his brain inhibited Ted from considering any other, more benign, explanations for Liza's actions.

The line snaked quite a distance from the door. Ted was in a good spot. Unless something happened he had not considered a window seat was assured. That relaxed him. Sort of a good break, he decided. Getting on the bus, getting out of New York, and sleeping for three or four hours was what he hoped to do. After some rest he would re-evaluate his situation. If he couldn't come up with any ideas to justify continuing to run he was beginning to accept turning himself in would probably be best. At that moment, more than lonely and abandoned, he felt helpless.

The door opened.

At about the fourth row Ted slid across the aisle seat over to the window and breathed a sigh of relief. He sensed he was more inconspicuous in that seat than since arriving in New York and that lessened some of his tension. He started to relax immediately. Aisle lights were on in the bus and passengers quietly worked their way down that path. Ted kept his reading light off, pulled his jacket collar up high, and leaned into the window. It wasn't practical to try to feign sleep but he hoped his position projected his desire to be left alone.

A stocky young kid stopped at his row and in a fluid motion slid a sizable backpack off his right shoulder to his lap and squeezed into the seat next to Ted. Ted barely acknowledged the kid's direct look and smiling nod at him. The kid fiddled in his backpack producing a hardbound book and popped on his reading light. Aisle lights dimmed and the bus began to move. Odor from a burst of diesel fuel wafted through the bus as it slowly navigated through the terminal and pulled out into the dark night. Looking out through tinted windows it appeared as though dulled city lights were guiding them through the emptying city streets.

Muted sounds of talking and occasional laughter in the bus were not disturbing to Ted. His seatmate made a variety of audible sounds, apparently reacting to his reading, but that did not bother Ted. Now he closed his eyes. Soon he was fast asleep.

* * *

"Holy shit! I mean ho-ly shit! I mean could that be true? Oh man, that's the fuckingist craziest thing I ever heard of!"

Was someone yelling at him? Was he asleep? What was going on?

"Hey man, you got to hear this." The kid was talking to Ted like he was sitting, awake, next to him.

Ted was awake now. His head throbbed. His throat was dry; his mouth felt stuffed with cotton. Was he nauseous? He opened his eyes, turned his head slightly, and stared at the kid speaking loudly next to him. The kid was animated, oblivious to destroying Ted's somnolence.

"So get this, will ya? So this book is about time travelers, you know. So this fucker winds up in some ancient times and there's this thing with eunuchs. You know about eunuchs right?" He continued right on.

"Well this fucker queen is worried whether the guys who are supposed to be eunuchs in her court are really eunuchs. You know; right? She's worried about her daughter, the princess. So she makes these guys, hands tied behind them, line up one at a time, naked, with a beautiful woman doing a strip right in front of the guy.

"Yeah, you guessed it, she wants to see what happens to these jerk's peckers. I guess those guys are not supposed to be able to get it up after being fixed, you know. But that's not the half of it." The kid's whole torso reacted, his arms flew up in the air, knocking against Ted. And his face expressed astonishment.

"She's got some apparatus set up so there's a sword hanging, swinging like a pendulum, just inches from the guys' peckers! Holy Shit! Can you imagine?"

Ted was up. He got the image and he had no idea if a true eunuch could ever get an erection, but he supposed not. What he did know was he wasn't going to engage this kid in any way. Nothing good could come of that. Who knew who was meeting the kid in Albany, and maybe this kid was crazy anyway. Ted stared at him, briefly, and then looked away. The kid was not done.

"I have got to draw this!"

With that he ripped open his backpack and started rummaging around looking for things. Along with a variety of personal and other items a drawing pad and charcoal pencils came out. Money, four or five bills, fell all over. The kid's lap was a mess. Ted reflexedly picked up a one dollar bill that landed on him and held it up for the kid to take. The kid started to sketch at a furious pace, chortling and grimacing as he worked.

That gave Ted a break but he was sure he would not be able to get back to sleep after all that. He had no idea how long he had been out but assumed not too long. 'Shit'. He closed his eyes but could not sleep.

In about twenty minutes he was jostled in his side by the kid.

"Hey, you have to see this."

Ted turned his head only. The drawing was good and it was scary.

The kid drew the back of a naked man whose head was twisted to one side to show his agony. A voluptuous, completely naked woman stood in front of the man smiling while a long scimitar hanging from a rope was about to pass in front of him. The attention to detail in the depiction of the woman in her natural glory in such a short time suggested she was an image he was quite familiar drawing. Ted stared for a time at the picture.

"I'm in art school in the City. A few of us are working on a new way to write books. We are calling them 'Graphic Novels'. I'm working on one right now."

Well, Ted thought, this picture certainly was graphic.

He couldn't fall asleep. He popped two Tylenol from the traveler's kit and struggled to produce enough saliva to get them down his throat. He kept his eyes closed and after a while he relaxed again. His thoughts turned to what he was going to do when he arrived in Albany.

* * *

Any method for gaining some form of control of his disaster continued to elude him. What was going on in the investigation? Information was what he needed first. Maybe there were developments that altered the dynamics of the homicide investigation. Maybe someone or others were sure Ted was set up and were working that possibility. Or there even was evidence for that which had already come out and changed the case dramatically, so that Ted should come in.

The bus rolled along the New York Thruway at a steady speed. It was completely quiet now. Even his seatmate had dozed off, although he left the overhead reading light on which was annoying. Except for that light everything Ted could see, inside or outside, was black. He sat back in his seat and considered his situation one more time. Ever so slightly more rested his head had stopped pounding and he was better focused as he ruminated on his predicament and pressed himself for options.

Two different thoughts competed in his mind forcing him to continue to feel he wasn't concentrating as well as he needed. What was he going to do when the bus arrived in Albany? And he accepted it was essential, a necessity, he get information to update the status of the homicide for which he was being sought.

Food also was a necessity. He decided when the bus arrived he would find out if there was an all-night diner he could walk to. From there he would have to kill time away from easy observation until he could walk to the main Albany Public Library where he assumed, hoped anyway, copies of the Burlington Free Press might be available. Ted Vallan made a simple assumption that reviewing that paper's stories about the murder would give him a complete update and, hopefully, maybe even confirm his wish he was no longer the one and only person of interest for the murder. He was satisfied with his hopeful plan and dream of exoneration.

Ted's eyes closed and he slept the final hour of the ride. Way too short but probably his best rest in two days.

* * *

UP ALL NIGHT/   Located in the bowels of New York City's Penn Station, around three a.m. it is often quiet in the central monitoring room for the Port Authority Bus Terminal and a few other transit spots. Both the Path Train Station and the bus terminal usually are slow then. So the staff takes some time then to update their databases, removing individuals no longer being sought and adding information on new suspects to be looked for. This night, after adding about fifteen descriptions and seven photos (some useless shots, some very good) the protocol called for a quick review of selected video or stills taken from about ten p.m. to one a.m. to look for the new add-ons. After about one traffic settled down and foot patrol worked through those who obviously were spending the night in the terminals.

Elmer Broadly, a cop very experienced at his job, had a miserable cold. His mates on the midnight shift had mixed feelings about him showing up for work that night. More work for them if he had called in but good likelihood he'd spread his cold in the confined quarters where they spent their workday. Either way they were going to lose. But Ted Vallan would have been pleased Officer Broadly went to work that night despite how crappy he was feeling. The officer was pushing buttons and turning rheostat switches, changing cameras and slowing or speeding tape on at least three screens while frequently looking up a few inches at the new photos, and less so, the new written descriptions.

When Broadly was sharp he was very good. The men in the cell, as they preferred to call their work room, kept a chart on the wall in a corner with a list of each of their nicknames followed by a length of bullseyes, tiny targets with a red arrow in the center, denoting the number of kills, as they liked to call them, for wanted individuals plucked off the streets because of a pick up by one of them. At the moment Officer sharpshooter Broadly's number of bullseyes was the longest.

Now and then Broadly slowed the pace of his scanning quite a bit, zeroing in closer; going back and forth; or calling up screens nearby the area of his immediate concern. In between a short sneezing fit, a man tossing his paper towel in a men's room caught his eye. Broadly wiped his drippy nose and compared that man to Ted Vallan's picture now resting on a board above him. Similar, but the thing was both guys looked so unremarkable. No look of malice like so many of the presumed perps they usually looked for.

Must be some white collar stuff the guy in that shot was wanted for, he figured. Broadly kept looking around in the neighborhood where that bathroom was. Nothing over the prior or next hour. Nothing at ticket windows either. Broadly had to admit the solitary bathroom shot wasn't great and the face was shaved and pretty unremarkable; no distinguishing features.

He stopped to turn away from the screens and coughed. Keeping the screens completely clean was one of their major commandments. While recovering he stood up and pushed a button to print out what there was on the face he might be seeing on the one and only shot he could find that might be that guy.

"Harris. Holy shit. Listen to this: APB on some just retired captain in the freaking Vermont State Police! Wanted for murder in Vermont…and a stabbing on west 133rd Street yesterday! White dude! 'Presumed armed and dangerous.' Well I guess so!

"Nah, but I ain't got him."

Then Broadly started to smile as he spoke but that was a bad idea.

"Gotta be drugs. Don' those cops get any pension or somethin'?" With that Broadly's words provoked an extended coughing jag and the conversation in the cell turned to whether or not he should go home.

* * *

After exiting the Thruway the bus's rapid turns and speed changes jostled Ted awake. It took minutes for him to become alert and re-integrate into the real world. The streets were deserted so the bus moved right along. The Trailways terminal was not large and buses were parked outside, only partially covered by a heavy metal overhang. Passengers began to stir when the bus pulled off the road into the gravel terminal lot. As soon as it stopped the aisle lights illuminated.

Ted's seatmate was up and ready to leave as the bus pulled in. As soon as the lights came on he maneuvered himself out of his seat to stand in the aisle until the door was opened. Ted was in no rush to exit the bus. His watch was gone but the could see a large clock in the terminal through a window. It looked like it was almost four a.m. Would anything be open at that hour?

While he was staring at the clock the door opened and the line in the aisle moved forward, initially only squeezing everyone closer together. Then, like a spring, it really started moving. Ted kept his head down, tucked into his collar but minimally turned to watch the exodus. Immediately his eyes fixed on a bill sitting on his departed neighbor's seat. Illuminated by the reading light above Ted could tell it was a Twenty. With that sighting his heart began to pound. What should he do?

Possession of that twenty would double his pitiful finances. Even only solving his food needs it still qualified as an immediate lifeline. What should he do? Should he pick it up and try to rush out to find the kid and give it to him? The kid might be back to the bus in only a few minutes after realizing the money was gone… if he needed to look for his cash to get where he was going. If not, maybe he wouldn't realize his loss until sometime during the day. Could Ted take the kid's money? Who would he give it to anyway if the kid was gone? For a fleeting moment he reflected on what he was happening to him.

He was still staring at the bill when an arm penetrated Ted's field of vision and was tentatively reaching down to take it. Reflexedly a dark scowl formed on Ted's face and his hand shot out and grabbed the bill before the extending arm could secure it. His eyes locked with the eyes of the man whose arm had attempted to swoop down and snag the bill. The arm recoiled sharply, the man quickly sensing the danger projected in Ted's expression. Fortunately it was not the kid.

What had he become? Ted felt a flush and a brief wave of queasiness. His descent seemed to know no bounds as he functioned more and more primitively. He was becoming like an animal, living a life of constant struggle for self-preservation; totally alone.

The man who was willing to lean in and take what clearly was not his hurried ahead and off the bus. For all he knew he had attempted to take Ted's twenty. But the brief episode resonated fiercely in Ted's head. How low was he going to descend? A savage on the streets fighting for scraps? How could he continue to live this way? How much more running could he do?

It was gradually becoming more clear to him. He was gaining little by running and perhaps losing his humanity and sanity in the process. For the first time a new and different understanding of his danger began to take shape and to crystalize in his mind: the risks of his behavior and actions now were probably no worse than the risks of finding some way or someone to get his story out about being set up. But how? And who? Who could he trust and who could he try to contact without drawing that person into risk and danger also?

* * *

Ted was moving more slowly than he wanted and was displeased he was the last person off the bus. He was hungry and knew he could afford something to eat. No one was hanging around the bus; certainly not the kid. The terminal building looked empty and the door was locked. No bathroom. He shuffled around the area near the bus, not sure what he should do. The driver, a portly middle-aged white man with a thin, silver moustache and a weary look, thumped down the few steps and onto the curb. He quickly figured out Ted's problem.

"Sorry pal, terminal's locked up tight for another hour. There's someone cleaning in there but no one will let you in."

Ted had to do something.

"Yeah, I see that. Maybe you can tell me if there's any place open around here to get something to eat?"

"No, nothing right around here. But listen, it's Saturday and I'm off for the weekend so I'm going home. During the week when I'm gonna drive my round trip again later in the day I usually stop at a place 'bout a mile away for something to eat before I hit the hay. It's on my way home, I can drop you if you'd like."

Ted was well aware the more direct contacts he made the easier he would, eventually, be tracked. But he couldn't figure any other way to avoid sitting at the bus station or walking deserted streets in the middle of the night. That wasn't smart either. He thanked the driver and accepted the ride.

"Not too far. Good place for breakfast. So, what brings you to Albany?" He broke out into a hearty laugh. "I mean besides my bus."

Ted was briefly dumbfounded. His fear of being exposed as a man without a good story appeared to be playing out much faster than he ever would have imagined.

"Well, I'm in town for a job interview. I…I came a day earlier than planned so I could look around the city some first. Can't get into the hotel booked for me till around noon, you know."

"Oh, I see." An honest sounding reaction. "What kinda job?"

The driver sounded like he was just trying to make conversation. Ted thought it unlikely he had any other motivation. He rapidly searched his brain. The meeting he attended a few years before in Albany was at the State University. He tried and tried to remember the hotel where he stayed if that was going to become a question also.

"At the University. In security" Oh shit, why did he say that?

But the driver had moved on. Perhaps in a more ominous direction.

"Travel kinda light, eh?"

Ted had no answer for that. How much bullshitting was he supposed to try to do? Now he was angry. Angry at himself for winding up in this guy's car and angry at this guy for constantly quizzing him. He struggled to stay calm and come up with a plausible enough answer. When would they get to where they were going anyway?

"Yeah, well kinda complicated. Wife coming from upstate; works for the state. She's got all our stuff."

"Yeah, I see you got a wedding ring on. Was wondering 'bout that. Yeah well none of my beeswax, that's for sure…Hey we're here. Nice little place."

Ted doubted the look on his face didn't leave the driver wondering. He was pissed and angry. If he was looking to catch a break he sure didn't sense finding that twenty was so great anymore. If he had so much trouble with a bus driver what would happen in a run in with any law enforcement officer?

The diner was tucked in a corner lot in an area with a number of small business structures all around it, on both sides of the street. It wasn't tiny but not large either. There was a sizable humming neon sign anchored on a tall pole at the edge of the street advertising 'Open 24 Hours'. Three cars were in the macadam lot; naturally, two were black and white patrol cars.

The driver eyed Ted with a slight squint. "There's Jim and Jose's squad cars. Usually see them here this time of night." He looked directly at Ted. "But they'll be pulling out shortly to get back on the road. Say, say hello to Maggie for me, okay? Tell her Ray says hello."

With that Ted offered as friendly a thank you as he could muster. But he was dazed; unhappy with the last five minutes and discouraged to see the police cars.

****

SATURDAY BEFORE DAWN

A KIND, LONELY WOMAN?/   Ted desperately didn't want to enter right away. There was nowhere else to go. Whatever he did outside would appear more suspicious than going in and taking a seat at the counter. He worried the bus driver was watching him. The driver sat for a time before pulling away. Would this Maggie or the cops have noticed the driver's car and expect Ted to say something about Ray, virtually insuring everyone in the place would know he just arrived on the bus from New York City, with no apparent luggage. Ted was terrified about the chatting that was bound to develop. Again and again he felt defeated by his circumstances.

Beside himself, he opened the door and walked inside. The breakfast odors and too warm environment did little to relax him. At the far end of the counter a black man in some sort of uniform was reading a paper as he ate. Ted decided his uniform was probably from the postal service, but he wasn't sure. Much closer to the door he just opened were the two policemen and a waitress, who was behind the counter.

One of the cops, probably Hispanic, looked like he had just stood up and Ted hoped that meant he was getting ready to leave. Both cops had their hats on. Each hat had been manipulated to have a depression from ear to ear in the center so that the front, especially, but also the back looked peaked, up. They reminded Ted of when he was visiting Chicago, where beat patrol cops had their hats that way. The Chicago cops also wore some of the nastiest, mean looking faces he had ever seen. He supposed that worked to their advantage in that city or so many wouldn't have looked that way. The Albany cops each had their hats tilted back on their heads, a childish appearance to Ted.

Of course his arrival was acknowledged by everyone in the room. Heads bobbed with nods from the cops, the man at the end of the counter looked over briefly, and the waitress smiled and spread her right arm as a sign to Ted to sit anywhere he wanted. Ted tried to return the smile but was consumed with what felt like agony to him trying to decide whether he should sit at the counter or a booth. He decided sitting in a booth would help to remove him from having to interact with the others and might also offer an easier opportunity to drag out his time in the comfort of the diner, if it turned out to be a safe place for him. He hoped the folks at the counter would be more likely to ignore him and let him alone in a booth. He kicked himself again for never getting a paper, or even a book, to further the chance others would leave him alone.

The cops got it and kept chatting with the waitress. She also left him alone while Ted gave the appearance of studying the menu intently. Ted did what he thought he should do in this place but part of him remained uncertain and alarmed. He was amazed how uncomfortable and nervous he was.

All he wanted was to save his own life. And yet he felt, and presumed appeared, as guilty as hell to anyone he came in contact with. Staying somewhere in New York City would have been better; easier, he decided. No more crowds here. Too small.

Was he losing it…again? Mostly, through it all, Ted Vallan saw himself and his actions more through the lens of a state trooper's experience than an innocent man on the run. He couldn't shake off his feeling he was the one on the wrong side.

To encourage his anonymity he had positioned his back to the cops when he sat in the booth. Now he sensed a slight sweat and that sick feeling again. He heard the heavy shoes and gear of the cops moving around somewhere behind him. He tried to anticipate their questions and consider responses. For a moment the idea of standing up and turning to face them and confessing ran through his mind. He was in a panic.

"So, decided what you'd like, hon?"

The patrol cars lit up the window as they fired up and then each backed away and out of the parking lot. Ted slumped down in his seat. His sense of relief was palpable and didn't go un-noticed.

"Hey, you okay, hon?"

"Huh. Oh yeah. Sure. It's been a long night. Just beat, you know." He couldn't even decide how fucking friendly he should be. He was a wreck.

She was middle-aged, long grayish blonde hair loosely tied in the back, with a nice enough figure, and a welcoming, friendly face. He guessed she was a good bet to want to chat.

"You must be Maggie. Ray said to say hello. He dropped me off on his way home."

"Oh yeah, thought that was Ray Smith's car pulled in then. Sweet guy. Pretty regular four days a week. Now and then brings someone from the bus. Guess you may not be one of those who does the up all night thing too good, huh? You and I ain't such youngsters anymore. Am I right?" She was just being friendly. Ted was still dizzy from all his worry but he began to relax. Ted smiled his agreement with an innocent look. He lifted the menu and ordered.

A few more customers filtered in over the next twenty minutes or so. Ted had ordered a lot and he enjoyed it, remaining cautious to eat slowly to let time pass. Maggie, with a pot of coffee seemingly wedded to her hip, came over to ask how he was doing and offer a refill. He thanked her. She smiled and off she went. A few minutes later, when Ted was the only patron left, Maggie put the coffee pot on his table and sat down across from him. He wasn't ready for more coffee yet and he figured she could just as well have gone into the kitchen to chat with the cook. Her move didn't cause Ted to panic as he did before.

Nothing threatening about this woman he decided. If he was going to stay out he had to be able to handle these kinds of situations. He felt some relief from anxiety and paranoia. As Maggie started to speak some of his resolve briefly melted. He felt a cold sweat. Maybe what he interpreted as relaxing was really another sign of his fading, like just before a drowning victim gives in to the inevitability of the end. Maybe his defenses were shot and it was useless to continue.

"It's Saturday morning and all I want to do is get off my feet and get some sleep. Used to do this shift better, you know. Kind of a trade-off. Day shift so busy really wears you out. Much slower at night but it's night, you know. Rest of the world lives during the day. No fun for me. Thank goodness for the VCR. At least can watch the shows I like when I manage to wake up."

She was sweet. Nothing pretentious. Friendly. She put Ted more at ease.

Maggie's appearance, her face really, reminded Ted of less formally educated women he occasionally crossed paths with in Vermont as a trooper. Actually he knew two types of those women, usually fated to spend their lives doing mostly humdrum work as they fought an endless struggle to scrape by, for themselves and their families.

Those like Maggie trended thin and commonly had drawn faces with a perpetually weary expression and pale, washed out, dry and damaged skin. Often smokers, they generally appeared older than their age and spoke with deeper, raspy voices. The other group was obese with round faces perched on top of round bodies. Paradoxically those women often appeared healthier than the ones like Maggie. Ted's experience with these types of women often came in the setting of a visit to a ramshackle home or trailer, the woman inevitably surrounded by hordes of children. Vermont is a poor state.

He was happy to listen to her talk about herself. Still he had not planned any story to tell her about himself. He gave an off-hand response.

"They say some people's internal clocks make them better at nightshift work than others. But you're right, working all night sure can mess up the daytime."

Maggie put him on guard but not exactly for what he had worried about.

"You know, I think it cost me my marriage." She looked at Ted with no particular sign of concern. "You keep covering up your wedding ring. Marriage in trouble?"

'Shit!' Nobody ever missed anything when it came to Ted Vallan. He meant to put the ring in his pocket when he got out of the bus driver's car but forgot to do it in the panic of seeing the patrol cars. In the diner he tried to fold his hands to cover the ring whenever Maggie came over. He uncovered his hand and decided he would not let her probe him.

"No. No, didn't realize I was doing that. Some aching in one of the joints. You know, aging."

He decided to try to move on.

"I need to go to the main library today. If it's hard to get to maybe you could put some directions on a napkin for me. I'd really appreciate it"

She sat back as though sizing him up and thinking. A short pause and then a tart but friendly wisecrack.

"If I thought you weren't married you and I could have done better than a trip to the library, hon." Almost a wink with it. "You and I each look like we could use some shut-eye."

Ted had no idea how to react.

"Kidding hon, jus kidding. No more married men for me. I can get you to the library. It's a walk but pretty straight." A little more serious tone after. "Don't know your story but you spend time in that library, especially at their computers, you better smell like a rose or they'll boot you. Colder it gets more bum…guys from off the street crowding that place. Not sayin' bout you and what your deal is but you don't want to raise a stink, if you know what I mean?"

Ted's brain was suffering a flood of disparate thoughts. He appreciated her advice. He wasn't sure if he should try to procure a shower and a clean bed if this women was giving him an opening to get her to take him home. Warning lights were flashing everywhere in his head. Computers? He hadn't even considered computers as another potential source for local information in a library. Ultimately, 'stay calm…go to the library' won out. 'Who knows what could happen with the waitress?'

"Maggie, you're sure an interesting woman. I better try to clean up before I leave. I know I'm a mess but have to do some work there today. Thanks."

More customers came in but it was slow. Not unusual for early on a Saturday morning. Ted lingered over succeeding cups of coffee with clear but unspoken encouragement from Maggie to do so. A little after daybreak, about seven, Maggie came by to tell Ted her shift was ending. He said he'd get cleaned up and go. She advised him to take his time and, whatever he did, he wasn't to dare leave a tip. His heart sank, but it was also a relief. A kind soul who understood more than she needed to ask.

In the small men's room he locked the door and determined not to spend any time looking at his sorry face in the stained and rusty mirror. He went right at it and took his shirt and T-shirt off. The idea of using a computer and what he might be able to do with it was percolating in his mind and diverted him, at least momentarily, from his fear and despair.

MORE THAN MURDER 91

A lot of wet paper towels were burned after he used the liquid soap all over his chest and armpits accomplishing close to what Liza would have called a sponge bath. He soaped and washed his hair but found no reason to shave again, after only eight or nine hours. He let some soap stay on his body hoping any odor from it might pass for body wash.

He had to put his coat right back so his shirt with the hospital logo on it was hidden. Warm or cold it must stay on, zipped up to his chest. He smeared some liquid soap on the shirt and jacket arm pit regions. As he was doing that he felt the bulge in a pocket and remembered the small travel kit from the City. There was a tiny stick of deodorant with a kind of sandalwood scent so he, dutifully, opened his shirt again and generously rolled some on each armpit.

When he finally emerged from the men's room he found Maggie had left. There was no check on his table. He caught the attention of the new waitress and asked for his check. The woman was busy but she stopped to quickly take in all of Ted Vallan. Her look suggested she was not impressed.

"Maggie took care of it, hon. Okay?"

Ted was shocked. His emotions were at a high pitch, easily moved within the tension of his situation. Tears welled up around his eyes.

"Easy hon. Don't think you're the first one, Okay?"

****

SATURDAY IN ALBANY, NEW YORK

DAYLIGHT AGAIN/   Paper napkin map in hand Ted headed
out into the fresh but chilly air of an early fall morning. Reminded
him of Vermont. Not commented on while he watched Maggie
draw the map, but clearly disturbing to Ted, was her use of a police
station next to the library as a landmark. Nothing was doing on
the streets of Albany so early on a Saturday morning. Paranoia
returned. Should he walk slowly or determinedly? He didn't know.
He was in no rush but didn't want to appear to be a vagrant either.

Arriving at the library well before he assumed it would open he was
disappointed to read on the sign at the street the building would
not open until ten on Saturday and would close at three. A short
day. The library was closed on Sunday.

With a lot of time to kill he walked away to a side street with some
commercial buildings. For the first time that day he thought about
what he would do after three. Where would he go for the night?
How could he keep kidding himself? He was getting nowhere. His
big goal right now, for the past few hours, was to get to the library.
What was that really going to do for him? He had no plans for
after. A mess.

Glancing at the level of the sun Ted assumed the time was about
eight o'clock. It was actually only an informed observation since his
prized engraved retirement watch was probably already on its way
to a landfill with other trash from the Port Authority.

He passed a Goodwill store which opened at eight-thirty and sat with a few others on a nearby retaining wall while waiting for the store to open. He listened to an intoxicated bullshitter loudly give his world view and found that vastly more satisfactory than letting his brain attempt once again to re-live the murder scene, thoughts of Liza, or the rest of his ordeal. He no longer could muster any sense of favorable options or views for his future.

When the store opened he walked the aisles slowly, looking everything over as though he was after a hidden object. He had time to kill. He happened on a minimally threadbare crewneck sweater for $6.25, plus tax, that fit him and solved covering the hospital logo on his shirt. He could barely afford anything, but thought buying that sweater was important.

There was more activity in the city around him as the morning progressed. Walking a circuitous route back to the library to avoid going in front of the neighboring police station his upset came over him again. The semi-urban feel of the area reminded him of some towns in Vermont. Watching a family of four go from their front door to their car in the driveway upset him. He was alone and terribly lonely.

Ted's thinking and actions continued to be severely hampered by recurring undulating waves of despair he could not escape. Try as he might to walk with some purpose and plan for a better end, his situation remained dire. Murder and more than murder the loss of the love and support of Liza, the person he shared most of his life with, was still unimaginable.

How do you recover from being suddenly jolted, from head to toe, by a massive force from out of nowhere? His mind betrayed him. He was wearing out. His hope was fading. The rapid and worsening toll from his exhaustion and ongoing poor circumstances amazed him. He guessed he wasn't so young anymore. He no longer felt like the Eagle Scout he once was.

Ted felt diminished as a man and that was the worst. He had lost control. What was the point of staying out any longer? His present path seemed to offer him no future. He had fallen into a hole and didn't feel he had the strength to climb out. He needed rest. Maybe another time or another day he would have energy to figure a way to climb out. He didn't realize putting off the struggle to climb out would only reinforce his depression and make it harder for him in the end.

Tears formed in his eyes as he climbed the steps of the stately main branch of the Albany Public Library. It was a little more than forty-eight hours since his ordeal began.

****

SATURDAY IN VERMONT I

TWO FOR ONE?/   'What does that asshole want now?' It was
Saturday morning, Shawn Barry's first time back in his office, and
when his phone rang there already was a lot to be unhappy about.
Barry spent the last two days in Burlington. That investigation was
stuck in several places. And his prime suspect was still nowhere
to be found. There was no question he had to work through the
weekend. His live-in girlfriend understood. It was harder last night
when he called his ex and explained he wouldn't be able to pick
up their son for the day today as planned. Even though years had
passed, whenever he first heard her voice his heart sank a little. He
never really got over losing her. For the thousandth time an image
of what his life might have been flashed over him and then landed
in the pit of his gut. What he had lost! Shawn guessed she was
aware of what was going on when he called but she resisted making
a comment and he appreciated that.

At first he felt better this morning as he settled into his familiar
chair and desk in the Waterbury Barracks. By the time he received
that call, about two hours later, his mood had already darkened.

Shortly after arriving he was quickly reminded of Captain Ted
Vallan's continued presence in that office. Seeing all that was piled
on his desk he recalled Ted's oft expressed acknowledgement and
then frustration with his requirement to be managing several
big cases at the same time; unable to solely concentrate all his
time, effort, or manpower on his biggest one, even if it was of

major importance. Shawn wasn't sure he could handle all this. He certainly didn't go to work that morning with a definite idea this case and his job were overwhelming him. But he wasn't sure. Vallan managed his responsibilities and Shawn Barry would too, he insisted to himself, despite the tinge of discouragement and uncertainty he recognized in his own inner voice.

"Shit" he spoke out loud, to no one. All the ME would say was he was uncomfortable talking on the phone. That was great. Then why didn't he come to Waterbury and save Barry the trip. Just wasn't done that way, he supposed. He told the ME he would be right over.

Even the trip to Burlington reminded him of Ted. From Vallan he had learned how to get to Burlington so quickly anyone waiting for him was always amazed how little time passed. A state trooper could cut a good ten to fifteen minutes off the trip. So many times, with Shawn's cruiser right behind Ted's, lights flashing (but no siren), staying in the speed lane on the interstate and, in decent weather doing up to ninety, the trip was quick. Who knew for sure what the regs were on that? But that's what Ted always did if no civilians were with him. He and Shawn often would play tag if the highway was pretty quiet.

He found himself almost in a dialog with the Captain, thinking how he would like to tell Ted his new cruiser made going ninety feel like seventy. On balance Barry remained angry with Ted. He learned from Ted and ultimately got his job but he didn't like the way it happened. It was probably Shawn's fault for getting too close to the Vallan family and he was sure, in his own mind, Vallan had never forgiven him.

Driving to Burlington and thinking about the Vallans reminded Shawn about his flipping, last night, through the first book Henry Vallan wrote about Ted Vallan's exploits years before. He tried to remember how he got that copy. Written on the inside cover it said, 'To Shawn, Henry Vallan'. He found the cold formality of that inscription annoying.

So did then Deputy Major Crime Investigator Ted Vallan actually murder someone? He didn't come near to reading the whole book. But he read that section over and over. He concluded, just from the book, he could not be sure. Now with Becker's homicide the history of Ted's behavior and actions were all suspect.

* * *

Indeed, the ME was surprised how quickly Lieutenant Barry arrived. His remark turned Shawn off.

"Shawn you must have learned some shortcuts from Ted to get here so soon." It wasn't what Shawn wanted to hear. He stayed all business.

"You know, Samir, I'm really busy; tied up with the homicide, finding the Captain, and a whole lot of shit I just found on my desk today. What do I need to know?"

Samir understood it from his words but mostly his tone. Either Shawn was overwhelmed or his anger about Vallan, of all people, being his suspect was getting to him.

"Sure, Shawn. But you do want to know everything I know about the homicide, correct?"

Shawn softened and nodded yes.

"Well, you remember at the post I told you there were some clinical issues with Dr. Becker's activities and oxygen levels the days before he died, right?"

Again Shawn nodded, this time mouthing 'of course'. Samir picked up some papers and looked at them. His face knotted, an expression of confusion and uncertainty. He was puzzled.

"Most of the tox report is back and it's quite a surprise; actually, startling."

Shawn sat up straighter in his chair across from Samir. 'Now what's happening' he thought. 'What more could be found in a man who was stabbed in the heart?'

"Shawn, Harvey Becker's body was filled with a morphine derivative. There are surprising levels of it in his body."

Samir was quite animated as he reviewed the report. He obviously remained very struck by the finding. Shawn didn't know what to make of it.

"Beyond my pay grade, Doc. What are we talking about here? How could this affect the fact he was stabbed in the heart and died?"

Samir responded earnestly.

"I'm not sure. I've been thinking about it since the report came today. What I can tell you is the amount of morphine in his body is well above what would usually kill a person."

"So he was killed two ways?"

Samir understood what Shawn meant. He slowly exhaled and continued.

"No. No, one of those things, or something, had to kill him first."

"You said he was stabbed to death and you even timed it to between four and six a.m."

"I know. I know. Obviously this doesn't all add up yet. But it's more than that also." He leaned forward at his desk. "I think if we look at the amount of the opioid in his blood and think about his continuing serious post-op weakness and failure to rehabilitate… and even his low oxygen saturation levels, there may be a correlation. Remember notes in his chart talked about depressed consciousness and low oxygen. His somnolence and probably depressed respirations causing the low oxygen could have been from the morphine.

"What I mean is if Harvey Becker wasn't murdered with a sudden massive dose of morphine what else could have been going on?"

Shawn appeared confused but Samir was looking off in the distance, clearly lost in what he was thinking and expressing.

"What if Dr. Becker had been on opioids for some time, maybe a long time before he died? Some of the effects of those high blood levels might have been modified as his body developed tolerance to higher levels for a while. Not necessarily free of side effects but still alive…Of course, eventually, despite some dose tolerance, higher doses of the drug would kill him, or anybody."

With those words Samir sat back. But his expression was still puzzlement. He was thinking.

"Doc, did this Becker die from an overdose or from the knife to his heart?" Shawn wasn't ready to open the bidding to any more potential competing possibilities. But Samir clearly was and ignored the Lieutenant's plea.

"So, if Becker could tolerate higher amounts of opioids because he was taking them over some time period before he died, that could explain some things but raises many, many questions."

Shawn was unhappy the ME planned to continue. He surmised whatever he was going to say would further complicate determining Becker's mode of death.

"You know Shawn, it's almost like…like; well think of it as a logic theorem. There are a few combinations or permutations to consider." The ME was into it now. He didn't speak or come across projecting his usual measured approach and cautious manner.

"Consider this: maybe Harvey Becker was given a massive amount of morphine as an act of murder and died from it right away. But what if Becker had already been taking morphine before this hospitalization; most likely long-acting then? That way he might not have required a massive amount of a sudden, short-acting dose to kill him. Or the length of time he was using morphine is unclear but maybe his actual clinical course in the hospital suggests an effort to kill him slowly, with gradually increasing doses. Could that have accounted for his poor clinical and respiratory status his last days?

"Were his meds being given in some way to cause the opioids to accumulate over time and surely become increasingly toxic? You know, we are unable to differentiate short from long acting morphine when we do a tox analysis.

"But, either way, I'll tell you, his level was so high, if there was a gradual, not sudden, overdose then he probably was taking morphine before to be able to tolerate close to the level we found and stay alive for several days."

Samir turned and, appearing more grounded in his thoughts again, looked squarely at Shawn.

"Then think about this Shawn: What if Becker was dead when the knife was plunged into his chest? Easier to kill if he was unconscious or, better yet, not breathing deeply. Was it planned to be that way? Or were the stabbing and apparent overdose completely unrelated; like you said, 'killing him in two ways'? You know, total serendipity."

Shawn drew some satisfaction from the ME quoting him but the fact Samir didn't appear to have run out of possibilities yet left him with a bad feeling about the whole exercise.

"But Doc, the guy recently had surgery and was supposed to be on some painkillers. It's in his chart. Wouldn't that mean he was bound to have some of that stuff in his blood?"

"Exactly. But the levels shouldn't have been so high. And because he was so out of it those last few days his doctors cut back on his doses. Didn't stop them but cut back. There really are so many possible narratives, Lieutenant. His blood levels were very elevated despite the cut backs."

Samir looked like he was ready to continue; to list more possibilities. Shawn raised his hand in a signal to stop.

"I sort of get it Doc, but it's a lot for me to digest. I think this is enough for right now. Doc, can you write this up for me in a way where you list all those different possibilities you keep talking about?"

The ME would not routinely be expected to be asked to do anything like that for law enforcement. But Samir understood the complexity of what he was introducing to the Lieutenant. He thought the request was not unreasonable or a major break in protocol.

"Yes, Shawn, I will try to put something together."

"Okay. Thanks Doc." He just wanted to get out of there. The ME had worn him out. 'Enough' Shawn thought. 'For Christ's sake, the poor bastard had a yellow handled knife in his chest; probably Ted Vallan's. Isn't that enough?'

Shawn walked rapidly to his cruiser and headed back to the highway as quickly as he could. This time when he hit the interstate he made no effort to rush back to Waterbury. After radioing in for messages he took his time on the road. He wanted, needed, time to think.

Again and again over the last few days Barry was practically forced by events to keep re-thinking what he initially considered a sure thing. Once again, after receiving potentially conflicting information, his first response was to remind himself that guilty or innocent the Captain had to be found and brought in. No matter what Ted Vallan was mixed up in this mess.

But that certainly was not good enough anymore. Barry recognized a good likelihood he needed to be looking for more suspects. Things were getting complicated. Could a bunch of people all think they were killing this Becker at about the same time? Or was it still all Ted? Leave it to being in a hospital for there to be a variety of ways to do someone in.

* * *

Shawn Barry was determined to have the ME's toxicology findings withheld from the public for as long as possible; at least several

days. He told the ME, his staff, and his superiors he needed time to
investigate all the possibilities raised by that development. He was
especially concerned about understanding the chain of custody for
controlled substances in the hospital. He said he needed to establish
how the pathways for handling those kinds of meds worked and
how many people might be involved with that in the hospital
setting. Once word got out he assumed the task of investigating all
those people would be more challenging.

He didn't tell anyone his thoughts about Kathy Conover. Early
on Shawn took notice she had been working per diem on the
overnight shift all that week; twice on the ward Becker was on.
His junior investigator was given the job of her initial interviews.
Shawn plainly didn't know how to go about something like that
with her. The passing of years made no difference in the level of
hostility between them; especially for Kathy, Shawn felt.

And anyway, in this setting, how could he not have some suspicions
about her. Her father being attacked publicly, for whatever, by
this guy Becker. Apparently Becker was really loud and aggressive.
Maybe there was something to his accusations and Vallan was
about to be in big trouble; maybe his reputation was in trouble.
Did Kathy decide to do something about that and kill that doctor?
At close to the same time Ted Vallan sneaked into his room and
stabbed him in the chest? In cahoots? No, not likely , but you never
know. If that's what happened it actually might turn out to be easier
to break the case than if neither had any idea what the other was
going to do.

If one of the possibilities posited by the ME was correct then a
plan by Kathy, to slowly boost Becker's levels of morphine over a
period of time, was a smarter one than Ted's. If she ever did such
a thing catching her would probably be very difficult. Kathy told
Deputy Investigative Trooper Dark she did per diem shift work
from time to time to make needed money. Many younger staff did
that. This week, although she was not staffing Harvey Becker's ward
the morning of his death, she worked every night. Maybe she felt a
crime of opportunity was staring her in the face.

Shawn Barry understood opening a parallel track for this homicide investigation meant undertaking a large, potentially complex effort to look at the people involved in every facet of the handling and distribution of controlled drugs in the hospital. Knowing that was happening would have been very exciting to Ted. It would, basically, be exactly what he was beginning to work on to better understand and, he suspected, find a diversion somewhere in that chain.

Shawn doubted he had the time or manpower to conduct such a complete probe in any reasonable period of time. He determined to start and, hopefully, end with Kathy Conover. He convinced himself it was a logical and practical decision. Barry prided himself for accepting the need for moving in that direction right away. Pursuing that path first was clearly going to be very personally challenging because of all the difficulty and stress he would face dealing directly, personally, with Kathy. He thought his decision was a sign of his integrity and, ultimately, the fairness with which he was running his investigation. 'Go first where there is fire.' That wasn't what Ted had in mind.

Barry knew a time would come when he'd have to meet directly with each one of the Vallans but first he had his deputy begin their interrogations.

* * *

LIZA VALLAN AND KATHY CONOVER GET INTERVIEWED BY THE 'B' TEAM/   Deputy Major Crime Unit Investigative Trooper Donald Dark was anxious for any direction from the Lieutenant. Eight months with the narcotics unit was not the right fit for him. It wasn't that he was unsuccessful. Actually he did well there. He didn't like the personalities of fellow unit members. Picking on his name was the least of it; he was used to that. He judged their comradery was based on absolute disrespect for the public they dealt with. That didn't help anything.

He felt much better about his four months as Lieutenant Barry's deputy. The work required using his brain much more and that was fine. The Vallan case was big for everybody but especially for him. The Lieutenant was planning to use him as his interface with all the members of the Vallan family. Didn't take long for Trooper Dark to figure out there was considerable bad blood between his boss and the Vallan family. He didn't know the details and didn't plan to ask.

So the Lieutenant and he sat together at times on Thursday and Friday and Dark wrote down a lengthy list of questions and concerns the Lieutenant asked him to cover when he interviewed those people.

Thursday's interviews did not go well. Liza was sobbing frequently and was so distracted she might have thought she just landed on a different planet. Kathy Conover had done her day job on Wednesday and worked eleven to seven over night; and then this. By the time he sat with her she was exhausted, although also notably angry with him and maybe everyone. Salty language and a bit nasty. Even in that state he thought she was quite attractive. Kathy was furious Dark wouldn't let her stay in the room when he interviewed Liza. All he worked on in both interviews that day was trying to establish some timelines for those people and the event.

Friday didn't go much better. The enormity of Ted Vallan's problem had really hit them. Dark gently pushed each of them, again interviewed apart, about their feelings about Dr. Becker and tried, with Liza, to probe how angry Ted was with Becker. Kathy remained notably angry and difficult. Liza mostly cried and verbalized fears about her husband's disappearance and well-being.

Saturday morning was different. Trooper Dark called Liza Vallan and she was courteous to him but very clearly told him her family was in the process of getting a lawyer. She was advised to say nothing more until then. Why this sudden change? What might be up? Raised Dark's and Barry's suspicions a little but far from unheard of in capital cases, especially when a loved one is the prime suspect.

The Lieutenant pulled Dark from his Saturday afternoon at home to go again to speak with Kathy because of the new information that morning from the ME about Dr. Becker's opiate blood levels. Barry put Dark on guard for a whole slew of possibilities that raised. In order to make it harder for her to blow off an interview the Trooper was advised not to call but drive to Kathy's place in his cruiser. The Lieutenant was suspicious.

Kathy, indeed, was not pleased to see the trooper for the third time in three days. Driving up to their rented house in his cruiser she and her family were outside doing some fall clean-up and playing. Now her family and her neighbors were having the homicide investigation brought close to home for them.

There was a good chance Deputy Major Crime Investigator Trooper Donald Dark was a good guy. But he was probably too green for the role he was being thrust into by the Lieutenant. Either he hadn't matured his skills or he was terminally literal about his interactions and investigations. More likely the former. Kathy Conover was smart and a force of life he had never encountered and was unable to understand.

She was furious about being interviewed repeatedly, especially in this way today. Sleep deprived from efforts to manage her family and two jobs, the events of the last few days left her simmering, 24/7. Her sarcasm was lost on Trooper Dark. Anticipating where his questioning was leading, she barked at him:

"Sure Trooper, that Becker was a real bastard. Everyone knew it. He picked on lots of people. So you still think what he was doing to my father got me so angry I wanted to plan to stick my father's knife in his chest. Sure, that makes sense, doesn't it."

"No… Maybe you are not aware but Dr. Becker was also poisoned with opiates two days ago, while he was in the hospital."

Kathy paused but only for a moment.

"Oh sure, now you think I poisoned the bastard. Oh why not? Shove pills down his throat and then plunge that knife into him. Makes sense, eh? One of those two should do it."

"What I'm saying is you had both motive and opportunity to

poison him."

"Wow. Trooper do you really think it's all that simple? Well then I guess my father isn't the only one gonna need a lawyer. Is that what you're saying?

"Go read the chart Trooper. Do your own fucking homework, okay? I'm the one who called the asshole surgical resident two times, and even the attending once, to get them to cut his narc doses back. The jerk was barely awake. Kept mumbling, 'give me my pills, give me my pills'. He was hypoventilating; weak. Finally they cut back a little."

"So, what does that mean? Ms. Conover that absolves no one."

"Then you know what, Trooper Dark, you're just going to have to figure all that out, won't you? If you think I've done something aren't you supposed to figure it all out yourselves; you and Shawn Barry? From now on you call my lawyer, not me. I'll get one fucking pronto. And I'll tell that guy to watch you guys, okay?"

That was the end of it.

Later, on the phone, Trooper Dark told the Lieutenant he thought she was angry and evasive. Hard for him to know why she said what she did. He told Shawn he was concerned. Shawn heard Dark's report that way, for sure.

****

FOOTNOTE — * * **THE AFFAIR FROM YEARS BEFORE THAT RUINED EVERYTHING**

LIVING HISTORY/   Kathy Conover was well aware she made a terrible mistake. The timing of her run in with Shawn on a street in Burlington was unfortunate for both of them. He, all of a sudden, was feeling his life greatly altered with a young baby and the notable impact that had on his wife. He acutely mourned a loss of spontaneity and a change in intimacy in their life. Just engaged, Kathy was wondering if it all was moving too fast; if she was really ready or wanted the pending restrictions of marriage. Sitting together for a quick coffee they seemed to bond as they talked about events pushing them; a sense of loss of control. One thing just led to another.

She knew she had to live with it and try to move on. But the episode hardened her feelings about her life and others in her life. Her change did not please her but she recognized it as a fact of her life. Barely out of her teens when it happened the brief miserable affair accelerated Kathy's engagement with both maturity and the real world. Happy go lucky no more. Some sweetness evaporated and even after the obvious trauma had settled many sensed she had become an angry person.

Even as years passed she retained some anger, in particular, directed at important men in her life. In her mind she was definitely seduced by Shawn, the older married man. Her fury directed at him was boundless. She despaired her father had placed her in a permanent purgatory and believed his lack of empathy plus allowing Shawn to maintain his career on the force was terribly unfair to her. A once unbreakable appearing bond between a daughter and her father was frayed. Her sense of rejection sustained some of her anger. She even still found herself, from time to time, angry at her husband, David, if only for his almost too easy acceptance of what happened and his ready forgiveness.

Working a full week as a nurse educator and taking frequent per diem nightshifts while raising two young children was taking a toll on her. If the Conover family was ever going to purchase a home Kathy had no choice. Dave had a respectable accounting job but no way to further supplement his income. That bothered Kathy also.

Kathy was never as clear in her own mind about her mother's reaction to the affair. Liza was empathetic and more supportive than Ted. But right from the start Kathy felt there was something unusual about the way she was, in some odd way, a bit distant or seemed to consciously temper her response to the affair. Liza, maybe even more than Kathy, seemed to want to put the affair behind them and move on. Kathy recognized some changes in her mother the last few years but Liza demurred there was nothing to talk about and Kathy determined she could not be sure anything was truly different.

* * *

THINKING ON THE JOB/   Until she walked into that room to administer his early morning meds four days before his death Kathy Conover did not connect the patient in 401, a private room, with the Becker who was viciously, publicly attacking her father so nonsensically. She barely knew Dr. Becker but had pegged him as a jerk long before. The way he was going after her father and the things he was saying only made any sense if you already knew what an idiot he was. She was at a complete loss as to why he was doing this to her father.

It was obvious to Kathy her dad was like a fish out of water from the moment he began at the hospital. She could see he wasn't happy. There was a void in their relationship but Kathy surely loved her father. Her heart went out to him seeing him so uncomfortable after his years of leadership. It seemed a shame for him to be in such a spot and then this jackass Becker starting up. It made her angry. And now it was her job to care for the bastard. For a brief moment Kathy fantasized about how a daughter might regain that unbreakable love of a father.

The human brain's remarkable capacity to allow or suppress vastly different thoughts and ideas is boundless. More so for some than others, of course. Did Kathy Conover ever also let herself toy with using the permanent humiliation of her father as a way to eliminate the hurt his modest condemnation supported for many years of her life? Or, would it be more likely she considered and then acted on ridding the Vallan family of this sinister idiot to aid her father and regain his unrestricted love?

****

SATURDAY IN VERMONT II

COMPLAINING TO THE NYPD/   That NYPD detective acted like a dick Friday morning and then, later in the day, seemed to attack him. It was obvious he was implying the VSP was withholding information, especially about Vallan and drugs. Shawn couldn't stand the guy. He was furious and had gone to his own superiors to complain. The Colonel was setting up a call for today with the NYPD Commissioner to make it clear the VSP was not aware of Ted Vallan having any drug connections and his quick apprehension by the NYPD was a huge priority for the VSP. All of a sudden Shawn was not so sure.

He was getting increasingly anxious about the pending update meeting with the top officers of the department before the call later. They wouldn't just want to hear him review the status of this very high profile case. They'd be looking for a clean case, certainly with no potentially contaminating drug component. The meeting might include some good friends of the Captain. Some at the top of the force would be hard pressed to accept Ted Vallan could be an obvious suspect for this or, probably, any case. Anyway, how on earth was he going to present any of this case after hearing from the ME just now?

Pulling into the Waterbury Barracks lot Shawn tried to decide if it would be best for his nerves to plan to do target practice at the shooting range before or after the meeting. He needed the release.

****

SATURDAY IN THE CITY

OVERTIME/   "Come on baby. Let him cry for a while an he'll fall back asleep."

As Detective James Wiley spoke she was already turning in bed and proceeded to put her legs over the side, starting to sit up. He reached out and touched her back.

"Not my fault I married a Puerto Riccan temptress." Expressed with a tinge of frustration; knowing the battle was already lost.

Wiley fell back in bed and Idelia picked up her robe and began to put it around her with her usual flourish, giving the illusion of almost tossing it in the air and it falling neatly, enveloping her body as it came down. The phone rang.

Wiley looked at the clock in the darkened room; 6:17 a.m. She picked up the phone. He figured she did it as a reflex in hopes of not further disturbing the child. Seemed silly since he was already crying. Usually Wiley picked up the odd hours calls. They were invariably for him. He was the cop.

Her face tightened but all she said was "Yes sir, he's right here."

She covered the speaker with her hands and with a serious tone whispered, "It's your Commander; Haworth."

Wiley sat up in bed and threw his legs over the side reaching for the phone while also flipping on the lamp next to him and looking for his pad and a pen on the night table. He tried to act calm.

"Yes, Commander, Jim Wiley here."

Deputy Inspector Howard Haworth's voice was never to be mistaken, unless, of course, you thought you might be speaking with James Earl Jones. His voice was booming, resonant, and full. And he had learned to use his words and phrasing to highlight it. He was generally an intimidating man.

"Wiley, some shit's been poppin' through the night about that *Vermunt* cop. Updated sheet with that Harlem business leaked to papers and TV. This here PD more leaky than a sharecropper's old roof. We got to move on this shit right away.

"The Commissioner supposed to talk to the head of *Vermunt* State Police sometime today." Haworth spoke in a parenthetical fashion. "Don't know what they call their top people there; maybe generals.

"We got to learn more about this guy but we also got to have stuff to give them. You been doing the grunt work on this one and I want you to be ready to fill us all in in about five hours. If it's all drug shit, that's fine, but we better be right." Haworth let the words flow off his tongue, "You understand?"

Wiley got it, just like he got it when he was subtly threatened by that Lieutenant Barry the day before. He wished he had tried harder to speak with Vallan's kid early last evening. Where was that shit? Should he say anything to the Commander? He had uniformed watching the kid's building now.

"Yes Commander Haworth I'm up and I'll check in. Got a couple places to go right away." You tried not to ask questions of the Commander. You waited and hoped he'd move the discussion.

"So Wiley, I told O'Rourke to assign another detective and have that person get a car and get to your building immediately. Move fast Wiley. You know Tessie, my personal aide?" Wiley nodded to the phone but Haworth continued before he could speak. "Call her if you need me and when you get stuff. Keep me apprised of your progress. I must talk with you by eleven, for sure. You got that? For now the word is to try to keep this rogue cop alive, so you pass that on and you do what you can if you get him. That's it for now Wiley."

"Yessir."

* * *

Wiley tried to think it through in the shower. 'Obviously whoever runs the Vermont State Police is going to great lengths to have this guy brought in. Fat chance they are truly looking to share info with NYPD. That Lieutenant has something up his ass about this guy. If he's such a fucking murderer why the smirk in the tone of that Trooper. Wonder if those assholes ever used to actually work cases together? Something missing in what's going on up there. His son was lying about contact with his father, but I hit him with stuff he knew nothing about. Totally shocked about his old man. This thing drags on maybe I should look at those books the kid's talking about.'

The uniform at Henry Vallan's building told him Vallan returned home around ten p.m. They told Vallan his building would be watched and that Wiley would be back in the morning to talk to him. No other activity. Wiley had no doubt Ted Vallan would stay away from that spot. Good chance he was out of the City by now.

Detective James Wiley, four months on the job as a full detective, finally began to feel and sense what being a detective, an investigator, could be. Working through the years in uniform and then the bullshit bureaucracy and detective training had dimmed his exciting vision from the past. Didn't seem to matter how well he did on the street or in the classroom. You worked to a top and then started the next level at the bottom and so on. Individual skill or ability seemed to mean very little. So he rose to the level of mediocrity that was expected of him and practiced by so many others.

This morning he felt different. Was there something different about this case with the Trooper? Why was his brain repeatedly thinking through a whole bunch of different possibilities or scenarios that could be playing out here? Why?... And why would Haworth tell him this case was bubbling up to top echelons but leave him in charge of filling it in for the NYPD? Never a hint Wiley ever caught that the Commander or anyone else ever thought he was ready or smart enough to lead this big an investigation.

As he opened the door to the unmarked he re-considered it all. 'Maybe not such a big deal. Maybe just a headache for the brass and happy to let anybody play with it for a while to satisfy Vermont law enforcement.'

Detective Joe Abell was the epitome of performing at a level of mediocrity. Well, maybe a bit below. He was senior to Wiley but he long ago realized he wasn't going anywhere and settled in to playing the system for another ten years or so. Working with him occasionally Wiley noted Abell's biggest efforts seemed to revolve around planning his eating through the day. He wasn't dumb, just incurious.

Abell was happy to have Wiley call the shots. Again, Wiley wondered now, but only briefly, if Abell had been instructed to be subordinate? 'Huh', He thought. 'Wouldn't that be something?'

Since Henry Vallan's status was known and he could get to him anytime Wiley decided to head first for the hospital in Harlem to try to get something from the knifing vics.

* * *

They agreed they should start in the ICU with the small guy named Johnson, the vic who was in critical condition. His time might be limited. But it was a waste of time. The man could speak but he wouldn't talk to them. Not a word. His eyes glared fire at them. His arms were all shot up and this guy was now, suddenly, totally dependent on hospital staff to dose him according to their protocols. The young surgical resident they spoke with told them the man only interacted about his narc dosing and his pain. After a relatively major abdominal surgery through the night he had become more stable and probably shouldn't be considered critical anymore.

Before the Detectives moved on to the next guy Wiley told the Doctor not to give any interviews or publicly state a change in this man's condition unless he heard from him. Abell wondered why Wiley wanted the guy to remain critical?

The young fat kid required a Big Boy bed. He really was big. The policemen walked in as he was being moved from his bed to a chair. The chair was oversized also. The kid, Sherman Molte, was also unhappy about his pain treatment, but looked fine to Wiley. Once he was settled in the chair and draped in blankets to cover him Wiley and Abell pulled over chairs and sat with him.

"Sherman, what's the deal man? You at the wrong place at the wrong time?"

The kid furrowed his brow. His face oozed unhappiness. But Wiley quickly noted an absence of wariness or even a hint of the last guy's anger and hatred. He could get somewhere with this kid; some information. But Molte said nothing in response to the Detective's opening.

"Sherman, I got feeling you lucky to be alive. Some shit was goin' on yesterday and we need to know 'bout it."

Wiley wanted the kid to explain as much as possible of what happened. Probably everyone around that bench shared in what went down to some extent. He wasn't even going to bring up anything about drugs. He wanted the kid to do it.

What Wiley had learned just before, over the radio, as he and Abell drove uptown to the hospital still left him less than neutral about the likely involvement of drugs in this mess. Foot patrol interviews in the neighborhood after the knifings found a street vendor a long block from the park who had sold food and a bottle of papaya juice to a white guy. Smashed to pieces near the park bench was a papaya juice bottle. It was so shattered no usable prints were found. The vendor got a kick telling the cop the guy tried to act like he didn't speak much English, using his arms and such to interact. After his purchase he wanted directions to the park. Everyone knows parks and drugs go together like meat and potatoes.

Wiley was planning to look for the vendor after he finished at the hospital. He had Ted Vallan's picture with him.

Young Molte continued to appear reluctant to begin talking.

"Sherman, you're not in a spot to stay quiet. You are in big trouble. Maybe very big trouble."

Molte's face remained impassive. But his eyes looked right at Wiley.

"Kid, that white guy who was around that bench with you is wanted for murder. Did you know that?"

A hit. Molte's face twisted in confusion. It put him off balance. It also made no sense to him.

"What were you doing in that park with a white dude, on the run for a murder rap, who stabbed the guy with you for sure and proly you before that?"

Molte's mouth had dropped open. He was incredulous. He started to speak.

"Ain't no story like that I know. No white killer, man. That dude a cop who wasn't s'posed to be where he was. You ought know that."

Wiley and Abell were floored. How'd this kid know he was a cop? Was Vallan on his own and bragging to low level punks? What? Or, was this episode the tip of something really big? Shit!.

"Molte, you best be square with us. You in a shitload of trouble. You know that. I want to know how you know this dude was a cop?"

A dietary aide knocked on the door. Apparently the posted guard was on a prolonged break while two detectives were on his man, who was shackled to the arm of his enormous chair anyway. The aide then backed into the door, opening it while carrying a tray with Sherman Molte's breakfast. Both Molte and Abell looked interested. Wiley took charge immediately. The kid's interest in the food was obvious.

"Sure, put the tray with breakfast on the bed, okay? We'll set him up with it as soon as we're done here. Thanks." Sherman looked over at the tray, repeatedly, for the rest of the time the Detectives were in there with him.

"So Sherman how you know he's a cop?"

Sherman was confused. His story wasn't a secret anymore. The people he didn't want to know he was talking to a cop already had figured it out and were about to kill him. For the first time Molte showed some anger. What was going on, he thought?

"Man you bullshitting an I don' get it. Cop NYPD narc and you know dat. Wha fuck you ast'in me? Ast him. Shithead had no biz showin' up dat street; goin' dat park. Shit! Get me killed sure. Woulda kilt him too if dey hadn't know he's a cop. Shit man! Wha the fuck?"

Wiley and Abell stared at each other. Wiley, anyway, rolled through a number of possibilities in his head that could explain what he just heard. This kid was a stooge. Too young to know how short a lifespan stooges have. Probably dead now no matter what happens next. A cop. But which cop? A narc or Vallan? Vallan working some covert program with ties to the City and Vermont? Drugs up there? Why not. Drugs everywhere. Involved in a homicide up there because of drugs?

Again, being a cop, Wiley still thought it a good bet Vallan was working the wrong side. But who the fuck knew? Could have been on the run and walked into a fucked-up situation and those schmucks mixed him up.

Wiley stood up so Abell did also.

"We gonna see you again Sherman. Real soon. Detective Abell gonna set you up with your breakfast now." He nodded to Abell and the man moved the tray from the bed to a table on wheels and rolled it to Molte. Abell removed the top and took a muffin as he and Wiley walked out.

* * *

Sitting in the black car Wiley called in to his precinct. He asked for Tessie and when she was on the line told her he needed to speak to the commander right away. Tessie sounded a little hesitant.

"Ma'am, I'm under real time pressure here. Commander said you'd know that. Some strange shi…stuff has come up an I'm never gonna get a quick answer without the Commander helping."

"Okay Detective. Sit tight a few minutes. I'll see what I can do."

While waiting Wiley concentrated on how best to present this new revelation to his boss and get it done efficiently. He was excited. Abell was working on the muffin, getting crumbs all over as he gradually peeled off the wrapper as he ate and continued to drive.

Commander Haworth called and asked Wiley what was up.

"Sir, we've got something new. It makes the situation probably more complicated, I think. We know this Vermont cop is wanted for a homicide in Vermont a few days ago. Maybe he fled to the City because his kid lives here. But maybe not. If he did, not sure what he thought that would do for him. Was on our way to talk to his kid again when this came up." Wiley was glad the Commander was hearing him out but suspected he better get to the point more quickly.

"Anyway, the guy's prints show up on a knife in a known dealer's groin in a drug spot in Harlem. Dealer probably gonna live. Another guy also stabbed. Bottom line is that guy, just a fat kid, says he was working with an NYPD narc. Kid says the narc screwed up and showed up bad timing and where he knew he shouldn't be. So this white guy could be our Vermont cop doing something bad or maybe part of some task force we got nothin' on…or…or a guy on the run winds up in Harlem and looked like a narc because he's white and sat down in the wrong spot to have a pretzel and drink papaya juice.

"I dunno Commander, before anyone talks to State Police in Vermont we better…"

"Yeah, find out if this *Vermunt* trooper could have been confused with one of ours. Shit! Wiley, you know how hard it is to get narcs and vice to tell the rest of us anything. Bastards keep their creeps hidden from everyone. Deep cover? Bullshit! That is bullshit!

"Glad you called. You move on. I'm going to go to the top and work down so we can get this done and get you to the guy you need, wherever, right away. I don't know if some of those creeps even check-in for days or can be found quickly. Shit! Keep your phone and pager close. You got that?"

"Yessir."

* * *

DARKNESS AT (ALMOST) NOON/   "Shit! Is the
asshole dead?"

Wiley wondered which asshole this narc meant?

He had given up on getting back to Henry Vallan before the meeting with the Commissioner. There were gaps he needed filled and he was not pleased with himself he wouldn't be able to get that done until later. Abell and Wiley were driving to the park at 133rd Street when the Commander called to advise them to go crosstown right away to the 23rd precinct on the east side.

At the precinct Wiley told Abell to go back but keep one eye on his pager. Time was bound to be close. He would page him with '!!!!' and that meant get to him immediately.

A man in civilian clothes was sitting on a desk a few feet behind the gated and secured duty desk that welcomed visitors to the precinct station. Wiley flashed his ID to the duty officer and the other man slid off the desk, let him in, and they trooped up a stairway. The man ushered Wiley into a windowless room and left. Not small; slightly larger than the Commander's office.

A small table, a few really small desks with secretarial chairs on wheels, and usual office paraphernalia. Also several flashing scanners and a big safe. Almost centered, at the small table, was a man on one of the small sliding chairs. And, in a corner, another man, was sitting on one of the small desks. Wiley got the picture right away; he was in a room with spooks.

The man in the center was the one who had spoken. He didn't look much like the picture of Ted Vallan Wiley now had. The two guys in that room could have been twins but neither was likely to be confused with his man.

Something strange puzzled Wiley. The guy in the corner was smoking a pipe, puffing out a strong, pungent, almost rancid odor. You couldn't be in that room and not have it soak into you. Hard to figure how that would be helpful for any undercover work.

Wiley responded directly to the man in the center. He decided to tell him the skinny one, Johnson, was critical and Molte was going to be okay. Said he didn't know anything about the other two.

Wiley thought he saw an eyelid go up on the talker when he mentioned the two who were missing. The narc spoke again.

"Yeah, that asshole kid was a bad bet from the start. Scared shitless all the time. Not up to it. They knew it too, those fuckers. One shitty mule. Useless to them and me."

Wiley pieced together the larger story without difficulty. Actually his only remaining problem was to establish what Ted Vallan's presence at that scene meant. In as few sentences as possible he briefed the narcs on the crime Ted Vallan was accused of in Vermont and the evidence placing him in the City the day before.

"Offi…" He didn't know what to call the man he was talking to. No greeting or exchange in any form had taken place. What to call this fucker? He decided they had to be cops so he'd stay with 'Officers.'

"Officers, do either of you recognize this man?" Both men had impassive faces. Who wouldn't be put off by the manner of these guys? Wiley would stay on guard, just like them, and provide as little information as possible. Not a sign of a very inclusive or supportive force he thought but that's the way it was.

He handed the sheet to the guy in the center of the room and watched him study it. After a short time that guy rolled his chair to the corner and handed it to the pipe smoker. No one said anything. By now Wiley had positioned himself on top of a small desk just off the door. He watched their faces and when the second man looked up Wiley looked back at the man in the center.

"No. No Detective. Never seen that guy." Then he looked over at the man in the corner. "How 'bout you? Anything?"

The second man cleared his throat. "No, me either Detective. No to your next question also. We got nothing related to that cop in the park or anything going out of town. No Vermont or Northeast connection to those bozos we're after; just local stuff."

He shifted in his chair.

"But your asshole sure has fucked up our work. Working a deal on his own or just stumbling into trouble he has us screwed. But we get it. That's why we're talking to you. Chance a way out of town rogue cop sits down with hard-assed dealers in that neighborhood by accident pretty slim. That bastard's got some story somewhere."

So they were doing him a favor to deign to take some of their time and talk with a straight cop and actually expose themselves to him. Almost talked to him like they respected him. Weren't they some guys. Spooks!

"Detective, we are very interested in how this story is going to play out. When you find this shithead we want to know how the blanks get filled in. Okay?"

Wiley stood and reached into his back pocket to pull out his card. He knew they wouldn't give him anything. As he started to open his card folder the man in the corner waved him off.

"We'll find you."

Wiley's pager went off. He was to call the Commander. There was a knock on the door and the guy who had walked him in told him his Commander was on the phone. Wiley barely tipped his head to those in the room; maybe those guys did also but hard to know. He moved out to the brighter stairway and down the steps.

As he descended he tried to decide what he had learned from those flies on the wall. Was Vallan a victim of reverse invisibility, having wandered into the wrong neighborhood for him? Not a bad bet. Molte was in trouble for stooging and so nervous he just assumed Vallan was his contact? Unless the Vermont cops knew something more about Vallan it was getting harder to connect him with drugs in the City.

"Detective Wiley? This is Tessie. There's been a change. The meeting with the Commissioner has been moved up. You need to get over here right away. Tell the desk sergeant to have someone rush you crosstown immediately. You hear?"

* * *

As soon as he was in the patrol car he paged Abell with the signal they had arranged. He worried that guy would stop for a bagel or something. So he called him on his cell. He was anxious now. It was unclear if he'd have any time to brief Haworth before the Commissioner showed.

"Abell? Get to the precinct right away. No stops, okay?"

"Coming Wiley. All set."

Wiley hoped he knew what Abell meant.

Getting crosstown, even with lights and an occasional *WUP, WUP*, took some time. His driver wanted to chat but Wiley waved him off as he tried to make a few notes and think this case through. Hopefully the Commissioner would be a little later than he just heard. If he was unable to tell Haworth what he had how would the presentation be managed? Christ!

They rounded the corner to the side street with the precinct and found it, as usual, parked and double-parked with patrol cars. At the station entrance there was a van from a local TV affiliate. That was unsettling. No obvious sign of the Commissioner's entourage.

His driver might take minutes to get through the congestion to the door so Wiley jumped out and walked rapidly to the building entrance. This all seemed to be happening too fast. What was he going to be asked to do at the meeting? Wiley told himself to calm down; let this business play out; just do only what he could do. But he was nervous. He turned to look at the scene on the street and take a breath. Halfway down the crowded street an unmarked kept flashing its headlights. He figured out it was Abell. He started back down the steps and out to him.

Tessie came out the front door and shouted to Wiley, stopping him in his tracks. He stood at the bottom of the steps. Abell figured it out. He got out of his vehicle and stood by his door, a minimal further delay to traffic. He shouted to Wiley. Wiley waved he understood and turned around to follow Tessie.

* * *

"Just sit here for a minute. The Commander sure hopes he can talk with you before the Commissioner arrives."

He wanted to call Idelia to tell her where he was and to be sure to watch the six o'clock news if he wasn't home. He didn't know if he had time. It wasn't a great feeling, at all. He was really tense. Wiley felt as though he was being pushed along, completely unsure what was going to happen or if he was going to be asked to say anything. With superiors he had had this feeling before. Subordinates usually were disrespected.

Wiley respected Haworth. Never really thought whether he liked him and assumed Haworth had no idea who he was. Today, about to speak with him and maybe have some involvement with the Commissioner, he felt conflicted. He guessed he had some anger for being put in this strange position. Actually, he decided his sense of anger was more from fear, maybe insecurity, than anything else. Superiors had most of the cards and could be real dicks.

His thoughts drifted to that Vermont Lieutenant who was after Vallan. What was his story? Vallan was his boss for years. Did he fear him or was there true anger? Or did he even hate Vallan? Would that impact on this case? Wiley was upset he still hadn't talked to Vallan's kid again. He really should have known more about this Vallan.

* * *

"James, Commissioner's group will be here any minute. Let's have a quick talk."

Haworth was all business and that was fine.

"Can you quickly tell me what you don't know?

That path surprised Wiley but he would try to answer it.

"Well, no one knows where this Captain Vallan is. Unless he's dead, which I doubt, my money is on him being out of the City by now. There's always a chance this Vallan has some connection with drugs and that's why he was in Harlem. That doesn't seem likely though, but this angle should be pursued further, especially with the State Police in Vermont.

"Frankly Commander, we don't know anything about the crime he's wanted for in Vermont. There was a homicide and they really want him. That's all they've told us. And, I guess, I, I mean we, need to know more about this Vallan's son but, so far, there isn't much. When I met with him he knew his father was on the run but I don't believe he knew why. I…"

"Have you checked the surveillance centers for signs of him at the terminals?"

"Yes. They had his info by early this morning and have reported nothing, including a back check when his sheet arrived."

"You've spoken to the perps and the narcs. Did this guy walk into an investigation?"

"More like the perps walked into him and thought he was part of the investigation."

Haworth seemed to understand. Tessie buzzed the office.

"Commissioner arriving Commander. I'll put them in the conference room."

"Okay Detective, let's go meet with them."

Wiley raised his hand slightly and Haworth nodded he could speak.

"One question. I haven't spent a whole lot of time on the phone with this Lieutenant Barry who's handling the investigation in Vermont. But I get a feeling he might really have it in for this guy, who was his boss for many years. Should any of that be brought up with the Commissioner?"

Haworth listened intently to him. His face showed a hint of a smirk. Who knew what superiors thought about how their troops felt about them…or if they cared? The Commander kept that pose for a few seconds and then motioned Wiley to follow him from the office.

* * *

Approaching the conference room Wiley still had no idea what he was supposed to do or say at the meeting. Almost at the door Haworth suddenly turned around and spoke to him.

"Detective what grade are you? You're not a sergeant are you?"

"No sir. Whatever the lowest detective grade is, that's me. Passed last exam four months ago."

Haworth flashed a look of uncertainty and then turned around and went inside.

* * *

MEETING WITH THE TOP BRASS/ NYPD Commissioner Arthur Ryan was standing beside a chair pulled back away from a conference table by an aide. He was on his cell and looked deeply involved in discussion. Besides the aide, the woman holding his chair, there were three others, all men. They were standing also. Two were in uniform. The tables in the room were set up to make a 'U'. Wiley followed Haworth into the room. The Commander pulled up a chair near one end of the 'U' and he pointed Wiley towards a chair and directed him to place it about a foot behind his on his right. Then Haworth walked over to the three standing together and they exchanged greetings and small talk. Detective Wiley stayed standing by his chair.

As soon as the Commissioner was off the phone he reached over to shake Haworth's hand and sat down. Tessie rushed into the room with a pad and pulled a chair to the table left of the Commander's seat. Everyone sat, so Wiley did also.

One of the uniformed officers looked at Wiley and spoke.

"Howard, who do you have with you?"

"Sam this is Detective James Wiley." Haworth's affected speech was not reserved for his subordinates. "He's been in charge of putting together whatever we can find about the man *Vermunt* is looking for. Detective, this is Commissioner Ryan, Manhattan Borough

Commander Inspector Sam Charles, Captain Skip Dawes of the Drug Task force, and Myron Smith of Inter-State Agencies Liaison. Janet Havier is one of Commissioner Ryan's assistants."

All offered a quick nod.

Inspector Charles spoke. Within seconds the Commissioner was bending away from the table and back on his phone.

"Myron, can you fill everyone in on why we're here today?"

"Sure Inspector. The Director of the Vermont State Police, a Colonel Blair, contacted my office after hours last evening to request assistance with the apprehension of a retired State Police Captain wanted for a homicide and believed to have entered our jurisdiction. I spoke with the Colonel and he told me the case is stirring up quite a fuss up there and finding this Captain as soon as possible is very important.

"Quite naturally, he is asking the NYPD to do everything we can to apprehend the fellow asap. The Colonel said our force had already determined he's in the City. Which is great for us. The State Police are requesting a phone meeting with the Commissioner to update our investigation."

Only Commander Haworth's head turned a little. All the officers knew about this request.

"Now that request is a bit unusual when agencies ask us to help find a perp. But it's Vermont. Who knows how they manage things up there? My sense is they are hoping this will get us to expedite our efforts. The call is set for three today."

"Thanks Myron." Sam Charles took over.

"So that's our situation folks. Little out of the ordinary, eh? The Commissioner has decided just to do a quick phone meeting with that Colonel. We think we can satisfy those authorities we're on it and move on. Can we get a brief review and update on this case? Howard?"

Janet Havier and Tessie were taking notes intently. Haworth sat motionless for a few seconds. Then he turned toward Wiley.

"Detective Wiley, would you tell us what we have?"

Wiley sensed this was coming. Haworth didn't know enough to handle it. Only he did. But how much did the brass need to know, or even want to know? Was anybody interested in whatever the story was with this Trooper?

Granted his last interaction with Lieutenant Barry did not go well. Was that the genesis for the Vermont cops to request the call? Was Barry angry because Wiley had gone after him about any possible drug connection? Or had Wiley actually gone a bit off the deep end by suggesting any of that so the Lieutenant gave up on him? And yet…that guy had something up his ass about Vallan.

He was conflicted about how detailed to be. Wiley moved his chair forward so he could speak, but Commander Charles spoke again.

"Detective, do we know where this fellow is right now?"

"No sir. We know early yesterday morning he had some form of contact with an adult son who resides on west 97th street. Probably was there very briefly. Then we have him ID'ed as being part of a probable drug related knifing that afternoon at St. Nicholas Park, off 133rd Street, around two or three o'clock."

Heads and eyes around the room bobbed and attention to Wiley and his words increased.

"This Captain was the head of a major crime investigating unit for that state so there are possibilities to consider about how his prints wound up on a knife stuck in a known dealer. My reading of what we know is there is a good chance the cop was wandering a city he knows very little about and happened to get mistaken for undercover and got into a fight."

Wiley had all their attention, even the Commissioner. He had assumed everyone knew all the details about the knife fight in Harlem.

"We don't know if he was injured in that fight. And we don't know where he is. If he's involved in drugs he may have some support down here and that's where he is. But my guess is that he knows no one but his son. My guess is if it were me, after yesterday, I'd have gotten out of the City by now."

"Anything other than prints on a knife detective." Captain Dawes asked?

"His sheet photo was ID'ed by one of the two knifing vics. That kid probably reliable but he did mistake this captain for his narc cont…, I mean undercover narcotics officer contact." Who knew how sensitive this Dawes might be?

"After the fight a uniformed on foot patrol checked the neighborhood for a vendor since remnants of a soft pretzel and a shattered bottle of papaya juice were at the scene. He found a guy who remembered selling that to a white guy. He took the vendor's license number and my partner, Detective Abell, was able to find the vendor this morning. That vendor confirmed our photo is the guy who bought the pretzel and juice."

All of a sudden the energy in the room changed. From the Commissioner on down everyone's face brightened. Wiley thought it was as if he had just told them a cop had split an atom for the first time. Inspector Charles spoke.

"That's wonderful. Just good, dogged basic police work, eh?"

"Janet, be sure to get the name of that foot patrolman. We want to recognize his work. Great; just great." This would be the memorable moment from the meeting for the Commissioner.

Inspector Charles spoke again. "So we have to figure out if he's still in the City. Hopefully before three. Detective?"

"Nothing from hospital ERs that fit him. No reports from the central screening areas of anyone fitting his description at the terminals from late last night on. I've asked them to go back a little earlier and look again when they have dead time tonight. Too busy now they said. Nothing very remarkable looking about this man. Won't be easy to find on a monitor."

"Well what should we tell them Detective?"

"I've spent a lot of time thinking about all this sir. Vermont State Police Lieutenant I spoke with off and on yesterday was hard to figure out. Told me this Captain Vallan was his immediate superior for many years before he retired some months ago. Seemed to get real mad when any possible drug angle came up. And didn't seem to want to share any details about the homicide in Vermont. At first he talked like this Captain is maybe not his favorite guy and case is a slam dunk. Later he got mad. Practically ordered me to find this man quick…and alive. Like he didn't trust us to do that."

Wiley paused. He wasn't sure if he should continue. No one looked bored or especially impatient.

"If drugs are a part of this story or there's other stuff going on I think that trooper doesn't want to talk about it. I don't know how that might reflect on what his Colonel wants. Or maybe that lieutenant is only focused on seeing his old boss fry. I don't know."

There. He said it.

"I'm set to talk to the guy's son again as soon as we're done here. I can call Commander Haworth when I'm finished. I just have a feeling that Lieutenant's interest is more complicated than only chasing a perp."

"Well Detective. Lots of cops would love to be after their boss for something like a Murder One." The Commissioner and all the others smiled at Inspector Charles' wry comment. "But I'm not sure NYPD needs to know more about this case unless there is a drug connection; then for sure.

"Get your partner to go up to the George Washington Bridge Bus Terminal and make sure they scan their screens again before three. Okay? My guess is, probably like you Detective, that if drugs aren't part of the story this senior cop, or trooper…whatever they're called, has high-tailed it out of this City by now. Probably realized not a good place for him." Then the Inspector moved his head just slightly, as in reflection.

"But, you know, as I think about it, you're right. It sounds like there could be a strange story there somewhere doesn't it? Myron, can you or your folks find out some more about what happened in Vermont and who this guy is? Not our typical perp. We need it quick.

"Then there's news media outside, Commissioner. What should we tell them?"

"Sam tell them we are tracking a retired trooper wanted for a homicide in his home state of Vermont involved in a possible drug related altercation in Harlem. The NYPD intends to offer the Vermont State Police as much assistance in this case as possible. Law enforcement throughout the City are on alert and will continue to look for this man until he is apprehended or found to be out of our jurisdiction…Something like that.

"Detective, I'd like you and your partner to be downtown at One Police Plaza at two-thirty."

The meeting broke up. Everyone trooped out of the precinct and re-formed on the front steps where Inspector Charles gave a brief statement to assembled television and print media. The Commissioner stood next to the Inspector and said nothing. Detective James Wiley was advised to stand in the second row, on the periphery of the group.

After the statement reporters asked for more information about the retired trooper from Vermont and, most pointedly, the altercation in Harlem. Inspector Charles responded only that a search and investigation were continuing. Then the Commissioner and the others walked away and the small crowd of reporters and onlookers also dispersed, clearly disappointed.

From the steps Wiley gazed up and down the street seeking out Abell and the black unmarked. Abell was far up the street leaning on the side of the car. Wiley had a nod from Haworth to resume his work and headed off for Abell's location.

* * *

FROM THE PAST?/   As Wiley reached the car an older man in a black top coat, carrying two coffee containers, appeared to be trying to catch up to him. At the car both Wiley and Abell turned and waited for him.

"Hey guys. Hold on a minute, would ya? Nichols, Jack Nichols. Detective Lieutenant, Tenth Precinct, retired. I think I know the guy you're looking for." Wiley was impressed this cop quickly had figured who was working the case.

All three climbed into the car. Abell and Wiley accepted the coffees he brought. Only Abell took one of the cheap cellophane wrapped powdered donuts Nichols pulled from his pocket. Wiley had a tremendous amount to get done and a short time to do it. He wasn't hungry for donuts but he was getting captivated by the story of this man he was looking for and knew nothing about. Something more than a slam dunk seemed to him to be going on. Now, what was this?

"Detective, we're in a real time crunch. What can we do for you?"

At that Nichols sat back and offered a soft sigh.

"Well I guess that's it Detectives. I once knew this cop, Vallan. Worked with him briefly on a case in the City, proly pushing thirty years ago. We stayed in touch a little after. Kinda felt I should come down here and see what's really goin' on, you know. Thing is he and I kept in touch from time to time and the guy, who was super green about the City when he was here, climbed the ladder up there in that Vermont. Had some big cases and had rep as a sharp detective; did what we do."

Wiley was interested and by now suspected this Vallan being a killer was a big deal in Vermont and for the State Police.

"So you're surprised to hear he's being sought for murder, and maybe more?"

"Sure am. Proly pretty straight guy but, you know, his boy wrote a book a bunch of years ago about that crazy case that Vallan came down here for."

"Yeah? So?"

"Well, that's it. After all these years hits me again. Vallan's actions at the end weren't clear to us cops. Asshole alone in a room with Vallan died. Not sure how. Nobody cared cause jerk was the worst. Wonder if anything like that played into what happened up there?"

* * *

WHAT A DIFFERENCE A DAY MAKES/   Abell dropped Wiley off at 97th Street and headed for the George Washington Bridge Bus Terminal. Running into Jack Nichols before he returned to see Vallan's kid was incredible luck, he thought. No matter exactly what Nichols was talking about he had a little more to go on with the kid. Wiley assumed the kid had found out a whole lot more about the story and circumstances of his father's situation by now. Deniability wouldn't fly this time. He doubted Henry Vallan knew where his father was but Wiley suspected the kid's attitude would now reflect his worry and fear about his father's situation. He would talk more.

A surprisingly large part of Wiley's interest remained focused on who this Vallan really was and just what he did to wind up in such trouble. Wiley didn't have a lot of time to interrogate his kid before Abell would pick him up to go to central headquarters.

Doreen Vallan worked part time as a copywriter for an art magazine and was working when Wiley arrived. So Henry, who worked at home anyway, was watching the baby.

The men spoke, in bland tones, for only seconds on the intercom. The door was open for the Detective as he came down the hallway off the elevator. Henry appeared at the door as Wiley did. There was a wariness in each of their eyes when they connected. It was also obvious Henry no longer looked clueless and Wiley was not angry. Henry indicated the baby was asleep which helped to reinforce the more mellow interaction this time.

"A lot has happened in the last day Mr. Vallan, hasn't it?" He wanted to get a gauge on how Henry was going to respond this time.

Henry tried to keep his expression flat but his tone and words were unmistakable.

"Detective Wiley, this is hell… I can, and will tell you what I know, but I don't understand or believe most of it. Doesn't make sense. Not my father. No way." Henry looked away, overcome by the strength of his words. "The guy who raised me and my sister was a fucking Eagle Scout, Detective. He ran a superior police agency, known throughout the region for incredible success with all kinds of serious criminal cases. My mother is a doctor and also is well known in our community. She encouraged Dad to run hospital security as a low key retirement job just months ago.

"The papers say my mom and father arrived at the hospital two days ago and were told of an emergency on a ward. That's when they walked into a room and a patient was dead, supposedly murdered with a knife. For some reason, my sister told me, my mom was shocked and indicated the knife in the patient was my dad's. But I told you yesterday Detective, she must have been startled and was frightened or confused because my dad never owned a knife like that.

"He ran away after that and I know that doesn't look good. You see, lots of people in the hospital apparently knew the man who died was very publicly attacking my dad for the last few weeks or so. I…I don't know what that was about. I…I."

Henry's head tipped down. He was out of energy. He understood why so much looked bad for his father. After a pause they talked about a few things. Henry reviewed the circumstances of his father's unannounced visit the day before. He told Wiley his dad was not himself and appeared very distracted. The way Henry described those moments with his father came out as quite an understatement. The setting and conscious effort to speak softly lent an aura of loss and sadness to the meeting. At some point Wiley changed the discussion.

"Mr. Vallan, I know you write books. Sorry I don't know anything about what you write. I just heard something about a book from before that's got your father in it. Is that right?"

Henry was surprised to hear this come up.

"Yes, my first book loosely followed an early case that involved both of my parents. The book took place in 1976. My more recent book used my parents again, but it was almost completely made up by me."

"I guess a question has come up and I admit, as I say, I haven't read your book. The question is if your father, Captain Vallan, in that first book, committed a murder on that case?"

Henry's head shot up and his back practically arched. Any accommodation he had felt for this cop appeared to be gone in an instant.

"What? What are you saying? Detective you'll just have to read the book. It's a big and complicated world Detective. Not everything always works out the way you want. You know that. You read the book; see what you think."

Even Henry was surprised how angry he was and how firmly he spoke; his voice rising beyond the level he wanted with the baby sleeping nearby.

Wiley extended both of his hands, palms vertically to slow Henry down. Wiley's face and body demonstrated he was backing off; did not intend to pursue this further.

"Okay, Okay. Gees man, I was advised to check that out." And then he redeemed himself to a degree with Henry. "I know books have to make stories, even true stories, be dramatic and sometimes things can appear to be ambiguous. I get that. Didn't accuse the Captain of anything."

Henry liked the way he said that. He relaxed and lowered his guard a little. But he was very unhappy; probably more unsettled now with the thought his own books might be considered any further evidence suggesting or linking his father to this Dr. Becker's murder.

It was clear to Wiley he better leave that topic or he might lose Henry Vallan's cooperation.

"Someone work in law enforcement all those years, like your dad, bound to have some enemies, huh?" Henry nodded. His face had a forlorn expression. His attention was fading. Time for Wiley to wrap it up already? He couldn't resist looking for a little more about the case and also that Vermont Lieutenant first.

"You seem to know a lot more now about your father's predicament and the homicide in Vermont from yesterday. NYPD really doesn't have much, at all, on any of that. Hope to find out more later today. This Lieutenant Barry and you; you must know each other if he worked with your dad for lots of years. What have you and the Lieutenant talked about since I saw you yesterday?"

For some time, then and after the interview, Wiley wrestled with trying to interpret Henry Vallan's reaction to that simple comment. There was something subtle, but definite, in his physical appearance that changed. And the timbre of his voice; its flatness, was noticeable.

"No, I haven't spoken with Shawn Barry."

"Really. I didn't know that Lieutenant was expecting NYPD to do anything more than find your father. You do know him, don't you?"

Slowly and blandly; barely looking Wiley's way.

"Yeah, I knew him pretty well when I was living in Vermont. I guess I wouldn't say Shawn Barry's considered any friend of our family much anymore for a while. I think I would have been surprised if Shawn had called me."

Boy! Then Wiley was surprised. The man that Trooper considered a slam dunk to be the murderer he was looking for had been in Manhattan where the guy's son lived. You can't just assume big parts of an investigation. Why didn't he contact this guy? Wiley thought that was really strange.

More and more he believed there were clear signs this Lieutenant and his only apparent suspect had their own complicated story. Even if that was a fact and maybe a problem for the Vermont State Police investigation, so what? It was none of his business. Wiley wasn't being asked to solve anything more than find that guy if he's in the City. If drugs really were any part of the mess that guy was in then NYPD might have to get more involved. Unlikely, he thought.

He decided there was no purpose in bringing up the drugs story to Henry. Stuff was in the news and anyone who could put two and two together could figure the possibilities. Wiley had decided that business in Harlem was an incredibly crazy fluke. Unless there was something about drugs on the three p.m. call from the Vermont police the mess in New York would probably die with the dead man in Vermont. Once this Vallan was caught Murder One would push whatever happened in Harlem to a forgotten afterthought.

****

SATURDAY IN VERMONT III

RETHINKING THAT COMPLAINT/   When Shawn Barry
returned to the Waterbury Barracks after his meeting with the ME
he sat at his desk and thought for a while. He was still trying to
make sense of the potential implications of what he had learned
an hour before. The place was quiet. None of the few troopers in
the building on a Saturday asked him anything about Ted and that
pleased him. After mulling over the new development for a short
time he determined it was best not to wait for the meeting with his
superiors. He better speak with the Captain and apprise him of the
new development right away.

Captain Steffens was startled by what he heard. He told Shawn he
would arrange a phone conference with the Colonel to talk about
the new findings and any range of impacts on the pending phone
call to the NYPD Commissioner. The upshot of their immediate
discussion was to consider a delay in the time of the call. The
Colonel and Captain came in around noon so the three of them
could meet.

The Colonel's wife sent him to the meeting with a basket of
sandwiches, a thermos of ice tea, and some cookies to be shared by
all of them. Being part of that group Shawn Barry tried to feel like
he had the best job in the world working on the force. But he just

couldn't relax, actually suffering acute anxiety amid the growing uncertainty provoked by unsettling information developing in this case.

About that same time the NYPD brass was asking Myron Smith to find out more about the case in Vermont. At first no one in authority at the VSP would take his calls. When Captain Steffens finally contacted him all he would say was the VSP was considering delaying the call to the Commissioner. Smith pointedly expressed more than disappointment to the Captain. Receiving that information after working through the night and all day to arrange the high level call with a bunch of people, including the Commissioner, made him angry. In truth, no one was happy. But If the call had gone through it would have raised more questions than it answered.

About one thirty Wiley got a page. It told him the phone call with the Director of the Vermont State Police had been cancelled by the authorities in Vermont and would take place 'sometime later in the week.' Wiley and Abell had to smile as they joked about the overtime they would punch for this Saturday work. Somehow the fire went out real quickly. Only Wiley wondered what happened.

* * *

The consensus at the meeting of high level VSP officers to cancel the call reflected the clear reaction of Barry's superiors to the most recent information, from Friday and today, presented by the Lieutenant. Putting pressure on the NYPD to encourage the safe apprehension of Captain Vallan was no longer such a fraternal goal. The VSP was not prepared to share information of any potential illicit drug component of this homicide with the NYPD for the foreseeable future. And so, unspoken, but obviously considered, a fatal conclusion to Captain Ted Vallan's adventure in New York City might be an acceptable or even preferred solution at this point. The call was to be put off and might never happen.

Without informing his superiors Shawn Barry did make one call after the meeting. That was when he had contacted Trooper Dark and directed him to drive to Kathy Conover's home to question her about the latest cause of Harvey Becker's death.

****

SATURDAY AT THE ALBANY, NEW YORK PUBLIC LIBRARY

WHAT YOU DIDN'T KNOW AND DON'T KNOW CAN HURT YOU/   The Albany library looked large enough that Ted hoped it would have the Burlington paper and it did. He was excited when he saw the familiar masthead as he flipped through some Northeast newspapers on a table off in a corner in the general reading room. Disappointment followed when he saw yesterday's date. Ted placed it flat on a nearby table so it was less likely anyone else would see he was looking at the Burlington paper.

Indeed, the bottom of the front page chronicled the occurrence of an apparent homicide in the hospital and the possibly related apparent disappearance of the new hospital Chief of Security, recently retired Vermont State Police Captain Ted Vallan. That was it. Old news to Ted. It was all only very preliminary information.

Finding Saturday's paper somewhere in Albany was probably possible but not for Ted. Maggie had given him the idea of using a computer in the library; another potential method to search for information about the investigation. He walked to the reference section, which was in its own fairly large room. Two rows of four carrels were set in the center. Only two were occupied. A guy at one already had his head down resting on his folded arms. A bum he guessed. Ted sat at the one he thought was farthest from the likely flow of traffic, but they all were exposed, placed as they were in the center of the room.

Ted wasn't sure how to start up his machine. Two laminated pages of directions, admonitions, and cautions were fixed to the inside of the carrel. Just putting his fingers to the keyboard alarmed him. He was shaky and unduly nervous. Was it fear of the machine and its recent history with him? Or a slowly growing realization of how connected these machines were with the world? Either way he wasn't even sure how to get online. There were a bunch of steps to go through to get there. Rereading both of the laminated pages was not helping. He sensed his patience and tolerance for any complexity was nil. He couldn't even get on the damn computer!

For almost ten hours he had focused on a library as a key for getting more information about the status of the investigation. Was that too much to hope for? His despair returned and began to roil him. He fought off tears and his desperation. Asking anyone for help was more than a double edge sword to Ted. He knew that. Looking around he could tell if he sought help it would have to be from either the elderly woman at the other occupied computer or the librarian at the reference desk across the room. Didn't look like anyone was going to wake the bum up; certainly not Ted.

* * *

ASSISTANCE?/   He thought about leaving. But to do what? Where would he go? One of the laminated cards, in bold type, encouraged asking at the reference desk for further assistance. It was his last hope.

Ted left his jacket on the back of the chair at the carrel he hoped to use and walked quietly to the desk. The woman at the desk looked up from her chair about five feet from the oak counter and smiled. Maybe only a man in Ted's straits would have reacted with such a range of emotions to this early middle-aged woman's friendly face and her welcoming smile.

Maggie's directness had alerted him to a slice of the world he previously barely knew existed. Was this woman alone also and looking for companionship? No matter what happened his wedding ring was no longer on his hand. Or was this only Ted's projected fantasy as he longed for the fulfilment of the fleeting images of rest, food, a shower, clean clothes, and companionship when Maggie teased him?

This woman was different, though. She popped up out of her chair with energy, displaying a well-groomed attractive woman with a pleasant figure. She didn't look lonely, but she also was not wearing a wedding band. She appeared to have sensed Ted might need more than a quick response to any question since she had noticed him sitting for a long time before one of the basic screens needed to complete access. Rather than speak from a distance from her desk she came to the counter.

"How can I help you?" Just above a whisper, the way librarians speak.

"Well I'm sorry to say I'm stuck and can't seem to get through all the screens needed to be online. I…I don't have a lot of computer experience. Especially on your machine here…" He spoke slowly and was guarded.

She burst right in, in a friendly and lively way. "Well they're not my machines as you call them. They can be a real pain. And often real slow, you know. But you just have to learn the routine to get where you want to go. Once you're on the internet it's usually okay. It's dead here right now so let's go over to your place and see what we've got."

She flashed a big smile when she said 'your place.' Ted was way too literal lately to let that pass. Surely she was joking but why would she say that to him?

She grabbed a piece of paper and a pencil, exited the desk area, and led Ted back to his carrel. She sat and he stood behind her. He hoped he didn't smell bad.

"Well, there, see? You're hung up right here." She pointed to a spot on the screen with her finger and periodically typed. Two more steps and an internet explorer home page for the library appeared. "There you are. Then, to do a search you use this bar here; type in your query or website, press enter and you should be on your way."

She made it look easy but Ted knew even on a good day it took time for him to adjust to a different machine. His face must have still evidenced some confusion. She spoke.

"You know…what's your name?"

"Steve… Steve Hart." He gave his middle name and Liza's maiden name."

"Steve's all I need, Steve. I can see you've got heart." She gave him a big grin. Innocent? Who could tell? She made him nervous. "But gotta say you look more like Droopy Drawers. No offense.

"So here, I'll write down the easy way to do the steps, okay? You may need to go to the bathroom and you won't want to leave the machine on when you're away, right? Listen, give it a go and see how you do. If you need more help I'll be at the desk till three, when we close today. My name is Roz, for Roslyn." She smiled and walked back to the desk.

She left the screen up he needed to do searches and there was no way he planned to start over to see if he could do it by himself; at least for now. He twisted the monitor so it faced more into one of the sides of the carrel to make it less visible to any passers-by. First he typed the name of the newspaper in. The Fee Press had no online news presence. What about the Boston Globe? He searched headlines and regional news but there was nothing.

Ted knew every computer had, essentially, its own finger print. And that you could try to erase where you looked but experts usually could track previously opened web pages. He started to get anxious and more upset again. Was that really true? How could he type in his own name or Becker's name, or whoever, and not worry it could backfire? If he went to a website could he be tracked from just being there? He doubted that but he did not know.

A day before he determined he had to solve his own case. Well not without access to information he wasn't. Arrested and out on bail, maybe. But they wouldn't have let him out even if he had walked to the Burlington PD and asked his friend, Wendell Partin, the Chief of Police to cuff him. No way on the inside for Ted to influence the investigation.

All the energy he put into getting into this chair in the library had brought him nothing. Even though it was a new century computers still didn't tell you everything. Mental exhaustion now competed with his physical exhaustion. He knew he was finished.

Well almost. There was still another use for the computer that had bumped around his brain today. It was only a relatively short leap from the idea of using a computer in the library for information to actually attempt to use it to communicate with others. That idea was instantly as appealing as it was frightening to him. What a risk and yet what a potential opportunity. He thought he should discard the thought because of the risk to himself and possibly others.

But did he really have any other options anymore?

Even if whoever he wrote told or showed the police what he wrote at least someone would know about his claim of innocence and the information he was uncovering in the hospital. If he wrote it all out, say to Henry, and told him it was okay if the police know about it Henry should be okay. He thought so but wasn't positive. The phone would be better but Henry's was unlisted and his business card, which Ted had saved when he tossed his wallet, only had his email address. Unknown to Ted, the card and a few contents he saved from the wallet were slowly becoming unreadable under the foot-bed of his left shoe, from the effects of moisture generated by his sweaty feet that had not been out of his shoes in more than forty-eight hours.

Ted assumed his private email was being legally tracked by now. Won't whoever does that be surprised if they've already looked, he thought. The account, set up about four years before, hadn't been looked at by Ted in at least three years. He had used his VSP account when he needed email and even that not too much. A court order was, indeed, in the works…for Ted's prior VSP account and new hospital account which he had barely used. The private account Liza set-up for Ted years before was not widely known and no one thought to ask Liza about Ted's email options yet. The request for that order was sent to a judge Tuesday morning.

He felt finished and physically ill. He was so tired. He wondered if he was making sense any longer. He wasn't sure if he could write something that would be understandable to anyone. He thought he had to try. He knew Liza's email but what would writing her do? He wanted to see her and talk with her. Messages wouldn't allow him to know, for sure, what her involvement in all this was. Without meeting face to face he would never know. He thought he had to try something, now.

His pulse picked up. He could feel it. He should do something. Ted felt so hopeless, it was difficult for him to think he was doing anything more than grasping at final straws before the logical end of this part of his nightmare. He felt for his shoe and realized he couldn't take it off and pull the footpad out right there. He'd have to shut the computer down first and go to the men's room. The thought of starting it again was frustrating. But he shut it down.

* * *

FOR WHOM THE INTERNET TROLLS/   In a stall in the men's room his sock was aromatic when he removed his shoe for the first time in days. He quickly pulled out the liner footpad from the shoe. The few things under it were damp. Henry's card was fading but his email address was legible. At his office desk, before he ran, Ted took the notes he had been making concerning his growing suspicions about possible diversion and carefully folded both pages beneath the footpad. The moisture from his sweat and the pressure from his weight on the blue ink on the folded hospital progress note paper left in his shoe for days must have had a dramatic effect. His heart sank when he unfolded the two pages of notes he had struggled to preserve through all this and saw large amounts of his ink handwriting were terribly smudged or gone. Could they ever be of any use now? He kept everything out and returned to the carrel hoping they would dry on the table.

Sure enough Ted was unable to get back online. He was angry and frustrated beyond a reasonable level. He tried to calm down but any, even minor, glitch in his life was now dramatically magnified in his brittle state. He was forced to return to Roz for assistance.

"Sure. Sure Steve. I'll give you a hand. If you're not used to it getting on can be tricky." They walked over to the carrel together. "You know this place is so quiet today I think you just want some conversation. I know I do." That big friendly smile again.

"So let's see. Steve why don't you sit and start it and I'll stand behind you and watch what you do?"

So Ted did that. He started with the key board then realized the ruined notes were unfolded on the desk next to the monitor. Useless to anybody, even him, but he stopped typing and folded them and placed the pages under his thigh on the seat. Another sign to him of the self-contagion of his sloppiness.

He actually got online without Roz needing to correct anything. She smiled and gave him a quick rub on his back which excited him and, reflexedly, he momentarily stiffened there.

"So Steve, you asked me all the way over here and you knew what to do all the time. Hmmm. Well glad to *help* you. You go back to your work and let me know if you need me again, okay?" Another friendly smile and almost a wink as she turned her back and walked to the reference desk. The room was practically empty, Ted had to admit. He watched her walk away.

* * *

Ted's private email was set-up by Liza almost four years before with a local outfit, Champlain Online, since bought out by a New England company who retained the original addresses. He remembered his was tvallanvsp@champ.com. Liza had picked his password and he had no reason to disagree with it. It was gOOdguy. Easy to remember.

Without much difficulty he found the homepage he needed and typed in his address and then password. How and what he was going to write were what occupied his mind. He was very uncertain of the wisdom of doing this. Whether or not his account still existed was also a concern. But it did.

Eighty-three *new messages* were listed next to a pictured envelope. Not bad for about four years he thought. His plan was to start writing to Henry right away and be done with it before he changed his mind. But curious, he clicked the new mail icon and was instantly diverted by the striking titles for a number of the entries on the list it contained. He clicked the most recent of the suspect titles and within a minute was absolutely astonished by what he read.

The three most recent were listed as sent by *hbecker*, all within the last three weeks. Becker! The most recent was just a week before. The title said 'Get out of this hospital now!' He clicked open.

You don't belong in this hospital. Well maybe as a janitor, or what they now call an environmental engineer. You have no skills. You are so inferior to everyone. I will expose your idleness and the way you waste your time and the hospital's money. Resign quickly or face a barrage of terrible public exposure of the bullying you do.

Your presence at the medical staff meeting was inappropriate and a poor attempt at intimidation of the doctors who rightfully should run this institution.

This is your final warning!

Becker

Sounded like Becker. 'That bastard' he thought. 'How did he get my home email?' Ted clicked to keep the email as new and read the next two. Both pretty much the same content. He was amazed at the lengths that asshole was going to needle and threaten him. Everything about that Becker, including this sequence of emails, suggested he was getting more and more angry and threatening. Ted assumed Becker truly did have something to hide the way he went after him.

It was natural for Ted to consider a link between Becker's taunts and his efforts to get deeper into his investigation of diversion since his progress had picked up over the last month. But he had to admit there could be any number of other factors at play with a jerk, and possibly crazy guy, like him. Becker seemed a man who really had difficulty controlling himself once he got warmed up. Could some of the doctors really be so angry about any crazy ideas of computers taking over the way they had to do their work they would threaten him, a messenger at best? Made much less sense to Ted than his first thoughts about possible diversion.

Ted reminded himself his goal was to quickly write to Henry. He was never certain if Roz or someone might tell him he couldn't continue to use the computer practically all day. There still was one empty carrel so he hoped he was okay for a while more but he should move on. Yet Becker's emails infuriated him.

He saved those emails, *keep as new*, and prepared to figure out how to write a message. Then he noticed the others with ominous titles, the most recent from a year before, all said: *DO NOT REPLY* where the sender's name was supposed to be. What was with that? He didn't have time to open all of them; there were too many.

Ted decided he would quickly look at three of those, one from each of the last years. He read quickly. He was devastated. They were brief and his eyes picked out something from each one which instantly led him to a terrible and sickening conclusion. His absolute worst fears appeared to be confirmed by the emails. He began with the newest and went down the list to pick out two more.

…She can't stand you. You're just a dumb cop. You don't even know how to try to figure out who I am. Get out of her life!…

…You must let her go. You are so inferior to her. She can no longer ever be happy with you. Let her leave!…

…She can't stand you. We cried together when we heard La Boheme…

Ted always felt affected by the unbelievable beauty of the music from that opera also. Tears formed now and one actually dropped onto the keyboard. His sense of sadness, abandonment, and jealousy were overwhelming. Suddenly, in only two days, he was no longer equipped to handle such an emotional shock. He knew there was no longer any reason to keep struggling to push away his thoughts about Liza's love. His suspicions were true.

What was the sense anymore in trying to do anything now that might save him? What for?

He sat and stared at the screen for a long while. In time his despair lessened slightly. As he focused on the screen he thought he saw something that began to attract his attention. These letters and Becker's letters contained some similar phrasing and actually the exact same phrase in one of them: 'You are so inferior…' What could that mean?

Becker's public threats were likely made to intimidate Ted to try to get him to leave the hospital for some reason. Possibly to stop his investigation of probable drug diversion? If the same person wrote both the recent *hbecker* emails and the *DO NOT REPLY* emails, which had been going on for years, then Becker's story might be much more complicated. And maybe, just maybe, Liza's apparent defection wasn't so clear either. He doubted that but he liked to hope so.

In his present state of difficulty concentrating the number of possibilities this raised seemed endless and therefore discouraging to consider. But the truth was there weren't that many different possible explanations. Fortunately Ted concluded he should still write to Henry and do it then. He seemed to understand he might be able to dissect through this new information better at another time; hopefully soon. He made sure he saved the emails he had just opened.

* * *

Henry,

I am okay. I'm far away from NYC now. I don't want to get you in any trouble. I expect this email account is monitored by the force. Maybe they can figure out where I'm writing from. I'm not sure. I will be leaving here very soon.

I had nothing to do with the death of Dr. Becker. I don't know why I was set up but I have some ideas. I was trying to get some experience about how computers work in the hospital. I believe I happened on something and was working on what looked like a medication diversion scheme. My investigation hadn't gotten too far when this happened. I don't know who might be involved. I never told anyone about it yet. I have two pages of notes but they are no longer in good shape and I do not know what to do with them.

Until today I had not looked at this email account Mom set up for me in many years. There are unsigned emails starting three years ago that are attacks on me and our marriage. I never knew they were there. A month ago I think similarly written but threatening emails started to come but were signed by the man who was killed.

Maybe you could hire a detective agency to find out who sent them if that's possible? After I finish this email I will forward several of those emails to you from years ago up until recently.

I know everyone must be upset but I'm okay. I don't have any good information about the homicide investigation and I'm afraid to write or contact anyone else even the Colonel.

Henry if this email brings the police to your door then you must tell them everything you know and give them this information. Please! Do not get yourself in trouble! I am okay for now. This is a nightmare but if I can figure out a way to influence the investigation maybe I can prove my innocence. I will check this account from time to time or get a new one.

Try not to worry too much

Dad

Writing the letter just about finished him. The magnitude of his fatigue left him feeling that despite his great upset over the sad new revelations and his frayed nerves he would be able to sleep if he only had an opportunity. His brain felt useless and his body was caving in. Sleep, hunger, getting clean. After the effort of writing the letter he felt he deserved something. It was like his last dying gasp and he was pleased he was able to complete it.

Ted kept reading it over, staring at the screen. He wanted to add more but he just couldn't do it. The energy required to do what he had done finished him. His success at that took away everything. He remembered how Liza once told him an observation of hers about desperately ill patients arriving at the Emergency Department. They struggled mightily to stay alive to get to the hospital. Somehow once they arrived and presumably assumed they would now be safe, and saved, some seemed to relax and that was when their bodies stopped fighting and they succumbed to their emergency.

He thought about the knifing in the City. No. What would he say? Ted was wiped out. He pushed the send button. It was done.

* * *

"Say Roz, I'm sorry. It looks like there's a way to print some things off the computer. I guess that costs some money. Can you help me with how I do that?"

How much was critical to Ted. When he was done at the library he planned to walk back to the bus terminal (if his feet would carry him there) and hope he could afford a ticket to somewhere; possibly Boston. A bigger city. But maybe a chance to sleep on the bus was what he was really thinking about.

An hour before he was almost ready to turn himself in. He knew he kept running partly because it had become rote for him by now; what he was supposed to do according to his original idea of thinking he might find a way to work his own case. But now he wanted to stay out at least until he, hopefully, would hear something from Henry.

Roz was out of her chair walking to him as he arrived at the counter and began to speak. She just looked nice. For a brief moment Ted thought he sensed a vulnerable look similar to what he had observed in Maggie also. He instructed himself to ignore any thought of it.

"Well Steve, I guess everything costs something, huh?" That friendly smile again. "Sure, it's a quarter a page. Pretty steep, huh?"

That sure was. He intended to copy some of the letters from Becker and DO NOT REPLY. Not at that price. He sensed Roz picked up on his reaction. That bothered him.

"You might want to keep your pages down with prices like that. Most people go that way when they hear how much it is."

She was sweet to try to lessen his worry about the impact of his reaction. Ted recognized he was barely able to think now but managed to decide copying one letter from each would have to do. Even little decisions were becoming challenges.

With a weak smile, he said, "Only two pages. That's all."

"If you've got quarters you're all set. Otherwise there's a machine but if you give me a buck I'll give you some quarters."

"Got the two quarters I need." He was careful not to pull his ring out with the change he produced from his pocket as he said that.

She pushed open the swinging gate keeping the 'Library Personnel Only' area from the public and led him back to the carrels.

"If it's two successive pages you can just print them. If each page is from a different spot the only way I know how to do it is to print one at a time. Takes a little longer with the back and forth of paying for each, one at a time. You know."

Ted indicated he would have to do one at a time. Roz appeared to make every effort to preserve the privacy of the page Ted teed up first. She stood away and cued him about what to do for each step.

After pressing *PRINT* he minimized the window and they walked a few steps just around a corner to the printer. Quarter in, the printer woke up and *hbecker's* letter was printed.

"I'll be good now. Thanks an awfully lot, Roz. Sorry I've been such a bother all day. I just have to forward something then I'll be done. I'll be leaving soon."

"Well sure you'll be leaving soon. It's almost three. You and I have been here most of the day and now it's almost time to close this mausoleum up for the day; the week, actually. We'll both be leaving."

There was that genuine, friendly smile. Ted was in no shape to be doing anything with anybody. Trouble every time before; sure to be trouble again. He was terribly lonely. She seemed so friendly.

"Roz you've been so helpful all day I feel I should get you a cup of coffee or something."

Instantly he regretted it. What if he wouldn't have enough money left to get far on a bus? What could he talk about with anyone? Saying anything he could dream up about himself was sure to be a mess.

Roz paused. She was thinking.

"Steve why don't you finish up what you need to do. I have to begin tidying up the reference area for closing. I live only two blocks away. We can stop at the café down the street or maybe get something there to bring back to have the coffee at my place. You look like you need some rest."

'Oh Shit.'

****

FOOTNOTE — * * * **HARRIET SUMMERS**

ANOTHER LONELY WOMAN?/   A year before Captain Ted Vallan retired Harriet Summers celebrated her fortieth birthday. It was a sad event for her. Not unattractive, she understood style and dressed nicely. But Harriet was terminally awkward and anxious around men; any man. Even after a drink or two she remained very uncomfortable just being touched. Her involuntary recoil could not be breeched. By now it didn't seem anyone was going to come around any longer. She hoped she was adapting to her solitary life. It was far from hopes and dreams now long in the past.

She first encountered the Doctor at an office visit for tingling in her right hand. He struck her as an odd man but she appreciated the time he took with her and when he held her hand to examine her she guessed the setting helped to allay her discomfort at being touched. He spent a long time reviewing the history of her complaint and appeared quite interested in what logically seemed the work related origin of the problem. He asked her for many details.

In a matter of fact way Harriet explained her role as a pharmacy technician in the hospital pharmacy. She routinely did several tasks but he, correctly, keyed on her unique method for pill counting as the likely culprit for her early carpal tunnel syndrome.

Harriet had devised a way of using a simple tongue depressor to flick pills she was counting and then distributing into different containers. She always used her dominant, right, hand. The maneuver required quick repetitive thrusts of her wrist. She counted a lot of pills in her job, she explained. In fact, Harriet had worked in the inpatient pharmacy for just over ten years and was considered and was, a trustworthy mainstay of the department.

He prescribed a splint for her right wrist and forearm and advised her to alter her pill counting and distributing method. He walked her out of the exam room and at the desk to check-out insisted she return for follow-up in ten days, a notably short time to assess any progress with her symptoms. Harriet didn't question his interest in her problem or his interest in chatting with her during subsequent long-lasting visits over the following two months.

Harriet became comfortable with her frequent office visits with him. She enjoyed his company and the dramatic intensity of his lengthy comments about most anything. To her, at least, he offered a self-deprecating twist to his use of the many fancy words contained in his endless recitations. He laughed when she dared comment on his wordy replies, calling himself 'loquacious', which he said was good.

The hand paresthesias essentially resolved but Harriet feared there would be no reason for continuing to schedule visits if she told him. So she didn't. They each joked that even though the problem was no longer a worry they should stay close in touch until everything was perfect again. The setting and the man didn't frighten Harriet. He never mentioned it but she knew he was divorced. Any level of expectation or anticipation had been so dulled by her many years of lack of virtually any relationship with a man she was slow to accept his interest in her beyond being a patient. He was at least two decades older and that also seemed to help relax her during the visits.

How he knew Harriet was interested in old Americana was never clear to her. But his insistence he shared a similar attraction excited her. When she mentioned the collection at the Sheldon Museum in

Middlebury he immediately suggested they arrange to make a visit so she could show it to him. One weekend they drove there and spent the day together. It worked out well.

How much they truly had in common was unclear but they got along nicely. She came to enjoy his predictable wordiness and need for inflections of intensity and drama in his speech. He was interested and opinionated about everything. He talked quite a bit about himself and assumed she was glad to hear his take on everything. Harriet reacted favorably to the way he was polite and courteous and put no pressure on her. As he held a door for her he might briefly place his hand on her back as she completed her path through the doorway, but that was about it. Harriet was not a formally educated person but she concluded she had stumbled onto a pleasant platonic relationship with a special man. And she loved it. Any effort he made to keep their budding relationship somewhat secretive didn't surprise her given his status as a physician and her low skilled position.

Even as his involvement in her life became gradually more important to her Harriet had few illusions their friendship would ever be more than just that. That they would arrange to meet beyond Burlington and drive to a dinner or a concert was fine with her. Harriet knew he was passionate about England yet was more than startled one evening when he told her he wanted to take her there to show her London, his favorite city, where he had studied for a year.

Right away he made it clear he was planning to pay for her. Harriet realized a host of potential implications from this turn of events. But she wanted to go. Half-way through dialing her mother to talk about it she impulsively slammed the phone handle down and stopped thinking about what she might be getting herself into. Family and friends were told she was taking a ten day tour of the British Isles with a well-regarded tour outfit.

After sitting separately on the plane from Burlington until they arrived in Newark they sat together from there to Heathrow. They slept in the same bed in a lovely hotel in Kensington but it wasn't until the third night they made love. Neither displayed any powerful passion but there was enough warmth for Harriet to be very satisfied. It was a dream come true. Anticipating the possibility of such an event Harriet had actually done manual exercises and learned the use of lubricants to allow intercourse. It was painful but she willed her success.

She marveled at her sustained relaxation. She hugged him through the night as she did with her large pillow at home. They made love again, briefly, on the next to last night. Harriet thought it was a glorious trip. He showed her so much and she thrived on how much he knew and his willingness to spend so much time imparting his knowledge to educate her. He was not always especially patient but mostly.

On the day before they were to return he spent a good deal of time describing an African safari to her and told her that's what their next trip should be. She was excited. In the afternoon, as they were packing, he asked her to sit in a chair. He sat across from her on the bed. Part of Harriet's world crumbled so quickly that what he was saying to her was not completely clear for several minutes.

His face looked serious but not grave.

"My dear, you have to know some things about me and my health. You can see how active I am. But, you know, looks can be deceiving. I have an ongoing infirmity that holds the potential to drain my lifeblood from me and leave me an invalid; even, perhaps, unable to work. You can imagine what my life would be like if I was unable to continue my practice. I can't even contemplate such a fate. It would be terrible. You know that." The drama in his speech was expected but Harriet still felt riveted by his words.

"WE, can't let that happen my dear. I must continue on." He looked straight at her. "Some years ago I had a fall and broke my back. I've lived with monstrous pain ever since. All I have to control severe discomfort are pills. I'll always be in pain but the pills are an essential aid for keeping the pain levels lower." His gaze dropped to the floor. "Harriet, I don't believe I would be allowed to continue my practice if the authorities knew about the medications I take to control the awful pain. I have been forced to surreptitiously obtain the precious medicine that I must have in order to continue my important work."

He looked up at her. She could see the pleading in his eyes. Not an expression she had ever seen from him before. Those few moments were like a strike from a bolt of lightning. She felt she had been punched in her stomach. She wasn't a fool. Never like this. Never after anything like their relationship. She had been asked before; offered money and all kinds of things… Was this all for drugs?

He stared off into nowhere. When their eyes next met she thought he looked like a little boy. Embarrassed. Maybe ashamed. Harriet felt confused. He spoke again, in a soft voice, devoid of the intensity and flourishes that were his usual pattern.

"Harriet, you and I are different than the others. We see and feel things in a very similar way. Yes, it's all very complicated and what I must do to continue to succeed means I have to live two lives; one secret. I think it's very cruel. If you and I are to stay together, a force for love and caring in this cruel and unfair world, then we must work as a team and live with our secrets. Will you help me?"

Harriet Summers was surprised how quickly she discarded any path to outrage or anger. She knew she might never be sure how truthful his words were. Right now he offered a strong antidote for her loneliness. If finding happiness in her life required some risks she quickly decided being with this man was worth it. She was convinced. She knew what she was being asked to do.

* * *

He was a pompous man, for sure. But he probably wasn't a fool, as evidenced by his continued acceptance as a consultant by the medical staff. He was, most assuredly, a determined person. Unknown to almost everyone though was the determination required to sustain his longstanding dependence on opioids, the consequence of an injury and the well-intentioned efforts of a colleague from some years before. Maintaining his usage required intense effort but, as with most everything in his adult life, he reveled in his success and prowess to get what he needed so anonymously. He knew he wasn't likely the only doctor who learned ways to access what he needed. And yet, it was never accomplished without risk or potential complications. He often thought someday, in more enlightened times, he would love to write his story with all the devilishly clever details of his success. Not now when he could wind up in prison for doing something like that.

*   *   *

Huddled together on the plane returning to the states they discussed opportunities and strategies for obtaining his medication. Oxycontin, a long acting form of the opioid oxycodone was highly addictive and tightly controlled. He presented an idea of substituting like appearing pills. Harriet knew every facet of the handling of the drug, from ordering from the wholesaler to sending the med to the wards in dose restricted apparatus. She understood his idea but had some other thoughts of her own.

A bottom line she had lived with for years was knowledge that diverting small amounts of controlled drugs wasn't really all that hard to do in a hospital pharmacy. The plan she ultimately put into action and continued to use cleverly altered records in the computer so if any tampering was suspected it would appear to be taking place on the wards. Nursing staff would more likely be at risk of being accused than anyone in the pharmacy.

****

LATER SATURDAY AFTERNOON IN ALBANY

REST PERIOD?/   "This fresh air is nice after being inside all day, don't you think? Of course I didn't have a choice today. Don't know about you though."

Immediately it was his turn. Damn. What a bad mistake. They were barely off the library steps. He had to say something. This was his idea.

"Well, I had to get some things done today and that meant using the library. You can see Roz, I'm trying to get back on track. Had a job problem down in New York City. Came up here without any planning a few days ago supposedly with a solid promise of something good." He intentionally feigned a look of disappointment. "But you know it turned out to be a scam. Never have had anything like this ever happen to me before. I think I've got things arranged to get back to the City now so I'll be heading back."

"Wow, that's unfortunate."

They walked side by side, probably slower than she anticipated. Ted was worn out, concentrating hard on walking straight. He hoped his bizarre storytelling would turn her off quickly so they would have something and sit for only a short time. Then he could head for the bus station.

At the café the counter glass display case held a variety of sweet options.

"Oh you know Steve, just get us that small coffee ring there and why don't we go on to my place so you can rest a little."

"Roz, no, you needn't do that. Let's sit here for a while. This will be fine."

"No, no Steve. Don't take it wrong, but I've been known to lend a helping hand before." She seemed to be joking. "Just usually to stray cats and like that." They each smiled.

The thought of putting his legs up and resting prone flooded his brain and went into fierce competition with the part of him frantically waving the red flag strongly cautioning Ted to find a way to shorten his time with this Roslyn, whoever she was.

The pastry cost almost nine dollars and eating it looked appealing. Roz didn't plan to get coffee and sit at a table.

"Come on Steve, you need a break, let's take the pastry and go." Friendly but no nonsense.

The final block to her apartment building was almost too far for Ted to walk. It was a nicely landscaped and maintained older brick two story structure with four units. He was dead on his feet from being mostly awake for somewhere beyond sixty hours. Walking the steps to her apartment on the second floor was a struggle. Roz motioned to the couch for him, but he carefully stepped towards the table in her small kitchen and sat. She put a pot of coffee on.

"Steve, I don't know what your story is but I can see you're out of character. None of my business. For some reason I'm not afraid of you." She went back to the counter to pour the coffee. "I can help you get some rest and maybe a shower, but then you'll have to go. Okay?"

"Oh no Roz, I…I…I can't put you in a spot like that…I"

"Steve. Eat something and drink some coffee. You're so tired it won't keep you awake anyway."

She was right. The revelations from his email and his decision and follow-through on writing Henry led to a collapse of any remaining fortitude. Each hour he felt weaker and worse now. After eating something she convinced him to lay down on the couch but he refused to take his shoes off and left his feet touching the floor. It didn't matter, he probably could sleep in any position; this was fine. Anything potentially incriminating was on his body, including the hospital lettering and logo on his shirt, now well covered by his new sweater.

"So Steve try to relax. I know this is kind of crazy but you do need to rest. I'll give you two hours. Then you can lock yourself in the bathroom and take a hot shower to get freshened up. Sorry but I can't help ya with your clothes. You can take care of that back in the City."

He was out in a minute. Hoping he never talked in his sleep was his last thought.

He woke up remembering pieces of a dream. It was a haunting memory. In his dream he was living part of the drawn image the kid on the bus had awakened him to see. He was naked, standing with his hands bound behind him. He managed to have his eyes fixed on two objects. One was the naked woman. The other was the slow motion movement of the descending sword. Ted was in fear but transfixed by the smiling face of the naked woman. Who was she? Was she Liza…or Roz? As dreams go it was frightening and the last thing he remembered before Roz's gentle tug on his arm brought him back into his challenging world.

As he was rousing, at first he wasn't sure, but then he noted there definitely was soft music coming from somewhere in the apartment.

* * *

He had a crushing headache. How truly restful a short one or two hour nap would be for someone in Ted's sleep-deprived state is open to question. Most might feel worse on waking. That didn't seem to be the case for Ted. With the aid of some Tylenol after about fifteen minutes he was feeling better. Not great but the fear of complete collapse was gone for the moment.

"So take your time in the shower Steve. I think I've got it all set up with everything you'll need in there. Sorry I don't have anything for a man to shave with."

He thought her kindness was unbelievable. His appreciation left him almost speechless. She hadn't peppered him with questions or suggested anything more than offering him a break from his pending collapse. Really nice of her and he told her so. He started to get up.

"I have a shaving kit in my jacket so I'm okay…Roz, I can't tell you how kind and helpful you are. You were right, I needed a break. I…I can't thank you enough."

"Shh now. Let's keep this simple, okay? Go take a shower now, okay?

Ted locked the door and began to peel his three day old clothes off. He placed them around the room hoping they might air out briefly. But his smelly clothes were going to be a continuing problem. Unconsciously he checked to see if his remaining cash was all there and immediately hated himself for the thought. He turned on the fan and then the water.

The shower was a delight; warm and forceful. Only when he turned the water off did he sense the beginning of the return of desperate thoughts and worries. Ted tried hard to key on his hope Henry would understand his letter and find a way to help him. He knew he'd try. Ted realized he had no idea, when he walked to the bus station on a Saturday evening, if he would even find a place to go and a bus to sit and sleep on again on his way to somewhere; preferably an all-night ride.

He toweled off and shaved. The thought he knew absolutely nothing about the middle-aged woman beyond the bathroom door who was responsible for his brief reprieve passed through his mind. Was she truly so altruistic or was a lady in a negligee and sweet perfume waiting for him a wall away? Could he even perform if it came to that? He wasn't sure.

Putting his soiled clothes back on made him hope that wasn't about to happen. He poured her scented after shower powder everywhere, even in his shoes. He cleaned the tub and sink and stowed the remnants of his shaving kit in his jacket. Before he left the bathroom he briefly argued with himself whether he could ask Roz later if she had any saran wrap or something like that he could use to put around the probably useless papers in his shoes. He turned off the fan and light, took a deep breathe, and unlocked and opened the door.

The living area was all lit up. Roz, in the same clothes as before, sat on the couch with a dour expression on her face, flanked by two large Albany City policemen staring intently at Ted. They spoke his name, Ted Vallan, and, just like that, it was all over.

Ted even knew where the jail was.

* * *

Maybe Ted wasn't able to find anything on the internet about the murder he was being accused of but Roz was a professional and she did. There wasn't much but enough. Seeing the letterhead of the Burlington hospital on the papers with scribbling he briefly left on the carrel peaked her interest. Later, she remembered seeing the name Becker in one article and then again on the email Ted was copying.

She wasn't a venomous or angry person out searching for criminals on the street. On the contrary she believed she cared enough to help this lost soul who was trying to function in a disaster beyond his abilities and was failing. She thought he just didn't realize it was time to quit, or how to stop. Roz truly believed turning Ted in was for his own benefit. Of course she was well aware once she had him over she had to do something. She knew what happened to Dr. Mudd.

"Good luck Ted. I hope those stories about you are not true."

But it should have been none of her business.

* * *

Very late in the afternoon, alone in his darkening apartment, discouraged and aimlessly poking around, Henry Vallan decided to check his email. Instantly he resolved not to tell Doreen anything about what he found. Their baby must be protected. She must not be implicated in any way. He had not the slightest concern for himself.

****

PART II - LOCKED UP

SATURDAY NIGHT IN ALBANY

HE'S IN THE JAILHOUSE NOW/   By the movement of the hands on the large institutional clock on a far wall an hour passed while Ted Vallan, arms and legs shackled, sat on a bench in an open area of the non-public access part of the Albany, New York Police Department. Saturdays might not be especially busy in the reference section of the Public Library but Saturday nights at the police station usually were. This Saturday was no exception. He sat like a fixed ornament with one other, neither barely moving while a parade of people moved back and forth in front them. His pockets had been emptied and his belt removed but otherwise he remained as he arrived. Everyone stared at everyone in this place. He had no idea if anyone knew who he was.

A tall and lanky black officer with a shaved head, not wearing a revolver, walked up to him with a wire basket that contained the manila envelope with the things already taken from Ted. He motioned Ted to stand which Ted did with some difficulty, reflecting the dual impacts of his weakness and his shackles. Ted followed him to a windowless room and noted the sound of the solid metal door being slammed shut after he was inside.

He was unshackled and told to take everything off; everything. As he undressed his jailer spoke few words but watched him closely. Underwear also. Ted didn't smell bad but his underwear did.

The intensity of the odor of his socks, shoes, and feet were only marginally buffered by the after shower powder he had dumped in his shoes. Everything went into the basket, shoes on the bottom. Ted was sure someone would examine his shoes but maybe not. He had to be sure his shoes or anything they found in them followed him back to Vermont.

"Hey pal. I'm talkin' to you." Ted had been preoccupied by his thoughts. "Up close and personal now. No crabs allowed, okay?"

The officer bent forward and shined a pen light on Ted's crotch. Said nothing for about thirty seconds.

"Now turn around, bend over, and spread 'em."

Ted anticipated something like this but he was unsure exactly what to expect. He had to put his arms out, touching the wall, to maintain an upright stance. The whole business made him dizzy. Apparently a visual examination was good enough, for which Ted felt grateful.

Some form of a paper diaper was offered as underpants. Then he was given a neon red top and bottom that looked for all the world like some of the various scrubs that sat in his closet, liberated from the hospital over the years by Liza. Foot wear was a type of a felt slip-on.

After dressing Ted was marched, without shackles, to a large, brightly lit, open room with at least ten other inmates lounging around, most watching sports on an old TV sunken in a wall with a solid piece of probably indestructible Plexiglas covering it. The Plexiglas made the picture appear distorted and gave it a yellow hue.

Ted wasn't happy to be in that room. It was not the typical holding cell he was used to. He wondered where he would get the adrenalin to respond to any likely challenge. He was too tired and discouraged to face anyone. Since his arrest he had barely spoken. A cup of some god-awful ginger ale was the sum total of his hydration or calories since being booked.

This all was bad and had a good chance of becoming much worse. The corners were all taken so he sat on a bench near the door. Cameras hung from the ceiling but any response to a fight would take the jailers some time to arrive; great damage could be done before then.

Before Ted's arrival could be meaningfully explored by his cellmates the door opened and Ted was plucked out of that room nearly as quickly as he had been put in. This time he was taken to another windowless room and told to sit on one of the two metal chairs in it. A small cot was in a corner. He felt sick to his stomach. Fear and anxiety were constants. Over these hours he regressed. Ted was once again no longer able to begin to think through parts of his situation that were important to him.

The entire process was meant to shame and belittle the prisoner. Demeaning. Ted felt acutely diminished. Even the false consolation of being free when on the run seemed preferable to this. He was living a nightmare that, impossibly, could still get worse. What more? Now he was light years from being able to influence anything in his case. If anyone offered him his one phone call that wouldn't even help.

To call Liza would risk suffering a final blow; stabbed not in the heart but in the back. What could he say to her anyway? He didn't have Henry's number and had no good thought who else he could talk to. Hiram Wouk popped into his sputtering mind.

'Sure, Hiram, you remember me, right? Listen, I need a favor; like tonight. Could you write down my email address and password and take a look at a pile of strange emails. All I want you to do is find out who the real senders were. That's all. And then find out how to contact my son, Henry, and get that information to him. Will you do that for me?' Fat chance. Where would he get that kid's number anyway?

What was the point? By now Ted thought he had a good idea of how a straight forward investigation would keep him as the main attraction for a long, long time even if he was eventually exonerated. By then what would be left of him? Could he survive like this that long?

He closed his eyes and his head gradually drooped forward. 'Droopy drawers' Roz called him. In this most uncomfortable position he dozed. That horrible dream. Whose face was that on the naked woman, smiling, maybe laughing, yes laughing at him? Why couldn't he recognize it? The fear he felt during the dream wasn't only because of the trajectory and logical consequence of the falling sword. His fear also was that face. It frightened him. That was strange because, although his dream didn't show it, he assumed he must have an erection or why else would he fear the falling sword?

The loud clanking sound of the solid metal door opening jarred Ted from his vexing and frightening dream. That was okay with him. He was sweaty and his neck was sore. He had to squint for a few seconds to adjust to the room light. A middle-aged man in casual clothes, a few years younger and slightly taller than Ted, walked into the small room and closed the door behind him. He had a serious demeanor. He extended his hand. Ted slowly, grudgingly reciprocated. As best he could Ted tried to raise his guard.

"Captain Vallan you may not remember me. I'm Paul Regardi, with the New York State Police. I'm a captain now too, but I was a lieutenant when we met at a conference at SUNY right here in Albany a few years ago. We spent some time in the same seminars and you also gave one of the sessions. I remember because you really impressed me and the others with your words and advice. You stressed the relevance and concepts of what you called the back room investigation. You really made that come alive. You taught how to collect and use basic details to anchor and build a case. Not glamorous but essential. Big impact on my career."

Ted looked up with a squint at the Captain. Back room investigation? Yes…success with learning and managing what he used to call the nuts and bolts of a case was critical. Now he thought he remembered the Captain also. Did they eat together a couple of times? A wan smile was all he could muster. Who would want to run into a colleague in Ted's situation? The Trooper spoke earnestly.

"Ted the New York State Police will be taking over the investigation of your time in upstate New York. I don't know much about your case yet but I intend to get up to speed in a hurry. Frankly, you don't look good at all. You need a lawyer. You know you will have to decide if you're willing to go right back to Vermont or make an issue about extradition. I and the State Police will do what we can for you."

Ted had thought about extradition. He saw it as inevitable. His first words were offered slowly and with gravity in his voice.

"Paul, I should go back to Vermont. It will be easier for everyone. If you can help me with three things I won't challenge it." He went right into his list.

"My son, Henry has an unlisted number in the City. I need to talk to him. Call it my one phone call…Then I don't want any publicity about me to get out until I arrive back in Vermont…And I need some paper and a pen or pencil."

He knew the writing implement could be a problem in jail and Captain Regardi reacted as he said it.

"I'm innocent Paul…Just like a doctor who wants to check his own heart this is what we do Paul. Imagine yourself in my spot. What would you do? I have to be part of my case."

Trooper Regardi was inclined to believe him, although Ted kept talking and maybe he should have stopped.

"I really don't know who I can trust, Paul."

Trooper Regardi looked long and hard at Ted.

"I hope you can believe you can trust me." Not really a question.

Ted felt he was getting emotional and he didn't want to come across that way. He gave a sniffle and exhaled audibly.

"Then you know what Paul? If there is any way you can keep some sort of an eye on what happens in my investigation…you might complicate your life but maybe save mine."

'Holy shit! What is this fucked-up looking run down fellow talking about? The Vermont State Police? No way.'

Before the NY Trooper spoke out loud Ted backed away with his words.

"I'm sorry Paul. Not your problem. It'll all get worked out. It will be okay. I'm sure."

"Ted, I'll do what I can. You need to get some real rest, soon." Ted did not react. "Ted I have to try to reach your Colonel now. What do you want me to tell him?"

Ted stared off at nothing for a few moments.

"Paul, I'd like to hope he believes I'm innocent. If I were you I'd tell Colonel Blair only that you've got me."

Ted wondered if maybe it was good he ended up in Albany after all.

* * *

EDUCATION BECOMES INVESTIGATION/   A turkey sandwich and a thin sweet liquid, probably what they used to call bug juice in the scouts, tasted fair. As down and discouraged as he was Ted determined to stay awake until Regardi was able to get him a number so he could call Henry. He lay back on the barely padded cot in his cell and battled hard to will himself to try to review his time working at the hospital. How did he get into trouble? His recollection came slowly but he thought he was able to roughly recall most of it.

The first few weeks as Chief of Hospital Security Ted concentrated on understanding and re-organizing the fairly basic police procedures required and utilized in that setting. He got to know his staff and studied manuals and guidelines available to him. Burlington PD Chief Wendell Partin and Ted decided to have lunch once a week for a while so they could design better coordination and division of responsibilities on safety and security issues generated in, by far, the largest hospital in Vermont.

He also set up regular meetings with Hiram Wouk. The meetings turned out to be tutorials in using the computer for information technology. Hiram was sharp and was glad to help. He kept any personal assessment of Ted's learning abilities to himself.

It was perhaps natural for Ted's interest to be piqued by an instance of a bad outcome for a patient that came to his attention as he was educating himself. His instincts as a law enforcement officer seemed to compel him to consider investigating such a case, but he really only planned to use it as an example for learning about hospital systems. That meant learning about the wards and the increasing use and reliance on computer IT systems.

With some guidance from Hiram Wouk Ted made a list of all the different IT systems being used in the hospital; a large number. Then he listed those systems utilized during the case he had chosen to review. He also looked at the medical record, including all the physician, nursing, and allied personnel notes.

The case he had chosen as a method for learning the utilization of IT and documentation in direct patient care involved an unfortunate, elderly woman with a long list of active medical problems. As best Ted could determine she was thought to have succumbed to the combined effects from several of her diseases. And that was a concern. Liza told him there was a conference where her case, and death, was presented and discussed. She told Ted the general feeling was the given explanation for her death was not considered satisfactory by the majority of those at the conference. He was surprised to hear that. That's when he decided to use her incompletely explained death to learn more about hospital systems and records.

It didn't take him long at all to recognize multiple layers of systems and protocols for patient care generated a surprising amount of complexity for him to understand. Just trying to follow the day-to-day clinical course was challenging for him. Then there were also daily, and more, inputs from all allied services such as mundane appearing entries, for example, from central supply to pharmacy divisions, and others.

So when he could find some time he took notes and read through the entire chart; notes from doctors, nursing, physical therapy, social service and others. After that he reviewed the formal records of components like vital signs, medication records, and other charting. He was much too busy to accomplish his goal in a short time. In fact, he was so busy this project went on for over three months. He was still evaluating his findings when he fled Vermont.

As he hoped, the exercise for understanding more and more about that patient's hospital stay was very instructive. But then it became more than just that. He found he needed to continue to dig deeper and deeper into hospital systems and her chart.

Four to six weeks in Ted worried he may have stumbled on criminal activity. It seemed obvious to him something was wrong. But, at the same time, what he was finding was so relatively easy to uncover he wondered if he had found anything at all. The written chart, in general, was kind of a mess. The computer systems appeared more organized. That bothered him. Many different people were inputting into the computer. In the computer everything had such an official look. Who knew how accurate those entries were?

The veracity of the documentation for the management of the patient on the ward clearly was rife with potential ways to manipulate what was charted, either written out or in the computer. Ted was trained to be suspicious when a human life was lost. His initial review suggested potential for a host of spots for errors or manipulation, in particular, on the chain of custody for medications. Of course he knew that included controlled substances. Early on Ted wondered about the possibility of an error, or even diversion. The systems and checks and balances he reviewed concerned him.

Ted continued to make notes as he proceeded. As he keyed more on the possibility, in some way, of misuse of certain medications, controlled drugs in particular, he wrote down the names of the doctors, nurses, pharmacists, pharmacy technicians, and others who had to document their role in orders and the progression of these medications from arrival at the hospital to ingestion by the patient. It was kind of a shock to Ted when he saw his daughter, Kathy Conover's, initials in the written record on two occasions.

Finding Kathy's name actually caused Ted to back off a little. It reminded him he was a novice at this type of investigation. He had his suspicions but he truly had no idea if he was really on to something or still didn't fully understand the systems and records he was evaluating. And yet he wondered if he could be playing with fire. Or did he simply not understand what he was looking at well enough to even begin to draw any preliminary conclusions of a criminal act.

Ted understood he might not be correct, but what he thought he found was a question of whether the patient was receiving the correct dose of an ordered controlled drug. Ultimately he decided there were several instances where written and electronic records did not correlate. Since he saw this several times the repeated finding may have lessened the possibility of an error and made an intentional act more likely. He suspected the listed administered dose somehow was less than it was supposed to be. At first that didn't make any sense.

He interviewed almost everyone: the Director of the pharmacy and some of his staff; then doctors and nurses who were part of the case. He decided he did not need to speak with Kathy since she was barely involved. Speaking with each of these people Ted didn't hint he thought there may be a problem. He interviewed under the guise he was using a case to inform himself about all hospital systems.

In his mind Ted began playing around with a theory he was developing. It was alarming. Nurses were signing for administering a certain dose of a medication. His suspicion was the given amount was less than what had been prescribed. Sure sounded like diversion. How could that happen?

The weekend before he ran from Vermont Ted distilled his notes down to two pages. He listed the pieces of his findings demonstrating likely medication misuse and potential places in the chain of custody for these medications where diversion or unlikely, but possible, errors could have occurred.

Probably useless now from being in his sweaty shoe. Large portions of his writing were smudged or dissolved to the point of being unreadable. With effort at the carrel he was able to decipher a few scattered words and sentences. He wondered where his shoes would wind up and if the papers below the removable foot pad remained in them.

He knew he was in no shape to begin to try to piece those notes back together. What was the point anyway? He had blown so much. Never sharing his concerns with anyone was a huge mistake. Taking that job was a fucking mistake. He was a loser for making so many mistakes. He was finished.

Ted sat up and started to get up. He was dizzy and thought he might fall. Quickly sitting again he didn't know what to do. Terribly despondent he tried to brush away a flash image of Liza. He didn't want to go back to where this began…again.

* * *

WHAT THE…?/   Was Liza really talking with someone when he came around that corner in the hallway? Couldn't have been that Becker. He was dead. Becker. Ted could think of only one possible connection to what happened and that Dr. Becker. He wasn't going to forget that. Shortly after he completed interviewing most everyone who had some involvement, in any way, with the case he was reviewing Harvey Becker began to attack him publicly.

Becker's nastiness and apparent vindictiveness was like a bolt from the blue to him. He had no idea who the man was who stood up and offered a stunning, lengthy public rebuke of him and the straight forward statements on IT and IT security he had just completed presenting at that medical staff meeting. It was awful.

For two weeks before the meeting Ted had labored on his presentation, notably anxious about having to stand before a large group of medical professionals to talk about anything. He was unaccustomed to speaking publicly to a large professional group like that. At first he assumed he must have said something wrong or incorrectly. Liza and a few others told him they couldn't understand the magnitude of the hostility in Becker's attack.

That evening, after Becker's tirade publicly shaming Ted, all Liza could tell Ted was many doctors were unhappy with the way they perceived computers were interfering with doctors providing care to patients. It was a future they distrusted. The way Liza explained the worries of many doctors Ted thought he could understand their concerns.

She described a changing world where many practitioners felt new and developing systems in the medical center were being forced on them. For them learning and working with new personal and hospital systems was like an uprooting; like having to work in a wild frontier environment. And why?

Liza presented to Ted the contrarian view of many physicians. Initially the systems and programs used were envisioned by researchers as a fantastic aid for data collection and analysis. Now a torrent of other health related uses were considered and being developed. As the government, already the major financier of medical research, had become the major payer for health services, IT services were the natural and mandatory place for monitoring and managing the enormous challenges that generated.

And yet, to hear many doctors tell it, the whole system, from data collection to now the beginning of the push toward the electronic health record, was more sinister than progressive. According to those who provided the care the main impetus for adopting that method for maintaining all records and notes was to create an unbelievably simple method for private insurers and Medicare and Medicaid to monitor and ratchet down billings. That what was happening might be inefficient for clinical care and poorly sensitive to documenting subtle patient health issues and dynamics meant nothing to payers. And, naturally, especially in early years, the imperative for the safety and security of personal data and important supplies was understood early on but not always so easily successfully implemented.

After that public meeting Becker took the time to complain about Ted in letters to three or four administrative committees, none of which had any notable ability to restrict or direct Ted's activities in the hospital.

Becker was repeatedly nasty and demeaning in the way he spoke about Ted, impugning his abilities and his character. Mostly he openly encouraged the administration and staff to challenge Ted's continuing employment. Because? Well it was innuendo and character assassination and Liza said there are always some who can be persuaded by such an authoritarian manner. There was some physician dissatisfaction Becker could tap into and try to make Ted a scapegoat. So there were some rumblings of dissatisfaction about him.

Ted didn't express anything to Liza but he never accepted Becker's malicious attacks on him were a reflection of any of that. Maybe superficially that made some sense and that line of disparagement may have allowed him to gain some of his support against Ted. Maybe Ted became a symbol for some angry doctors trying to paddle upstream against the inevitability of the future. But Becker's over the top efforts to get rid of Ted must have been generated by something other than that. He was pretty sure.

Kicking himself some more was easy in his state of despair. It now seemed like eons before but it was only a week ago when he committed his growing concerns to the two pages of notes. That was when he first began to wonder if there could be a connection with Becker and the potential crime he might be uncovering. He had nothing more to go on than the apparent coincidence of his investigation, basically the interviews, and the sudden onslaught by this difficult, wordy man. Nothing else made sense to him about Becker.

During those last days in Vermont he still never said a word to Liza or anyone else about his suspicion linking Becker to his investigation. What would he have said? Talking to that intimidating asshole or going after him, in any fashion, never occurred to him. And he certainly hadn't considered planning to resign.

He lay back and tried to turn on his stomach so he could shield his face from the fluorescent light bank that apparently was going to be on eternally in the windowless room. He had no idea what his memories were going to do for him. Remembering all that was difficult but also settled him a little. Shortly, he succumbed to his great fatigue and dozed off.

Fifteen minutes later he was jolted awake by the stinging sound of the clanking steel door opening again. A deputy roused him and then offered an arm helping to stabilize his gait and walked him to an open area with a desk and a phone. He placed Henry's phone number in front of the phone and helped a bleary-eyed Ted sit down.

****

FOOTNOTE — * * * * **CHASING FREEDOM?**

A COLLISION AND.../   While Ted Vallan was on the run another drama of human life, one he knew nothing about, was playing out. At times of great personal distress, like atoms colliding randomly, the fate of his and another life became entwined.

Harriet Summers wondered if she was trapped forever.

Even a lonely woman might have limits to her tolerance of a bad situation. Over the course of a year Harriet became increasingly aware of the bind she had been drawn into. The man she was repeatedly committing a felony for could destroy her life in a minute if she failed his requirements or if he was exposed for abusing drugs. As the year passed she grew unable to stand him and feared his behavior and threats to expose her if she stopped or said anything. She correctly judged to be considered an enemy by him was a dangerous thing. He seemed to have endless energy, ability, and interest in his battles (wars would be his description in his own mind).

The continuing small diversion was not a great concern; she was managing it well. He, the boisterous, somewhat paranoid doctor who, over time, less convincingly kept professing his deep love for her was the real problem. She knew it, but she was trapped.

* * *

When Ted Vallan, the new Chief of Hospital Security, showed up in the pharmacy one afternoon Harriet Summers was terrified. She was surprised how quickly and almost hysterically she reacted after all the time she had lived with the crime she was committing. She was one of three in the pharmacy he interviewed. His questions to her did not seem particularly specific or especially probing to lead her to suspect he was truly on to her method for diversion.

After speaking with Harriet and the other workers in the unit he sought out the Director's office. As the thirty minutes or so he spent speaking with him passed Harriet became increasingly anxious and upset. She worried her co-workers would sense her discomfort. She started to sweat. Ted Vallan exited the Director's office and immediately left the pharmacy. She remained beside herself.

What was she going to do? If everyone was about to be watched more closely or more stringent audits were about to be instituted everything would change. If she had to stop what she was doing, even for a short time, what would he do? How would he get his drug? With his supply suddenly at risk or even gone Harriet could only imagine what he would try to make her do and how he would behave.

She was terrified and went home to several sleepless nights. Predictably, he was infuriated when she told him about the new Chief of Security's apparent probe. If he was frightened he didn't let on to her. Instantly he went into a war mode. He instructed Harriet to continue what she was doing and told her he would get Ted Vallan out of the hospital. He assured her whatever investigation that man was doing would end when Vallan resigned or was fired.

Harvey Becker's public campaign to discredit Ted Vallan was immediate and nasty. A number of colleagues on the staff respected the Doctor and right away he had several of his small group of like-minded colleagues speaking out in support of his claims; like they always did. It all seemed crazy to Harriet. She worried he had gone too far too quickly and the chances of his attacks failing, or even back-firing, seemed great. Within a week his behavior betrayed his great fear as far as Harriet was concerned. She doubted his efforts would succeed. She also realized the emotional impact of trying to maintain the diversion was having on her now. She was increasingly paranoid.

Continuing to rest poorly, not eating well, and fearful of even calling him to try to talk about her fears, she wondered if the trap she was forced to survive in was finally overwhelming her ability to cope with her daily responsibilities. Lying in bed, tears forming in her eyes, a strange thought came into her head. Maybe circumstances could help her to find a small crack in the cage that had trapped her for a year now.

* * *

DESPARATE MEASURES?/   He had significant prostate problems and had to do something about it. For months they planned a strategy so he could adequately maintain his addiction while in the hospital for surgery on his prostate. The procedure was scheduled two weeks from then. If something happened to him while in the hospital was there a chance this Security Chief who he was defaming and insulting would be considered a suspect if Becker died in suspicious circumstances? Maybe his death in the hospital after surgery wouldn't even be considered suspicious, she fantasized.

Harriet Summers at least felt some relief and direction pursuing such an outlandish possibility. He tears dried up. As she mulled it over she recognized the magnitude of the anger and hostility she felt toward him. Even a slim chance at being done with him… forever… and hopefully free of danger of arrest would be like receiving a great gift. What other options did she have?

At first she assumed it would all be too much for her to figure out much less implement. But as she thought about it more and more her resourcefulness impressed her. She gained motivation rapidly and ideas came to her. Harriet wrote down notes which she dated when she was interviewed by Ted Vallan. Her written comments reflected concern the Security Chief had pressed her to give him examples of methods for how drugs coming from the hospital pharmacy could be used to overdose a patient in a criminal act. She placed the notes in an envelope labelled 'to be opened if I am arrested or something happens to me' and locked it in her jewelry case which she kept hidden in a false drawer in her dresser.

Harriet told him he was not being aggressive enough in his attacks on the Security Chief. He should go after the man and even his wife to make the attacks more personal. And, perhaps most importantly, he needed to figure a way to create the impression his attacks began before Harriet was interviewed. They each agreed there should be no obvious connection between the interviews by Ted Vallan and his efforts to discredit the man.

He was pleased she had come around to working to help solve *their* problem. He had difficulty coming up with some indication he had started after Ted Vallan before the new Security Chief had gone to the pharmacy. He didn't tell Harriet he planned to work on that and figure a way to implement a solution while he was in the hospital recuperating from his surgery.

It was far from perfect but Harriet felt there were no other options for her. She proceeded with her plan when he was admitted. She had tampered with the pills and delivery mechanism well beforehand. Once the expected orders arrived in the pharmacy she made final adjustments. Her plan was simple and logical but unproven.

Instead of the standard short acting opioids for post-op pain, typically given every four to six hours, he would receive the long acting formulation, which she substituted. It was common sense to her if he was given a version four to six times each day that was supposed to be given every twelve hours the drug would gradually accumulate in his body. She had no doubt he would ask for pain pills frequently. Over time, along with the Oxycontin he brought with him, Harriet assumed he would be overdosed.

The surreptitious changes were all teed up and all a nurse had to do was administer what the nurse presumed was ordered each day by the doctors. Harriet felt no regrets. Her entire future was on the line.

****

FRIDAY IN VERMONT

HOMICIDE COMPETITION IS NOT HEALTHY FOR ANYONE/ The morning Harvey Becker died on Thursday Harriet Summers was in the pharmacy doing a routine inventory. Suddenly the room was alive with everyone chattering abnormally loudly for the usually sedate surroundings. She knew it could be that day or one of the next, but it would happen. Harriet calmly walked toward the buzzing crowd. On its periphery she stopped to hear what the commotion was about and her jaw dropped open. A co-worker was excitedly telling the assembled group a doctor, Dr. Harvey Becker, was just found dead in his hospital room with a knife sticking out of his chest.

She could have been free!

* * *

...AFTERMATH/ Devising a method to siphon a relatively small amount of Oxycontin on a continuing basis had never been all that difficult for Harriet Summers after working in the hospital pharmacy for ten years. There was always risk but the constancy of the limited amounts helped her to meld the thefts into the pharmacy routine. The plan for Harvey to bring and hide twelve pills while in the hospital for his surgery had been manageable. (And he used them all.) The idea of overdosing him and obscuring any possible path to implicate the pharmacy was much more challenging.

Harriet's plan for causing the level of oxycodone in his body to gradually increase until it was fatal was based on her thinking it might make the determination of an intentional overdose appear less likely. That was her failsafe thought. What she assumed would happen was Harvey's death by an overdose would be determined to be a murder with the new Chief of Security, maybe working with his wife, a doctor, the likely suspects.

For a few hours after the murder was discovered she tried to convince herself there might never be any search for toxic substances since the cause of death was so obvious. Harriet stumbled through the day. Becker's death should have been her release, the freedom she had longed for and dreamed about for months. Instead she was miserable and increasingly afraid.

Harriet isolated herself from the excitement in the pharmacy. She barely managed to last through her shift, desperate to leave and go home. But even outside in fresh air, finally away from the hospital, she felt no relief. Her, as they say, hopes, dreams, and desires all were gone. She had failed. The glimmer of companionship and love with Becker failed and now her more limited reach for freedom from him had come crashing down around her also. It was only a matter of time until they would come for her. She was sure.

That evening at home she could not eat. Harriet was unable to sustain any hope his death was the end of her torture. Her panic was growing. She lay in her bed but was unable to sleep. The blood would be tested and the overdose probably would be found. Why would this Vallan, or his wife, or anyone else want to kill him twice? It just didn't make sense. Eventually the police would look beyond that Vallan for a second murderer. Now her plan seemed foolish to her.

By the light of day Harriet believed it was all inevitable at this point. Just like the suffocating trap he kept her in for a year with no recourse in sight. She was finished. It would only be a matter of time before she was caught. His planned death and now hers were the price of trying to squeeze out of his trap. She now had few illusions her thefts would escape a serious and comprehensive search for diverted Oxycontin.

There was no support for her. Her life with him left her almost friendless. Supplying his habit encouraged her to shun others for fear she might say or do something in an unguarded moment to expose her deeds. Even her parents became expendable in her effort to insulate herself and others, for their safety, from the trap she lived in. Her apartment was just an extension of her cage, her small cat her only remaining confidant. Harriet couldn't bring herself to go to work on Friday and called in.

She worried through the day. Within hours she decided calling in probably quickly branded her as a suspect. Everything was going wrong. She couldn't be saved. Her fear and panic slowly dissolved into an acceptance of her fate.

Harriet must have previously considered the possibility of everything blowing up. Months before she spirited out a small number of benzodiazepines and short acting opioids, assembling what she assumed was a lethal cocktail. At the time she hoped she did it for the possibility of serving it to him. But even then she recognized it could be used for her.

The images in her mind she feared for so long: being walked before crowds flashing cameras and yelling; the drip, drip, drip of the endless embarrassment of public prosecution; the horror of her family's suffering; the remainder of her life trapped, physically, in a locked cell. It was more than she could bear. She had tried. She thought there was a chance, but she failed.

Harriet filled the tub and took a warm bath. For a moment she thought about taking the cocktail and then toppling the candles she had carefully arranged around the room and burning her apartment. But then her cat would die. That wouldn't be right.

No note; no final contact. She had tried and failed. She slowly took all the pills and lay back on the inflated plastic pillow attached by a suction cup to the tub.

*   *   *

News about the dramatic details of the murder of Dr. Harvey Becker flooded the state. There is no twenty-four hour news outlet in Burlington but whenever there was news that was the story for the next few days. Harriet Summers' parents called her Friday evening to talk about it but there was no answer at her apartment. They had become used to difficulty reaching her, especially on weekends, when she was often away. Her parents had been almost frozen out of her private life, an endlessly upsetting development for them.

Earlier in the week Harriet had agreed to a rare visit for a late lunch on Saturday; a hopeful piece of her dream for beginning her life again. She never arrived and calls to her apartment remained unanswered. Her father called their son and he agreed to check her apartment. It was around six p.m. when he entered and found her underwater in the bathtub, her cat crying plaintively on the floor.

****

SUNDAY IN THE CITY

Sunday was to be Jim Wiley's only day of rest this week. Saturday had turned into a lot of work, and thinking, probably for nothing. Unless there was some kind of a Ted Vallan sighting in the City Sunday his involvement in that case probably was over. On Monday he would find out if Haworth wanted him to tie up any loose ends on the Vallan business or, more likely, move on to other assignments.

Breakfast was breaking up and the expectations for Jim were clear. This was a day when changing the baby, bathing the baby, and managing a long walk and maybe ten other things were his responsibility. He got it but he was tired. He always thought, on paper, how much work could a twenty, twenty-five pound kid be? A joke. Once he got into it he usually enjoyed it. How soon could he introduce a baseball to his boy? That's when the fun would begin.

The phone rang. A Sunday morning call never was good for a cop. This one left the Detective even more tied up in his thoughts than his musings about child rearing. He finished with the precinct and put the phone down. He turned to Idelia.

"Never trust the judgment of a fucking first year surgical resident."

His skinny, recovering knifing vic, Johnson, had died an hour before. Wiley called the hospital. The death was sudden and unexpected. Not until later in the week did Wiley learn Johnson had a shitload of drugs in his body including a notable level for cocaine. Tethered to his bed in a guarded room in a hospital how did he get coke? His death was from a heart attack. When that was determined would his death still be considered a homicide?

By the time the tox and autopsy information came out at the end of the week it didn't matter anymore for retired Vermont State Police Captain Ted Vallan.

*   *   *

Wiley tended to the baby and completed the necessary chores before he and Idelia launched their walk with the baby neatly tucked into the stroller. There was no mistaking the early morning news energized him. He wasn't ready to be done with Ted Vallan and searching for him. Maybe he was making more of the story of this ex-cop than there really was but the whole business was strange. He suspected this was one with all kinds of twists and turns, far from that Vermont Trooper's self-proclaimed slam dunk.

Walking in the park on a pleasant early fall morning Idelia Mendez-Wiley picked up on his mood very quickly and wasn't sure what to make of it.

"Jimmy, you look excited. Haven't seen you so interested in a case maybe ever. You know what? I like seeing you thinking about things in a case; wanting to get things settled out. You know, staying with it. Not just punching your ticket every day."

Jim smiled and readily acknowledged Idelia's observation.

"You're right babe. Since this case got complicated, and maybe since I got mad at another cop, my mind has really gotten into this. I don't know where this case might go and how I might be involved but it does feel good. You're right, this is the kind of stuff I used to think being a detective is all about."

There was excitement in his voice. "Man, this is gonna be challenging. So many different threads to work on and try to understand. It's murder, now in the City also, and maybe more. Just have a feeling about that. Bad in my business to base too much of anything on a feeling, babe, but that's how I feel. You know?"

Wiley's cell put out a fairly loud electronic sound, like repeating ripples in water. He was glad he answered with his title.

"Detective, this is Tessie. Commander Haworth asked me to track you down this morning just to let you know the Commissioner's office heard late last night that Vermont State Police Captain you've been looking for is in custody. Last night in Albany."

A million thoughts ran through his head as he thanked her and hung up. The three of them continued on the stroll but Idelia could easily see Wiley was lost in his thoughts. Neither said anything. Only a few minutes later his cell's odd ring sounded again. Once again he decided he should answer with his official title and did.

"Detective Wiley, this is Henry Vallan, Captain Ted Vallan's son. The man you have been looking for. I'm terribly sorry to be calling you so early, and on a Sunday, but I need to speak with you." There was an obvious urgency in his voice; and worry.

Wiley was uncertain why Henry Vallan would be calling him. He should know by now his father is in custody.

"Yes Mr. Vallan, what can I do for you?" Idelia pushed the stroller and they continued to walk. "Your father is in custody now, you do know?"

The more Henry spoke the more desperate he sounded.

"Yes, yes, I know. That's it Detective. I talked to him last night. He continues to insist he was set-up. And Detective Wiley, he told me about some strange emails and some possible drug diversion he was working on at his hospital. He's terrified the local authorities are turning a blind eye to all that because it looks like they have such a strong case against him." Then his voice lowered and softened.

"Detective I don't know what to do. I don't know what to do."

Wiley looked Idelia in the face and showed a frown. But she knew he was acting. She could see the activity of the morning was exciting her husband. Two years ago she wondered if marrying a policeman meant living with someone who was also married to his job. It hadn't worked out that way. Maybe until now.

"Mr. Vallan did your father tell you anything about the knifing in Harlem."

"No, nothing."

"Did you know one of the knifing victims died this morning?"

"Oh no!"

"Where is your father now?"

"I believe the New York State Police have taken over the investigation in Albany, but I think my father agreed to go back to Vermont and expects that will happen sometime today."

"Listen, Mr. Vallan. We should talk. I need to speak with my superiors and, hopefully, someone in the New York State Police. I imagine you're planning to go to Vermont. I…"

"Yes. I want to leave later today."

Wiley looked off toward the Hudson river and thought through a few ideas.

"Vallan, can you hang on a minute?"

Jim turned to Idelia and asked if she thought junior was good for another hour or so. She nodded 'okay'.

"Say Vallan, we're not too far from your place. Walking the baby in Riverside Park. You think you could come over, or even you could bundle your kid up, and we meet up on the main path?"

"I'd really like to talk with you Detective…but I can't let anyone, including my wife, know what's going on. If she ever got implicated in anything…"

"Whoa, whoa Henry! I get it, but you shouldn't worry. It's almost like the slate is wiped and everything starts over now your dad's in custody. But I understand. Listen my wife, Idelia, is with me and the baby. The ladies can be off and chat while we talk a little distance away."

They planned the likely range of the location they would meet up and the call ended.

"You know this Vallan's kid got a baby coupla' months older than Jimmy junior. Maybe we can talk some while we push our strollers. Know? That Trooper Vallan still alive, but he's in a heap of trouble, babe."

* * *

GOIN' UP COUNTRY?/   They headed south. Wiley still had his cell in his hand. He dialed Tessie and asked her to apologize to the Commander but he needed to speak with him as soon as possible. It was Sunday so he might be hard to reach. Since he got a message to Wiley earlier through Tessie he hoped Haworth was reachable. The Wiley family arrived near the planned meeting spot and sat at a bench. Haworth returned his call.

Wiley was so caught up in the rapid sequence of the morning's excitement he forgot the unspoken rule of waiting for the Commander to structure the discussion. Instead Wiley spoke up right away.

"Commander I need to make sure you are made aware this case with the retired Vermont Trooper is still active. One of the men in the hospital from his knife fight died this morning." He continued before the Commander could speak, if he was planning to. "Just now I was given unverified information about a possible drug diversion this ex-trooper may have been investigating in Vermont.

Even if it's true I don't know if any of this could have anything to do with that knife fight, but who knows."

"Hold on Detective; hold on a minute."

Wiley froze. He realized what he had done. Haworth assumed control of the conversation. But all the Commander wanted to do was slow the discussion down and be able to speak using his paced sonorous phrasing.

"I think I follow what is giving you your concern here James. Yes, our investigation will have to continue." He paused, a bit longer than usual. His words had a dramatic effect on Wiley. "James I guess you need to find who to speak with in the State Police in Albany and…" A pause again. "Suppose an interview with the suspect in *Vermunt* should be completed soon; before the poor bastard gets overwhelmed with his Murder One. Okay?"

Wiley had learned yesterday Haworth was not the man to go over details with.

"I will ask Tessie to arrange a caar…"

"Commander, I…"

"Wiley, work out the details with her, aw right?"

"Yes sir."

The Commander told Wiley to make his plans with Tessie and, almost as an afterthought, asked to be kept informed. But it was already getting complicated. The Detective shot a glance at his wife sitting beside him. He would need to find the right moment to tell her; but soon.

* * *

Henry and Wiley wanted the formalities to be brief so they could talk. There wasn't a lot of time for either of them. Doreen mostly understood why Henry had been keeping her in the dark. His newly expressed hope and interest in Detective James Wiley gave her a good feeling and respect for the Detective. Idelia Mendez-Wiley was impressed and pleased at the way the Vallans acted towards Jimmy. It made her feel good about her husband and his profession, her marriage, and herself. She felt a responsibility to be gracious to this couple in trouble and actively engaged Doreen. Actually, the young mothers had a lot in common.

Henry and James walked about twenty feet behind them. Before the two men spoke specifically about Ted Henry handed Wiley copies of Ted's emails and his letter to Henry. He didn't give Wiley much time to look at them before he started to speak.

"Detective, my father's call last night was terrible. He kept telling me I was his one call; the one call a prisoner gets to make. I don't know if they were rushing him but he seemed to be in a hurry. Some of what he said didn't make much sense.

"You know, since I saw my father early Friday I haven't slept well, at all, and I bet he hasn't had any good rest since Wednesday night. He sounded confused. He talked about some 'notes'. Something about them 'melting' in his shoes or something. Detective I don't know what's happened to him. I've never heard him talk like that… It's so sad…"

Henry kept walking but he looked away, towards the river. It was obvious to Wiley he was crying. What could he say? Maybe this older guy had gone off the deep end and his kid was going to have to be a witness to his end. But there was a good chance Henry was correct; that the dark perils of being on the run and bad sleep deprivation had caught up to the old guy.

"Henry, I get your father's email to you, but I don't have any frame of reference for the others. There's a lot that's not very clear in this case, from start to now. If your father was really set up he's already paid a terrible price. I'm not sure what the NYPD or I, can do for you or a fellow cop."

He paused and took a breath. Henry's head was down as they walked slowly, the ladies now farther ahead.

"For better or for worse the NYPD still has a stake in your father's nightmare Henry. The death on 133rd Street is still my responsibility. I don't know if I can be completely objective about your father.

"I just talked with my precinct commander. He's asked me to contact the New York State Police and he's given me a tentative okay for a quick trip up north to interview your father."

Wiley hadn't presented this information in more than a matter-of-fact tone but Henry took it as a kind of victory. He looked at Wiley and Henry's face showed a slight sad smile. It was a beginning. Wiley interpreted Henry's look correctly and knew he was probably far from the savior the Vallan family was hoping for. However, this case had uncovered Wiley's buried passion. Whether it would play out in some way so he also aided the Vallans was very unclear to him. Wiley knew Henry hoped it would.

"Listen Vallan, I guess I'm gonna drive up to your Vermont later today. Unless you got your own plans we could go up together. Give us time to go over everything. Two, three hours?"

"No Detective, more like five hours."

One of Wiley's eyelids drifted up, reflecting his surprise.

The whole situation should have been much more awkward. They barely knew each other. It wasn't a stretch for either of them to assume they came from very different lives. City boy and country boy, and so on. And it wasn't at all clear they shared similar motivations about the case that was bringing them together. But since their rocky introduction two days before so much seemed different now. Their goals may not have been exactly the same but now they were closer to a unity of purpose. Later, in the car, it came out that besides both having young babies, Wiley's father had been a cop also. They got along surprisingly well.

Henry's number was now in his cell for later contact. James called ahead to the ladies and suggested they turn their strollers around and each family head back home. Henry pulled a brown paper bag from storage space below the Vallan's stroller. It had copies of his two books, each in some way tied to Ted Vallan. Real or imaginary stories? Either way Detective Wiley already had his first homework assignment for this case.

* * *

"But babe didn't you tell me 'round Christmas you were going ta let your license lapse since you hadn't really driven in a year and there always seemed to be a uniform or a partner to do the driving?"

Well, he had. He was supposed to have a license but he had been lazy.

"Yeah, you're right" He stopped his packing and thought about it. "Know what I think I'll do? I'll have Vallan drive. And anyway, car will be NYPD unmarked and I got my shield and I'll have all kinds of ID. It'll be fine. I'm not gonna worry about it."

There were a number of arrangements to be made; for both of them.

It was decided Idelia and the baby would stay with her parents. Any plan where James didn't have to be with his in-laws was a good plan for him. They each were in good spirits. An important job needed to be done and the Wileys were both up for it and hoping for success. Neither presumed any likely danger although Idelia watched him put his small off-duty revolver in his coat pocket. A patrol car waited downstairs to take him to the mid-town police garage.

He kissed the baby and he and Idelia shared a lingering kiss and hug Wiley would continue to recall for a few hours. Things were finally the way they were supposed to be. He believed he had skills and he was all-in on figuring this business out.

* * *

"Shit! Shit!"

"Stop that Henry! The baby doesn't have to hear that. And I don't either."

"I can't find my driver's license. It must be in Vermont. I sure hope so. And you know what? I bet it's expired. Shit!"

"So Detective Wiley will drive anyway, at least until you get home. Then you'll just do the best you can. Really. It's an emergency. You'll just have to be careful. I wouldn't worry about that right now."

Doreen Vallan didn't say much more. She was well aware Henry had to go; and immediately. She would have to make whatever arrangements she could to maintain their life in the City. She had no relatives in New York or Vermont (other than the Vallans). Going with Henry wasn't a good idea with everything that was going on. She would have to be resourceful but the family hadn't been apart since before the baby.

Henry recognized the challenge for Doreen but he was at loose ends and wished he was already in Vermont. There was so much he didn't understand. It was all so suddenly serious; and dangerous. Wiley coming with him gave him a boost. He decided he was coming with his own private detective; the only good thing that had happened in days.

* * *

Standing outside his building waiting for Wiley to arrive Henry thought about both his parents and the impact of this unfolding disaster on each of them. His father may have actually lost it. What about his mother? Her mood also seemed to be drifting lower. He had some fear for her also. Living alone in the house while this horror was unfolding was not good for her. Her comments often were not very helpful and she, too, like his father, seemed stuck on how any of this could be happening.

How on earth would he ever find a way to ask her why she said what she said in that hospital room? What would he say to the Detective when Wiley asked him why she said that? Maybe he should wait and let Wiley ask her himself.

Wiley pulled up to the curb at Henry's building in a black unmarked. Henry went to the passenger back door and placed his things on the seat. He noticed the bag with the two novels he had just given Wiley sitting there. Not likely much time for reading right now. Wiley lowered the passenger window as Henry started to open the front door.

"Vallan, you know where we're goin'. Why don't you do the drivin'?"

Henry froze. He was desperate to get home. No delays. He would be careful. And he was with a cop.

Unconvincingly, "Sure. Sure. I can do that." With that he walked around to the driver's side as Wiley got out and walked to the passenger side. As they passed in front of the car each offered a quick wink. They were off to Vermont.

****

SATURDAY NIGHT/SUNDAY MORNING IN VERMONT

911/   Seeing a naked body completely submerged in a bathtub the initial investigating Officer from the BPD immediately assumed drowning, intentional or accidental, the likely cause of one Harriet Summers' death. She could have been drowned by someone but there were absolutely no signs of any type of disturbance in the apartment. Perhaps accidental. She looked far too young to have had a sudden heart or other organ event. But you never know. The Officer was also well aware people who overdose in a bathtub often die and slide down below the water line giving the appearance of drowning. A half empty glass of water was sitting on a small table abutting the top of the bathtub.

Her place would have to be searched in detail to find out if she was a user. Her brother denied the possibility but, to the police, that was only his opinion. A quick search turned up nothing. A more complete effort would have to wait until the morning when more and better trained manpower would be available. In the meantime she would be packed off to the Medical Examiner's office for an autopsy, probably also on Sunday.

Sunday morning several officers and technical lab personnel arrived at her apartment around nine-thirty. Yellow crime scene tape blocked the door. Early on in their search not finding any personal valuables was a signal they were missing some form of hiding place used by Ms. Summers. The team stayed with it and less than an hour after they began the false bottom of a drawer in her dresser was located.

In that space they found jewelry, a jewelry box, and a few papers but there were no pills or signs of drug paraphernalia. Underneath jewelry in the jewelry box there was an envelope with a startling inscription: 'To be opened if I am arrested or something happens to me.'

****

SUNDAY IN VERMONT

Late morning Lieutenant Barry received a call from the Burlington Police Department Chief.

"Right…Right…Oh my, Chief Partin. Yes…Yes, everything is happening very fast. Did you know Vallan is in custody? Yeah. Got caught in Albany. Should be on his way to Vermont as we speak."

Shawn was thinking as fast as he could. He was about to leave for the correctional facility in South Burlington to greet Ted Vallan.

"Listen, Chief, please ask someone to make some copies. I'll get in touch with my deputy and have him go to your headquarters to pick up the original and a copy, okay?"

Chief Partin knew Ted Vallan's name was on his DOA's note. It sure seemed that letter could be involved in some way with the homicide the state police were working. For a fleeting moment the Chief wondered what bringing the criminal misuse of drugs into the mix of this case might mean? Didn't the guy die with a knife in his chest? He had no idea of any other details of Harvey Becker's death or the information Lieutenant Barry possessed. The State Police were the primary investigators.

"Sure Lieutenant, that will be fine. I'll let the duty officer know to expect him."

Shawn Barry sat in his office in the almost empty Waterbury Barracks and stared out the window. "What the fuck does all this mean?" Initially, as the Chief was speaking, he felt a rush hearing of a new drug connection. On quick reflection he realized if that woman wasn't a suicide it sure wasn't too likely Ted Vallan was the person who killed her. Determining when she was last seen alive and how long she was dead would be important.

In short order his thoughts drifted to Kathy. Kathy Conover and Ted Vallan together conceiving a way to kill that Becker? Did this new information make something like that more likely? Maybe. It suited Shawn Barry's mindset to think so. He was on the right track. Fresh evidence kept coming in. He knew he had Ted. To implicate Kathy might take more time and work. It was looking more and more like she could be involved so he had to move forward, even if it turned out to be a much more complicated investigation.

Without spending much more time considering the new report Barry returned to thinking about Ted Vallan's pending arrival back in Vermont later in the afternoon. Yes, the case was moving very fast. Now that Ted Vallan was about to be in confinement in Vermont Shawn was no longer in a hurry. He wanted to be sure, in custody, Ted Vallan would suffer and feel humiliated, much as Ted Vallan made him feel for years. The Vallans were offering him an opportunity to put salve on long-open wounds that caused him hurt for years. Shawn Barry intended to make the most of these moments.

* * *

Shawn called the duty officer at the correctional facility in South Burlington to get an idea when Ted would arrive from Albany.

"Lieutenant, the Captain should be here within the hour." In a tone that indicated 'of course,' "I guess you'd like us to find a spot in the single cell unit?"

Shawn started to say "Yea…" Then his tone changed to a firm "No. No, put him in general holding… at least for now…Let him sit in there for a while." To himself, 'Vallan should be welcomed home really uncomfortably,' he decided.

* * *

With the passing years Shawn tried to believe his ill-fated affair with Kathy Conover was her fault and the cause of his subsequent long, messy, and financially disastrous divorce which led to the loss of the one woman he truly loved. Captain Vallan's condescending tolerance of his continuing work on the force was a steady humiliation that never stopped. The Vallan family had made his life so much more difficult. He sure as hell wasn't going to let them get away with murder.

* * *

A CHANCE TO TALLY THE TROUBLES/   It was already afternoon. The day was clear and bright but it would be getting dark earlier now. Some of the trip would be in the dark. Wiley quickly determined there was no use trying to remember the route they were traveling to make his eventual return trip easier. Maybe Vallan would come back with him. But not likely.

They each knew there was work to get done on the drive. Wiley needed to know much more about Captain Ted Vallan, his angry, judgmental pursuer, and probably a lot more. Yes, good chance a lot more. There was much Henry guessed James, and even he also, still didn't know about what had happened. Henry Vallan figured Wiley was expecting him to spill any and every detail that might even remotely play some role or part in what was going on. Some of it would be painful. What should he do? He barely knew the man sitting next to him. So much was unspoken.

Ted Vallan was a criminal investigator all his professional life. One way or another he always succeeded. From even his brief contact with him the last few days Henry suspected his father was beyond helping to solve anything for now. The Vallan family was desperate for assistance. Hoovering over everything was the apparent commitment of Shawn Barry to direct circumstances towards his father's guilt. Henry would be best to begin with that painful story. They had hours to go.

* * *

Wiley moved the discussion almost immediately.

"Henry, I'm supposed to call Captain Regardi from the New York State Police between eight and nine tonight. Talked to him for only a few minutes before I left and he said he wants to talk things over more tonight after we've had a chance to see where your father is and how he's doing. And, get this…how he's being treated. What the hell do you think that means?"

Henry was listening as he navigated the large sedan north on the Westside Highway but his mind was still mulling over how he would explain what he knew to Wiley. He desperately wanted his help but Henry was a private person. Discussing family issues, surely important for this case, was difficult for him. Wiley continued to talk.

"My father's a big reader. Always reading somethin'. And, you know what, he reads all kinds of stuff. Everything. After this business is over I'm sure he'll want to read your books too. He says authors are 'astute observers of human nature.' Of course when he talks it comes out like 'ass-toot' but he means it. He would have loved it if I became a writer. Maybe we got the wrong fathers, eh, Vallan?"

This guy was something else. Henry couldn't help but be impressed with the way he was setting him up to tell his story. And maybe that was part of the problem for Henry: Henry might be so focused on reading people and emotions his view and perspective of the story had more emotional depth than others in the family even realized about themselves. Maybe it was his tendency to highlight and maybe make more of his family's flaws and weaknesses than a less observant person would…or should? 'Bullshit' he reacted. 'Just tell the cop what you know and you'll see what it means to him. How much worse could this all get?'

"You know I'm officially on my way to Vermont to interview your father about 133rd Street, but you're hoping I can help you shed light on the whole picture. You also know I been stuck on the guy who's calling your father a 'bastard' and the homicide they got him for a 'slam dunk.' You got to know this guy if he and your dad worked together for years, right? Let's start there, okay?"

Soon they would hit the Tappan zee Bridge and the traffic would get lighter.

So Henry told Wiley as much as he knew about Lieutenant Shawn Barry. That required him to give a short history of the make-up and responsibilities of the State Police in Vermont. Henry remembered exactly when Shawn became his father's deputy investigator and when his parents attended Shawn's wedding. Until then Shawn was around a lot. Ted was always the one in charge but they appeared to work well together. Even Vermont troopers with administrative responsibilities usually went into the field and Ted and Shawn often went together. Henry recounted one episode where Ted always said Shawn probably saved his life in the forest.

Wiley listened patiently. He had inklings of a solid partnership gone bad at some point.

Finally Henry began to speak about his sister. From the timing of her showing up in his narrative Wiley immediately suspected trouble was coming. Henry started to describe Kathy in some detail but then stopped. He wondered if that was important or necessary for the tale he had to tell. Was he also, like his father, judgmental in assessing her role in what happened? He decided he should keep it brief.

"I guess if there is anyone in the Vallan family who could be considered a free spirit it's Kathy. She's very bright and I think my parents thought she was going to be a doctor, like Mom. She's cute and lively, and that's coming from a brother whose life she often made a living hell. I mean she was tough on me like siblings are. She went to UVM, that's the University of Vermont, in Burlington. She quickly decided she could have way more fun in school going into nursing and not having to study so hard. She'd get a four year degree so no one argued with her. She played hard and got out of the house into an apartment as soon as she could. A good time girl I guess you could call her. I really don't know if she really was actually very promiscuous.

"Smart enough to breeze through school but my parents worried she was doing a lot of partying; maybe too carefree and too interested in having fun at college. But she seemed then, and still does, like someone capable of doing it all. She got good grades and had a part-time job so there wasn't much my parents could complain about. Senior year, like many coeds do, she got into a steady relationship with a real nice guy. They got engaged less than a year later. It all seemed good. If you had asked me who the fellow reminded me of I would have to say my dad. Kind of the opposite personality for the way Kathy was living during college. A young accountant. And that's the way he seemed. Know what I mean?"

Wiley smiled. He kept listening, very patiently, as they continued to the New York Thruway, across the Hudson.

"I guess Shawn did well on the force and he and my dad worked together well. At his wedding I believe his wife was already pregnant but I remember Mom reminding everyone they had been together a long time and she insisted they were very much in love.

"The story goes downhill from there, as I imagine you've guessed. Kind of murky but the party line is Kathy was housesitting the dog while we were away for a weekend and she either called Shawn about a problem in the house or he showed up for reasons only they know. He's married with an infant and she's engaged with a pending wedding date.

"Within a month one of Kathy's roommates spilled the beans to Shawn's wife that he's been at the apartment twice. Apparently she might have overlooked a solitary stay but not repetition."

Wiley kept looking at Henry, who maintained his matter-of-fact presentation with a bland expression on his face.

"It all blew up quickly. Other than Shawn's wife my dad seemed to be the most angry. You might be surprised but in Vermont these kinds of things can stay pretty quiet if that's what people want. But Shawn had a terrible time. His wife was furious and she divorced him as quickly as that kind of thing can be done. And it wasn't good for him on the force. Getting to the higher ranks after an episode like that was uncertain.

"Dad was beside himself and furious with both of them. Interestingly my mom tried to be a moderating force. That just made my father's response look more dramatic. I think he's a bit of a prude anyway but the optics of this affair made it a sordid disaster to him: his engaged daughter and his, newly married and a father, long time deputy sleeping together. He took it really hard."

Henry was amazed at how patiently Wiley continued to listen. He knew James was putting all this in a context related to recent events. It was like talking to a therapist.

"So then, and I guess ever after, everyone has been angry. Life goes on. Kathy and Dave did get back together and Kathy matured, I think. She finished college and became a nurse educator and they have two cute little kids. They seem happy to me. But my father has never truly forgiven her for what happened. He may hold her more responsible for that affair happening. Not sure. Whatever, he, and I guess to some extent she also, can't get over their feelings, and he can't forgive her and move on. It's a shame."

"And Shawn Barry?"

"Similar. I think he thinks Barry got what he deserved with his wife leaving him. Why he continued in Dad's department and eventually replaced him isn't completely clear to me. I think Dad felt Shawn's career shouldn't hinge on Dad's personal reaction to his behavior with his daughter. Shawn was qualified for his professional role and Dad left it at that. I don't know how it went in their work on the force. I know Dad tried never to talk about him at home and he was never around anymore. Knowing Dad, wouldn't surprise me if working with my dad became pretty unpleasant from then on. I wondered why Shawn stayed. I remember Shawn barely put in an appearance at Dad's retirement dinner. He looked sour. And yet Dad's recommendation was necessary for Shawn to take over his job."

"I guess the signals coming from the Lieutenant the last few days pretty much tells the tale on how he felt working those years with Ted Vallan. High on Barry's shit list, eh?"

Henry sorrowfully agreed. "Yes, the fallout from that brief affair was a big deal that scarred a lot of people."

Who would have considered, he mulled over in his mind, impact from that mess years ago crashing like this in his father's life today?

They rode silently for a while. Henry was surprised how little Wiley asked during or after his recent words about Shawn and Kathy. Was he waiting for Henry to bring up other parts of the story?

"So Henry, you haven't told me much about your mother. Isn't she the one who ID'ed that knife as your Dad's?"

As he had decided earlier, Henry told Wiley all about his mother's career and her strong and caring personality. He shared his confusion about the report of her words at the homicide scene. But he had decided he was not going to say anything relating to his long-standing speculation about any private events in her life. This was not the time for that. And he truly was uncertain. He told himself, not very convincingly, it was his responsibility to query his mother about any of the events at the homicide scene and anything else, not Wiley.

* * *

The trip went comparatively fast. All the traffic was opposite them, going south. That direction was congested, almost a continuous stream of vehicles and headlights, the entire trip. Henry explained the traffic was from folks who lived in the metropolitan area, mostly New York, Connecticut, and New Jersey returning from an early fall weekend in the Catskills, the Berkshires, the Adirondacks, and Vermont.

There was some urgency. Captain Regardi was their ticket to get to see Ted that evening. He and the trooper who brought Ted from Albany had spoken with the duty officer at the correctional facility and firmly insisted an NYPD Detective be allowed a brief interview today with Vallan after he was settled in at the facility. It was unclear if anyone was aware Captain Vallan's son was with the Detective. Captain Regardi had cryptically left Wiley with 'I want to know everything you see there, Detective.' The duty officer had given them a deadline of no later than eight o'clock to arrive and out by eight-thirty at the latest.

If Shawn Barry had known Henry Vallan was with the NYPD Detective it's not likely he would have approved the somewhat unusual evening interview. It was also very possible Lieutenant Barry was unaware the NYPD Detective coming to the correctional facility was the cop he had unhappily spared with a few days before.

At Albany they left the Thruway and began the Adirondack Northway. At that junction they got off, briefly, on Wolf Road to stop for gas and some snacks. The highway circled the outskirts of Albany, which didn't appear very large to Wiley. Their next fifty or so miles on the Northway belied the true beauty of that ribbon of highway as it cuts through the Adirondacks farther north on its way to the Canadian border. Long deservedly touted as one of the most scenic roads in America, James Wiley would miss the splendor and majesty of its Adirondack vistas when he and Henry exited the highway at Lake George.

There was ample time to talk and speculate in more detail about Ted's email to Henry and the two threatening emails which Ted had forwarded. Wiley tried, again, to get Henry to open up more about his mother when they reviewed the leave her note, as Wiley called it. Wasn't it obvious, he thought? But Henry wasn't near ready to draw a firm conclusion.

Henry said he thought both the letters were probably from Becker, suggesting the animus he had for Ted greatly pre-dated their more public row. He thought that made more sense given the apparent gravity and subsequent escalation of their feud. From the little he was able to find out about the feud and this Dr. Becker he told James he believed any obsession Becker might have had with his mother was bound to have been one-sided only; very unlikely his mother would have been any part of it. "Someone would have recognized something at some time; wouldn't they?" he expressed.

Wiley backed off…for the time being.

After snacking in the car it was quiet for an extended period. Henry was buried in a myriad of thoughts and worries. Was there anything else going on? At one point Wiley broke the silence.

"I'll tell you this Henry, not likely any strangers wandering around that hospital ward at three, four, five in the morning."

Henry was impressed James was working the case all the while during the long ride.

****

FOOTNOTE — * * * * * **CAN 1 LOVE 2?**

THE STORY OF LIZA AND SPORTIN' LIFE/ Their beginning, many years before, was almost predictable. The intensity of child-rearing lessened and her medical career took off. Liza became a minor star in the local medical community, well regarded for her skills and empathy. As she gradually allowed her practice to grow she was continually sought after by patients. He, known as kind and caring, was also well regarded, and busy. Clinical practice is extremely time intensive and the two were regularly around each other for long hours. A clinic facility can become like a second home. So they bonded, but just as Liza bonded with others who she shared the long hours with in their office. She was careful to guard her comments and support as he went through a divorce. But it was obvious to her he made efforts to get closer to her over time. It was true they had much in common and she was impressed by how intellectual he was.

Did his gradually professed love for her encourage Liza to look more critically at her own life? For decades her push to succeed personally with Ted and her family plus her medical training and career didn't seem to allow much time to reflect on any of it. When her career took off and she began to make enough money to have a dramatic impact on the life of her family Liza was very slow to understand the impact of that on Ted. After years with his job as the major source of family income her salary quickly was double his and altered the Vallan family economy dramatically and forever.

With her success in so many ways, Liza's lack of awareness of how unsettling changes like that might be to Ted may have been emblematic of her own changing feelings over time. How impactful was the wooing by another man on all that? For some time Liza found herself cataloging problems with Ted and their relationship. Was Liza willing to believe Ted was responsible for a variety of minor problems in their life? What marriage couldn't be bruised by constancy and routine over decades when challenged by images of sweet, greener pastures? Was Ted becoming expendable?

Liza was a doctor. You don't exactly marry your in-laws. But both Ted's parents had health issues that were scary and probably offered a hint of what might be to come for Ted. His mother died in her late seventies after a prolonged, sad, and difficult decline with Alzheimer's disease. His father died shortly after from heart failure but he clearly was developing some form of dementing process at the same time. Liza accepted what her role might become with her husband and, rightly or wrongly, it colored her views about how to live her life now.

He, Sportin' Life, was after her for years and for many of those years she enjoyed their lively repartee where he verbally cleverly attacked and petitioned and she, equally cleverly, pushed him off. That's what happened at the office and at occasional hospital meetings and events. She knew he was much more serious about them becoming a couple than she. Liza did, however, make an impression on him, the staff at the clinic, and on Ted as she spent more time on her appearance; attention to her grooming and her clothes. She put more effort into trying different perfumes and finally deciding on one that pleased her than she ever would have dreamed in the past. At first she told herself it was because she could finally afford those things.

His persistence and the growth of their relationship from something casual into more than that was not unappealing to Liza. She knew she enjoyed him being around and got to looking forward to their limited relationship…and his wooing. Ostensibly attending something like an all-day medical meeting one hundred miles away from Burlington, in a place like Montreal, they were occasionally able to spend a few hours together at a museum or even a movie. They once saw *Porgy and Bess* on a large screen. It was in English with French subtitles. Liza was struck, in particular, by *Sportin' Life*, who kept tempting Bess until he won her. Liza decided she would call him Sportin' Life since that was his goal with her.

* * *

Eventually, some years later, after months of on and off considering, agreement and then not so firm nixing, Liza ultimately did not abort their gradually developed plan that led, once and for all, to proving their relationship was more than platonic. They were finally at the meeting they had struggled to arrange to be at together in Seattle and had slept together for the first time ever the night before.

Despite their long history of expressions and verbalizing their affection for each other, becoming naked together, essentially with a stranger, was brand new; certainly for Liza. She retained some ambivalence about things getting to this point but, correctly, doubted that was the case for him. There was some anticipation. Since she was there Liza had to accept she shared some interest. Prior to leaving, knowing getting pregnant was impossible for her, but who could ever know about a venereal disease, she managed to procure some condoms. It turned out he did the same. Coming up in discussion in their transition to the bed it worked to relieve some of the tension. At least they were on the same page on that level.

Liza was sure she did not want to get naked in front of him, but assumed, correctly again, he would like her to. There were no visual images she longed for. She found she did long for his arms. Hugging and softly stroking each other's arms and backs might have been good enough for her as a next step in a possible continuum to further commitment.

But there was more to do. Neither gave any sign of being in a rush.

They literally had all night. They kissed and that aroused each of them. Liza was surprised by the effect. Her goal for the night was to relax. Alcohol probably helped but kissing was nice. After slowly collapsing onto the bed they remained sitting, lips and arms entwined. He was clearly more goal directed. He spoke softly and sweetly affirming his pleasure and devotion as he gently pulled them both to a prone position on the huge California king they would luxuriate in while they committed physically to each other… or committed adultery if you wanted to see it that way.

Running actively was a part of her life forever but all bodies age and Liza's was no exception. Being naked in front of anyone besides Ted was not a comfortable thought for her. The sagging of her breasts and other changes seemed more acutely unfortunate to her at that moment.

He solved the problem of undressing by slowly undressing her in the barely lighted room. He spoke and they kissed and she accepted his desire for her to be passive and let him live what she assumed was a long time fantasy or anticipation. After she was fully naked he delayed doing the same for himself. Liza wondered if he was waiting for her to do that for him, but it was not going to happen.

He talked a little more, which she found unusual, but okay, and he gently played with most every part of her body. She gave in to the pleasure it gave her. His chest was heaving and she could sense his rapid pulse when they were bound tightly together. Momentarily Liza worried if he was all right. His breathing was slightly rapid but rhythmic. She assumed he was excited but fine.

He lessened his embrace some and relaxed his breathing. He said he would undress and place the condom. His activity and turning his back to her allowed Liza to sprint from the bed to the bathroom. Liza Vallan was no longer a young woman. She was hell bent on preparing for sex, especially peeing first and then inserting lubricant, which would assure a more pleasant experience for each of them. Pre-coital concerns attended to she dashed back to the bed, only then realizing she never brushed her hair or her teeth. He didn't care.

He was in heaven. He even stopped talking. Once again they kissed and stroked. If he was expecting or hoping for more than stroking of his erection he would be disappointed this night. But they each did okay. He gently stimulated her and it aided her arousal. They made love in the missionary position. He surely had dreamed of this day for a very long time and in his dreams they moved from position to position. It's doubtful Liza would have wanted to change much at all but it never became an issue.

Foreplay lasted a fairly long time. After he moved on top of her and they kissed as their bodies moved together, slowly but rhythmically, his excitement and pleasure was obvious. Liza tried not to be distracted by his rapidly beating heart. He was unable to control himself and that's how the missionary position became the only position for that encounter. Ted knew what to do to arouse Liza to orgasm. She expected sex with another man would require a learning process to succeed. Not tonight and that was fine with her.

He began talking again. He told her he was not disappointed and hoped she wasn't either. He actually quoted some famous literature. He wondered if he had too much or, maybe, too little to drink and that had an impact. He said he wanted to do it again, soon, that night. But he was older than Liza and that did not happen. Just before dawn he wanted to try again but Liza was out and seemed to respond to his gentle efforts at waking and arousing her in a way that made him realize he wasn't the only person to have been rejected in that setting by her. In the morning they had to appear at the conference early anyway.

By dinner the next day Liza was more than torn by the experience. She thought thank god she never had to deal with such emotions as a young person. All night and still today her brain was a jumble of rushing thoughts and emotions. On balance guilt was predominant. That she was too old for all this ran a close second. Sex had no longer been so exciting or pleasurable for her for some years. Actually, Ted's continuing desire to make love fairly often was a minor annoyance to her. Last night wasn't much different but he really seemed to enjoy it. He flooded her with admiring words before and after. At least he was quiet during intercourse.

Sitting at their table in a trendy place in Pioneer Square they were getting along well. She thought he really was a fine person. If anyone was the bad person she felt it was she. He placed her on a pedestal. Together they enjoyed racing through assessing the world in what she took to be the wry, clever way of cultured people. A fantasy, she knew, but a pleasant one. Not the Left Bank but not Vermont either.

A brief flush and anxiety came over Liza as she noticed a colleague from Vermont, who knew both of them, starting to walk towards their table. Then the colleague stopped and abruptly turned and went in a different direction. Liza relaxed; then more than that. She decided to interpret the colleague's maneuver as both acknowledgement and acceptance of her affair. Amazing how a brain can work to spin even itself.

So it was okay. One more night.

The second, and last, night of the trip wasn't completely similar. Not an old familiar couple but far from the passion and sexual commitment of the evening before. This time he thought it best to drink more earlier. All that did was delay his ability to maintain an adequate erection for sex meaning they each drowsed off a bit until he could wake Liza and prove his ability. Even then he didn't last much longer, not that it wasn't pleasurable for each of them. They were tired and had a long day ahead returning to the east and home, which played on their minds.

* * *

Of course the weekend in Seattle was a fairy tale. Liza loved her family. And yes, she loved Ted. About a week after Seattle Liza developed periods of sudden cold sweats. What had she done? Slowly, over the following weeks, she began to see how she used her worries and concerns about a myriad of things in her life, especially with Ted, to think she could justify her affair. Guilt and regret ran rampant in her life for weeks. How could she have let it all go so far?

The consummation of their affair happened in Seattle. This penultimate evidence for him of their love and need to be together had the opposite effect on Liza. Ever after she often longed for the relative innocence of their time before. She truly cursed herself for agreeing to go to Seattle. They used to have such fun in the office in between battling the daily challenges of their profession. Liza could never leave Ted which, to her, would mean her family also. She may have loved him but she loved Ted also. She began to develop a realization there was no reason, especially now in their lives, she couldn't encourage Ted to help fill the void in their relationship she had made him the focus of for her. Now they could do things together, like travel and more. They could broaden horizons for both of them. Why not?

* * *

THE TALE OF THE BUTTERFLY AND THE FRUMP/

How could Liza have forgotten that story? In med school she, and a few others, mostly the four other women in the freshman class, had been outraged about it. That's the way she remembered it over the years. At that time it was their problem. Very few others cared much that in the US men were the doctors and women could choose from nursing or a host of other allied health professions but were discouraged from becoming doctors.

So her anatomy professor nor the vast majority of the rest of her classmates didn't as much as blink when he offered social advice he presented regularly for many years early in the first semester to his young doctors in training. He told them to be alert to a great challenge to marriage in school and training for young physicians. In the early years they would find they had precious little time for anything but their education. A marriage in that setting meant constant support by the wife; especially if there were children. Any further education for the spouse had to be put off while the woman generally worked or managed the family, or both and, presumably, did little else.

In his telling the quite natural result of this difference in roles, often over a long number of years, was the gradual blossoming or molting of the doctor into a strong and beautiful butterfly with special education and boundless opportunity. Meanwhile the wife remained limited by her prior non-glamorous role, and implied, banal persona. She would not grow so was endangered and could remain a frump, whatever that was exactly. The prof made it sound like the spouse was practically a shut-in in life. A woman who naturally would have lost her allure just as he, the vaunted physician, had gained his allure. Well it was obvious where the prof felt those marriages were likely to go.

Sexism still wasn't a frequently used word in medical schools in the early seventies but Liza knew that's what it was. He was cautioning the medical students to help their poor wives fight to avoid becoming nothing in life at the same time the wives were serving them.

So Liza was amazed when that prof's inane caution popped into her head so many years later. This time she recognized she actually had bought into some of what he was talking about. Her full tilt dedication to medicine accounted for much of the good feelings she had about herself. She often felt more positively about other medical professionals than even her own husband. Ted was bright and actually very successful…extremely successful, in his own career and well respected in the community. But he wasn't able to be much involved in a large part of the life she embraced so totally.

He certainly accepted his role as a supporter and enabler in the early years of her med school and training. How could she have drifted so far from continuing to invest in their relationship? But he wasn't ever a frump. Was he? It wasn't a perfect metaphor for her. Ted was a butterfly but not her butterfly. Liza had to believe there was time to learn to love only one man…again. Why not?

Well, one problem with that was the clever, empathetic, worldly lover she had grown together with over some years. Liza should never have been so naïve about the effects of love and relationships. Plainly, he loved her for years. Her declaration after Seattle that it would never happen again and, more than that, she would never leave her husband so he must stop having ideas or plans for that, meant almost nothing to him. Despite years of protestations he once had successfully seduced her and he saw no reason to respect her words now. But years passed and it didn't happen again.

As this story played out, over a very long time, years in fact, despite her sustained resolve after Seattle, Liza was occasionally still uncomfortable with her thoughts. Early on she found herself wondering if it was possible to love two men at the same time? Gradually there was some acceptance. Then, of course, she recognized she was living the impossibility of such a life and began to wish there was only one man she loved in her life. Even after ostensibly rejecting Sportin' Life, in occasional dark moments, she wondered which man she truly wanted and how it would be so much easier if one of them was no longer around.

He still tried to play Sportin' Life in the office but he was desolate. Despite the years that passed he refused to admit the obvious. They were unlikely to recapture the fun of the chase ever again. When he tried to put pressure on Liza she showed some anger. She wanted him to believe it was over for her. There was never again anything more than their less frequent efforts at modestly spirited verbal sparring in the office.

Life went on but he continued to have difficulty accepting how close they had come to being together; maybe forever, and then it was gone. He never managed to move on. He still adored her. When Liza told him she was encouraging Ted to take charge of security in the hospital he said nothing but he was upset and deeply offended.

****

SUNDAY EVENING AT THE CHITTENDEN REGIONAL CORRECTIONAL FACILITY

A LAND OF ANGRY PEOPLE?/ It took almost two hours after they left the interstate to wind their way, on local roads, to get to their destination, the correctional facility in South Burlington. Henry pointed out that much of the worn out, depressed appearing countryside they had passed was still in New York. Vermont was mostly farms as best Wiley could see in the looming darkness. He figured no one was out because it was Sunday night. He assumed all the metropolitan area city folks had gone home greatly depleting the population and activity. Was this place mostly a vacationland?

Henry and James exited the car and started to the jail. Halfway to the building they crossed paths with Dr. Samir Balasubramanian, Dr. Sam as Henry called him, walking from the facility. He was steaming. The introductions were very brief. It was clear Dr. Balasubramanian was furious. He was beside himself with anger. For a moment Wiley wondered if anger…no, more than that, fury, was the default mood in this sparsely populated, lonely appearing land. Almost everyone he heard about or met was really angry.

Dr. Sam and Henry were well acquainted from years of interacting in various ways related to youth soccer and as a friend of his parents. The ME was modestly moving his arms and head and fidgeting with his fingers; distracted. Wiley had no idea the man was known for his hyperactive appearance but even Henry was startled by his level of discomfort and anger.

"Listen, Detective and Henry, this is not going well. Henry you're not going to like what you see if you're even able to get in to see your father tonight.

Henry and Wiley's eyes locked.

"You know, I think I've had enough. This case hasn't gone right from the start. At all. I get mixed signals from Lieutenant Barry. I think he's trying but you know he and your dad had a tough last few years. Barry doesn't have to like Ted but he still should respect him." The ME was furious. "This is bullshit! What's going on in that jail is bullshit!"

They were standing in the parking lot, about thirty yards from the building. It was getting darker and cooler. No one else was around. Wiley was suddenly fully alert and quickly saw an opportunity to query a major player in the case. Dr. Sam's aroused sympathies towards the accused might allow him to feel he could share important details with them even though their involvement was far from official. James directed them to the unmarked. He, intentionally, placed Dr. Sam and Henry in the front. By sitting in the back he hoped Dr. Sam's sympathies with a Vallan would help sustain a flow of information. Henry looked like he sort of got it.

Henry was getting a feel for the Detective's style and manner and was observing closely. Wiley was calm and very patient. Maybe he hadn't been so patient back on West 97th Street but, as he did then, he was very good at maintaining control and subtly directing the interview.

Wiley gave Dr. Sam time to vent his anger and frustration, which was directed most immediately at Ted Vallan's placement in the facility. He was being kept in the general holding area with other felons and whoever. Dr. Sam was astonished and furious seeing Ted like that. He was sure Ted's absolutely frightening demeanor had to be, at least to some extent, a reflection of those circumstances.

The Detective listened to Dr. Sam and both he and Henry knew something wasn't right. But as much as he shared the ME's disgust at what seemed to be happening to Ted Vallan on his return to Vermont, Wiley was more interested in hearing the ME's perspective about the homicide case. He felt he had a window of opportunity that might not last long. Wiley also knew he had a potential time crunch for seeing Captain Vallan and getting back to the New York State Police Captain as they had arranged.

"Doctor, I think Henry and I will get the Captain to where he should be. The New York State Police have just that concern and are waiting for my report. I'll have them call the jail. I have to call them very soon. If you could give us a real quick review of your take on this tragedy I think I can help better."

Dr. Sam was still hot. Wiley came across as calm but riveted on the situation; a take charge effect reassuring to both the Doctor and Henry. But Dr. Sam really didn't know who this guy was and why an NYPD cop was even there with Henry. His upset over the past few days was acutely magnified by what he had just seen and he did what he probably should not have.

Dr. Sam turned towards the back seat and spoke softly but deliberately.

"I have to say I don't think it's completely clear how Harvey Becker was killed, much less by who."

Henry's chin hit the steering wheel. Wiley choked on his own saliva. To Wiley it was a statement without parallel in a case he already thought had bizarre elements. This topped them all. 'What did he say?' Dr. Sam knew what he was saying and was ready to follow-up on his words as soon as Henry and Wiley started breathing again.

"Yes. I know he was stabbed in several great vessels and his heart and he was given fatal amounts of an opioid. He probably was dead before he was stabbed but it's difficult to know. Either one would have killed him."

Completely astounded, the two New Yorkers stared at each other. Henry recovered first. He was eternally directed towards trying to pluck out anything that might be considered good news.

"So that knife could have nothing to do with the death. Is that right?"

Before the Doctor could respond Wiley wanted to gauge the Doctor's reaction to his responsibilities with the case.

"Doctor, you must know Ted Vallan was involved in a knife fight with a drug dealer in the City a few days ago. Did…"

"I heard something but I don't know much about it. What I do know is I did a post this afternoon on a pharmacy tech at the hospital, a young woman whose death I think will turn out to be an overdose… Nothing is simple here. The Burlington PD officer who brought her over told me this morning Ted might be involved in some way in that case too."

Henry felt as rapidly deflated as his hopes had briefly been raised. There was no audible sound in the car except soft breathing.

* * *

FIRST MEETING WITH TED VALLAN IN JAIL/   Both of them were diverted by thoughts generated by the brief run-in with Dr. Sam. They almost missed Ted as they were being shown down a corridor to the room where they would meet with him. They walked by a large long window which made the holding area visible. Henry wasn't sure at first. It was Ted, being walked from the room to see them. Henry was shocked. He moved slowly, like the old man he looked like would. Head down; stiff; shuffling.

In the room Ted sat immediately and Henry knelt beside him and put his hand on his wrist. As he was touched Ted looked at the hand and regarded it like he wasn't sure what was happening. Henry had to hold back tears.

As he slammed the door behind him the guard yelled into the room, "fifteen minutes. That's it. Got it?"

Henry was furious. Wiley stayed near the door to give Henry some time with his father. He guessed everything was worse than he thought. Henry stood up and stepped back, trying to think.

Ted barely moved and he certainly didn't get up. He lifted his drooped head up slowly and offered a blank stare at Henry and Wiley. As they watched his eyes fix on them they each wondered if he was all there. It was clear his words were meant to reflect his utter despair.

"So…is this the fucking cavalry?"

Henry reached down deep, battling to control his emotions. He couldn't let this get any worse.

"Of course it is Dad. Maybe it would've been better to show up sooner, but you know the cavalry; Got to arrive at the last minute, right?"

Ted just sat. Henry told him he was going to stay until the whole mess was straightened out and Ted was home again. Everyone was going to help. He told him a lawyer was in the works. Ted never asked, but he told him he planned to stay at home with Liza and help her also.

Time was short so he introduced Detective Wiley to Ted. Ted stayed stone faced. A slight motion of his eyes was his only acknowledgement of the man.

Necessary but unfortunate, Wiley spoke softly and explained to Ted he was officially there to get information about the stabbings in Harlem. The subtlety of his also coming perhaps to help the family was lost on Ted. The brief, bizarre fight in the City was barely a memory for him.

"Captain, were you there in Harlem for a reason or anything to do with drugs?" Wiley felt like an idiot even asking that.

Ted's expression didn't change.

"Lost. No idea where I was." Ted looked at Henry. Detective Wiley was dismissed from his thoughts.

"Dad, we'll be back in the morning. Please try to sleep and in the morning eat a good breakfast." Now Henry felt like an idiot also. He was trying to rescue a man who was disintegrating before his eyes.

* * *

Henry's voice rose as he questioned why Ted was in a holding area. Wiley shoved a paper with New York State Police Captain Regardi's information in the Officer's face and told him he was about to call Captain Regardi who had been assured what they had just seen would never happen. The Officer, contritely, apologized and said the Captain was on his way to a special private area. He got it.

They drove to the hotel in silence. Wiley checked in.

* * *

THE FAMILY THAT MATTERS/   Kathy picked them up at the hotel and drove them to Richmond. She had some Kentucky Fried in the car. The smell made Wiley realize how hungry he was. The chicken odor bothered Henry, whose appetite was gone. Wiley sat in the back. The majority of the conversation was about Liza's poor state of mind and neglect of herself. The lawyer left only an hour before and Kathy said his words greatly upset Liza. Liza had no intention of going to work on Monday but had put off calling anyone and now it was getting late. One of them had to call.

Wiley got only a brief feel for Kathy's anger and sarcasm, her attempt to cover up her fear and upset. She and Henry said surprisingly little to each other in the car despite this being their first time together since the episode began. Kathy keyed on her worries about both her parents and had choice words for Shawn Barry…and his deputy. Henry reminded Kathy they had to come up with some strategies to get everyone, including themselves, through what was bound to turn out to be a protracted and surely difficult time.

Arriving at the Vallan home Wiley and Liza only had time for a
brief introduction. Immediately Wiley got on the phone in the
kitchen and spoke with Captain Regardi. Even though Ted was
moved to a solitary cell after they met with him Wiley advised the
Captain to call the jail and make some noise about where they put
Ted through the afternoon. Regardi became another furious person.
He and Wiley briefly shared some thoughts about the Vermont
State Police that should have been unthinkable. The Captain then
called the facility to let them know that was not what had been
promised. He made it clear he was going to speak with the VSP
Director in the morning. Monday morning Colonel Blair's office
arranged for the Colonel to speak with Regardi on Tuesday.

When he walked back from the kitchen to the living room Liza
was sitting in a chair, crying; Kathy and Henry kneeling beside her.
It was an awkward moment for all of them. Henry gave a look to
Wiley indicating he was not going to attempt to ask his mother any
of the questions he knew Wiley was waiting for.

Wiley gestured back, using his hand and fingers to simulate a
telephone handle. Wiley was insistent Henry get his mother to help
them with something they heard from the ME. Henry had told
him Liza had a distant cousin who worked as the administrative
assistant in the ME's office. Wiley wanted her called.

It was after eight and Liza, unhappy about being asked to it in the
first place, told Henry it was too late. He led her into the kitchen.
Kathy and Wiley stayed in the living room where they listened and
did not speak.

"Mom, it's time to break the rules. Please don't start to cry again
but we're in a very tough spot. You know that. We're beginning to
work with the lawyer but you know I happened on Detective Wiley
and he's trying to help. I don't know what else to do so I'm trying
to follow his advice. His even coming and staying here hasn't been
easy for him. I believe he's really trying.

"We live here, Mom. Vermont is our home. We know so many
people because you and Dad have devoted yourselves to this corner
of Vermont. If we have to fight this ourselves we will get as much

help as we can. Don't be embarrassed. Please call your cousin. See what she says. You can tell her if anyone asks she can say you or I called her. No secrets. Please do it."

Liza's mind was in many places. Fighting with her son was not what she wanted to be doing. She would pick up the pieces sometime in the future. Susan Joiner probably wouldn't tell her anything anyway. She got up, found her address book and a pen and piece of blank paper and called the number listed.

"Susan, it's Liza Vallan. I'm so sorry to call so late. I…"

"Liza, I'm so sorry for you and Ted. This is all so terrible. Is there anything I can do for you?"

"Susan I need the name of the young woman mentioned in today's paper who was found dead in her apartment on Saturday. You can tell anyone I asked you, I…I will be responsible. I…"

There was silence on the line for a few seconds.

"Harriet Summers, Liza." And she hung up.

Henry packed up some chicken for Wiley and Kathy drove him to the hotel. On the ride over they didn't talk too much. Wiley asked about the hospital. He had Kathy describe the general layout of the different parts of the facility. It passed the time during the ride and helped Wiley construct an image for some of the recent events. But very little. Kathy dropped him and continued on to her home in Burlington. He figured her a hard person to know.

* * *

"Hola Abuela, it's Jimmie. Is Idelia still up?"

"Yeah, sure. Hold on James." Formal and no idle chatter.

"Jimmie!"

"Hi babe, hope I'm not too late? You and Jimmie doin' okay? Somethin else up here."

"We're good. Papi and Jimmie had a great day. They're both out for the count." Some concern in her voice. "I hoped you would call. You okay?"

"Oh guess I'm fine. This business up here, it's a mess. Last thing anyone's gonna care about up here is the homicide on 133rd Street. Not sure coming to Vermont was a great idea. These people got their troubles.

"I mean that Lieutenant running the investigation; I told you about him. Well he still sounds strange now that I'm here. Expect I'll meet him tomorrow and ain't looking forward to it too much. Nasty guy but I have to say this Vallan, maybe his family too, they got their troubles. Bastard that Lieutenant is, got to say there's plenty looks bad for that Captain. Bad news just keeps coming. Some things 'bout his family may not be right also. Wonder if even Henry might be holding back on me. Maybe not.

"Dunno babe, maybe coming here wasn't a great idea. Thinking about one more time with the Captain tomorrow and maybe coming home. Let them try to figure out their own mess. I don't know. Not sure what I want to do. You know, maybe the guy is innocent but maybe someone else in the family isn't. What does figuring that out do for anybody? You know?"

"Oh Jimmie, that doesn't sound too good. You do what you think is best. But we're okay here. Really." Idelia paused and the line was quiet for a moment.

"You know Jimmie you are up there and that Henry is hoping you can help some. Know what I think I might do in your spot? Maybe take a shot, maybe it's a long shot, who knows, at guessing the ex-cop is innocent and then considering who else could have done it and let the chips fall wherever. Then get out of there and come home in a coupla' days to me and Jimmie, junior."

At that moment Wiley didn't think much about what she said. Was he already homesick just hearing her voice? He couldn't remember the last time at night they weren't together in the same bed.

****

MONDAY, MONDAY

A night of restless sleep followed and he was up, showered, and dressed early Monday morning. He was staying in a nice place, the Catamount Inn, on the eastern border of Burlington, very close to the hospital. Henry was meeting him at nine so they could go back to the correctional facility and try one more time to get something from Ted Vallan. Then they would meet with the enigmatic Lieutenant Shawn Barry in Williston, wherever that was. Right away Wiley wanted to talk with Henry about how serious and committed he was to getting the whole truth.

Idelia's words came back into his head early in the morning. Her idea might be good. Check-out everyone else. He figured that meant they really should try to learn more about the emails to Ted. Maybe talk with an expert about how to try to find out who was writing them. One person? more than one?

* * *

THE LAW IS THE LAW/   Courtesy of the NYPD Wiley ate too big a breakfast in the coffee shop. He assumed a real cop would have gone for a run instead of stuffing himself. He paid for his big meal with belching and some indigestion throughout the morning. It was a cool, overcast day. Rain was likely at some point.

When he arrived Henry looked down and totally serious. He had driven over in his father's car. He said nothing about his family. He offered no quick response to Wiley's words about possible risks of seeking the truth. Henry left it up in the air if after meeting with Barry they'd drive to Richmond to see Liza and Kathy.

Wiley burped his way outside to the hotel lot where they each walked towards the other's car, parked close together. Wiley stopped. Henry explained James needed to learn how to find his way around. Wiley hesitated but didn't argue.

Together in the NYPD unmarked, with Henry directing, Wiley pulled out into the traffic on Williston Road. A quarter of a mile up the road he misunderstood what Henry said and made an obviously illegal left turn onto Spear Street. They had gone a half-mile farther down the road when they heard *WUP,WUP* and could see flashing lights coming from behind them. In unison they each said "Oh shit."

Officer Andy Smith's expression broadcast his anger. For the traffic division this vehicle's violations were adding up: a dangerous, illegal left turn in traffic, missing a right brake light, and did not signal (or faulty left rear signal light). Of course there were additional unofficial points for having all this with New York plates.

"License and registration please. Just made a really dangerous illegal left turn. No signal either and I see a brake light out."

Well, Wiley had a registration but no license. Wiley produced the registration and his NYPD ID and shield for Officer Smith. It was all he had. Henry was astonished. They both were increasingly uncomfortable.

"Step out of the vehicle please."

Wiley got out. Henry was pissed at Wiley and himself. They brought this on themselves. If Henry had known he would have had Kathy drive them today. Officer Smith looked in the car through the driver's door as James got out.

"And who are you?"

"My name is Henry Vallan, Officer."

That raised an eye. The name was almost poison in Vermont right now. It held maximum notoriety at the moment. Reacting to the sudden burst of information generated by this stop Officer Smith stepped back, possibly constructing a bigger picture in his mind as he mulled it all over.

Officer Smith was torn about his anger, his duty, and the need to consider courtesy to a fellow law enforcement officer.

"Mr. Vallan, I suppose you have a driver's license, right?"

"Well actually Officer I live in New York City and got home to Vermont last night and found my license is expired."

"Mr. Vallan why don't you step out of the vehicle also."

This was getting bad. He couldn't let either of them drive.

Two Vermont State Police cruisers, traveling at a fast clip, started to go by coming from the opposite direction. They slowed and each put their lights on and turned around pulling up behind Officer Smith's patrol car. Traffic slowed to a crawl in each direction.

Lieutenant Barry certainly knew Henry Vallan. Minutes before, at the correctional facility, he also had just looked at a copy of the name and photo ID of the NYPD detective who signed in to see Ted Vallan the evening before. He was still disturbed the Detective turned out to be the obnoxious cop he had spoken with a few days before. Henry softly whispered to Wiley it was Shawn Barry walking towards them. Officer Smith missed that. He was still busy reacting, first to stopping a fucked-up NYPD cop, and now two state troopers showing up. Not to mention someone from Ted Vallan's family in the mix.

The Lieutenant and the Detective sized each other up. It wasn't really a contest; not even close. There was a time when he first became an investigator Shawn wore a suit for a while. Ted had always pushed for wearing the uniform. He told Shawn the VSP uniform had a variety of useful effects on the public. And he was right. At this moment Shawn looked fit and sharp. He had a smart appearance. Wiley was swallowing occasional burps. His suit was wrinkled and exposed his early paunch. Not anything to look at. This was Shawn Barry's territory anyway so he was probably bound to be the master of this interaction no matter what he looked like.

Officer Smith filled in the Lieutenant and his deputy on the situation. Barry and Wiley stared pretty consistently at each other. Notably, Shawn did not really look at Henry. Without any formal introductions or even a handshake the Lieutenant seemed to make his decision about how this was to go and announced his plan accordingly and publicly. It started to drizzle lightly.

"Officer Smith you've uncovered a big problem here. Detective Wiley and I have been in touch about a case in New York City and he's up here to interview a suspect in a City homicide. I guess the NYPD a little too hasty planning his trip; defective vehicle, unlicensed driver, and such. But I do think we need to let the Detective quickly complete his business here today and get back to his city."

With that he turned to his deputy.

"Trooper Dark would you please write something out to allow the Detective to stay in Vermont until midnight tonight with his defective vehicle and without a driver's license. After that, and in other states, you will have to be on your own Detective.

"I guess I'll see you in about an hour or so at the Williston Barracks to review notes about Ted Vallan's time in New York. Okay?"

Lieutenant Barry turned to walk back to his cruiser. Wiley nodded and said a clear thank you as Barry walked away. Barry never acknowledged that or Henry Vallan's presence. If this was a win the Lieutenant wanted he got it here. Wiley wasn't going to try to wrest anything from this mess. The get out of Dodge order seemed like something from the old west. Wiley figured he'd worry about that later, if he had to.

He really couldn't fault the Lieutenant for their own stupidity and carelessness. But man, the guy looked happy to have dominated him and undoubtedly wasn't planning to work with him. That seemed for sure. Wiley wondered again, especially then, what he was doing in Vermont? He decided to give it the day and see what happened. What was he going to tell the Commander? Tessie, anyway.

As Wiley and Henry climbed back into the car they looked at each other and successfully fought any temptation to get into a verbal row about how both agreed to drive without licenses. Not their best move and had to cast doubt, even for them, on the investigative effort they were supposedly teaming up for. At first they turned around and started to go get Henry's car. After some almost laughable back and forth they decided Wiley, with his timed free pass, would drive his car…slowly. The major fuck-up, unbelievable to each of them, actually drew them closer together.

They were both flustered, but Wiley held onto his purpose and aimed to get as much from Ted Vallan as he could.

* * *

JAIL TIME 1 – FIRST MOVE GOES TO THE STATE/   The Lieutenant and his deputy were returning to Williston after making sure they were at the correctional facility early to interview Ted before anyone else, including a lawyer, met with him. It was damn important to Barry to have Ted answer some questions before the case got any more contaminated by the cop from the City.

From what he had seen watching Ted on the live closed circuit feed from the day room late in the afternoon yesterday the man looked pitiful and withdrawn. What he heard from the jailers about the Captain's meetings with Dr. Sam and then his son and the cop in the evening suggested Ted was kind of out of it. Unlikely most anything happened to interfere with the case he was building.

Today the Lieutenant would sit on the other side of the two way mirror while Trooper Dark interviewed Ted. Shawn assumed

Ted was aware he was being watched but doubted it would be an impediment to the interrogation.

In an interrogation the initial path of inquiry can be the most critical. Trooper Dark's opening was an immediate error which instantly made the entire meeting slow and mostly meaningless. His first question brought home to Ted his complete failure and a rush of despondency over-came him. It was not the first time.

"Captain Vallan, why did you run? What did you think that would accomplish?"

Ted shrunk, visibly, farther down in his chair. The Lieutenant, and even Dark, knew it was already over. How could Ted answer a question that became nonsensical after he had tried to live it? Tell them he was going to work his own case?

He could have said he knew he was set-up or had panicked; or, if he was guilty, to get away. But his mind was far from understanding what was going on. He was bathed in despair. Head down, Ted barely moved so his eyes could meet the Trooper's.

"I dunno."

It never got any better for Trooper Dark's interrogation. He rambled on with his questions and Ted mumbled one or two word replies. Nothing to benefit either of them.

At one point Dark asked a long question about Ted's apparent effort to study one case to learn about hospital systems. He reviewed for Ted what he knew and his question was about his interviews.

"If you picked that case at random to study why did you ask so much about controlled drugs and how they are managed in the hospital? And why did you ask how much narcotic it would take to overdose someone? Dark never should have put those two separate questions together.

Ted understood it as one question and obviously answered the first.

"Wasn't sure. Maybe diversion. Not sure."

Shawn knew they had no business talking to Ted like this. And he wasn't getting anything anyway, for all the risk. He heard a lawyer was in the works. Ted was barely answering and seemed confused. Who knew if he would or wouldn't be able to respond better to a lawyer, or even his family, when he talked more with them? He had an officer pull Dark out of the room and went after him angrily.

"Listen, just ask about his daughter and get out of there. You got it?"

Dark accepted the scold and went back in. Ted hadn't moved; he looked frozen; a statue.

"Captain, when you went through that case you must have been aware your daughter, Kathy Vallan Conover's, name appears on that chart. Why didn't you speak with her about that case?"

This time Ted looked up more directly at the Trooper. His face remained glazed over. Ted had no idea why he was being asked that question. At that moment his answer did nobody any good.

"She's my daughter."

Dark might have tried to follow-up but he didn't and ended his effort. Shawn was pissed. Afterwards Ted thought some more about the question. He thought it should have meant something to him about the State Police investigation. At that moment he was unable to put anything together, but it stayed with him.

Even in a deep depression there can still be thinking. How clear?... Kathy? Ted could not figure out what role Liza played in all of this. He hadn't thought at all about Kathy. Could she be involved? Ted pushed himself to wonder if she would ever do something thinking she was helping him...or did she hate him so much for the way their relationship changed after the affair? Could she have done this to hurt him and get him out of her life?

Of course not. She would never do any of that, he knew...Ted's face turned red and his lips and cheeks sank. If only he could cry. What had he done to his daughter? At a time when piling on more signs of his failures in life was his predilection, adding his conduct with his daughter to his long list was not difficult. But this one Ted felt was a revelation that was long overdue.

He had no idea there was an overdose component to the homicide.

* * *

JAIL TIME 2A – THEN THE DEFENSE/   This time when Henry and Wiley arrived at the front desk at the correctional facility the officer on duty made it clear they would not be allowed to see the Captain together; only one at a time, for thirty minutes max. They each probably had different agendas anyway. Henry was to be first and before he went in they reviewed some questions and who might pursue what. Wiley advised Henry there was a good chance someone would be listening to the interviews.

Ted didn't look much better. New outfit but he hadn't shaved which made it unlikely he had a shower. He didn't respond much differently either despite appearing a little better rested. Henry was upset at Ted's appearance but also somewhat frustrated at how it remained like dental work getting him to speak, much less really cooperate. The whole business remained terrifying.

Henry told Ted Wiley and he thought Shawn wasn't handling the case correctly. Wiley wanted to get the State Police leaders to understand that. Wiley said he had some ideas but had to be careful how he handled contacting them. He also told Ted the New York State Trooper, Captain Regardi, was following along also. What Henry was saying would have raised Shawn Barry's interest but, in fact, there was no listening device on. Nothing he said seemed to arouse Ted's interest.

Henry spoke, venting some frustration, then immediately greatly regretted what he said to the tired old man sitting before him.

"Dad, don't you think it's time for you to be coming out of this?" He made it up. "We're making progress and I think you're going to be okay. Don't you? We need for you to bounce back. You could be helping more, you know."

Ted was still stuck plumbing the depths of his depression and despair. It was far from over yet in his mind. Worry over what the next disaster would be continued to preoccupy his mind.

* * *

JAIL TIME 2B – MORE FOR THE DEFENSE/ Henry's time with his father did have an impact on Ted. Just a day before he lay on a cot in the Albany jail and reviewed some details in his mind. Now there was a young cop sitting across from him asking him questions he had wondered about also.

Wiley was done with New York City. Today he wanted to try to better understand some of the emails, especially if there was any basis in fact for any of them. He heard how Becker went after Ted publicly and had seen the emails.

"What went on at the medical meeting that got that Becker so angry at you in public and his emails?"

Ted didn't visibly react to the question. Later Wiley would describe his expression as stuck on glum. He stared off at nothing; his face looked flat. Ted felt he had done poorly on the run as a perp and now he wasn't sure he'd do any better trying to help his own investigation. He was continually distracted. He worried he had yet to mine the extent of his despair. He continued to constantly fear what would happen next.

Finally though, this was the interest and help he had dreamed about days before. He tried to believe Henry and this Detective were not going to give up on him. But attempts of others at reassurance just hadn't cut it.

If Liza had been around at all, in short order, she would have told the others and tried to explain to Ted he was suffering major depression; a well-defined, function impairing clinical problem. But Ted would not see or speak with Liza.

Within his limitations it was Ted's intention to be helpful. He did not mean to complicate Henry's or Wiley's efforts. He spoke without moving or emotion. His words came slowly and haltingly but his thoughts were expressed much more easily, almost in sentences. Both he and Wiley were surprised.

"Told me was routine meeting of medical staff; doctors… Surprised there were not a lot of people there… Liza was." He stopped for a moment. His brain drifted. The man he saw Liza with in that hallway couldn't have been Becker, right?… "Was there so Chief of Staff could introduce me. Told them I was new Director of Security and hospital computer systems security. Before got up he told them I retired from the force… Remember he gave them long version of formal title when I was with the force. Remember now…thought made it sound like hired to investigate hospital… And said I was husband of 'Doctor Liza Vallan'… I recall that.

"Remember what I said because worked on it for two weeks before… Stood up. Reminded those doctors computers were revolutionizing many aspects of what happened in hospitals, from direct patient care to service and business areas…Told them patient privacy was a major concern… Reminded them every computer terminal was linked but each had a distinct footprint and could be tracked… Ended telling them importance of all this meant new regulations and even laws coming out to guide in using this technology safely and legally… Sat down after."

Ted looked exhausted from the effort to remember and speak.

"I know you're tired Captain, but that's really helpful. Doesn't sound like anything that should have set anyone off, 'cept maybe, like you say, got some there uncomfortable they'd be getting watched, you know. Captain what about this Becker and the stuff you were working on with that case in the hospital? You seem to think there could be a link there, right?"

Ted, looking like he had almost instantly regressed, nodded yes.

Wiley took a piece of paper from his pocket and unfolded it in front of Ted. He asked Ted to look at it. He very simply asked Ted if he recognized the name on the paper as one of the people he had interviewed for the case he was reviewing. Ted looked puzzled but, again, nodded yes.

The name was Harriet Summers.

Wiley thought to end with a few questions about Shawn Barry. If the Lieutenant was listening it didn't worry Wiley. He knew Barry was aware of how he felt about him. If he ruffled Barry's feathers a little more that might be good. Make him nervous.

"Captain, Lieutenant Barry isn't talking to you or anyone in your family. If he's in charge don't see how he can work a case without personally speaking with the folks involved. You think he's working the case honestly? You and he talk at all before this?"

"Shawn called every few weeks to ask some advice… Bad situation. I should never have let it happen… Worry he won't be fair? Sure."

Wiley had to leave. He was surprised he couldn't bring himself to ask something about Liza. Too difficult for him also. So he tossed out a last query.

"We all make enemies over a lifetime. Captain, anyone out there who's name hasn't come up who you think could have set you up?" Wiley was pretty sure only someone with access and well known to hospital staff could have plunged a knife in that guy.

Ted's head dropped down. Was his mind elsewhere? Very slow speech again.

"Too hard to say… Too hard to say."

The words trailed off each time. What did he mean? Was he saying he couldn't think of anyone, or did he mean it was too hard, too upsetting, to talk about someone?

* * *

The ride to Williston was short. Wiley was stuck on why Becker went after Ted so publicly at that meeting. Henry and Wiley looked at each other. Henry tried to stress if that was what he said, Ted's words didn't sound especially provocative.

"That's looking at it backwards, Henry. Our job is to figure out why what he said did set off Becker. Even if it wasn't Becker who wrote that email." He didn't say it but he wondered if none of that was the real story. And he wasn't sure what any of this might have to do with Harriet Summers so he left that for now.

They quickly drifted to Ted's sorry appearance and limited interest and apparent inability to assist them much. Henry was startled his mother hadn't seen Ted despite what he assumed was his father's desire to shield her from the condition he had devolved into. Henry was surprised his mother accepted that. That was not her style. She would live and die a take charge woman, he thought. He could see she was different since he arrived. Kathy defended her actions. She told Henry their mother was living in a daze; clearly not herself. Kathy thought their mom was in shock and didn't know what was the right thing to do anymore.

They were clear Ted was still stuck in a deep hole ruled by the depths of depression and despair. Obviously this was far from over yet in his mind. He barely ate and his efforts at sleep were fitful, at best. No one had taken charge to aggressively manage the care and feeding of an episode of traumatic physical and mental exhaustion. And Ted was right, it wasn't over. Eventually Henry and Wiley realized this couldn't be called post-traumatic stress because it wasn't clear the stress was over. They would have to work within Ted's continuing limitations. Wiley added one more victim to his growing list.

* * *

Back in his cell Ted's review of the day's interviews was not kind to him. Why should his repeated failures stop now? Ted allowed himself to be consumed by visions of his failures. It pulled him lower; farther down. He thought he failed his family. He failed to be able to stay out on the street. He failed to put any pieces together to even begin to figure out what was going on in his own case. And he recognized his continuing abject failure to adapt, in most any way, to his incarceration. What greater sign of failure could there be for a man who devoted decades of his life to being a law officer than being locked up?

He may not have thought so but a bigger failure may have gone unrecognized by Ted. Was that an inability, from the beginning and continuing especially now, to accept others would, along the way, step forward to help support and seek to extricate him from his nightmare and solve this case. Why couldn't he have assumed that from the start? Too late now?

* * *

A PROFESSIONAL VISIT TO THE VSP WILLISTON BARRACKS/   One of the growing local suburbs, Williston, is minutes from downtown Burlington and also the Chittenden Regional Correctional facility. The State Police headquarters for the Burlington region is located there. As they pulled into the parking lot of the Williston Barracks they talked strategy. James advised Henry not to say much, or even anything. On arrival at the Barracks it was clear they were expected. The woman at the desk announced the Lieutenant would only meet with the Detective. Perhaps another time with family; too busy at the moment. Wiley offered a knowing glance to Henry. He was not surprised.

Wiley was shown to a small conference room Barry was using when he was working in Williston. This time Lieutenant Barry was slightly less cold to Detective Wiley. He stood up and offered his hand. Why shouldn't this guy be cordial, Wiley thought? This was all his turf. Wiley wasn't sure but thought there was a good chance Barry thought Wiley already owed him one. He guessed maybe he did. And the Detective's time in Vermont hadn't proved especially useful so far. Going home and leaving a lost cause was on his mind. The meeting turned out to be brief.

"Lieutenant, you were right… things don't look good for that Captain Vallan. Looks like he's in a heap of trouble."

"Detective Wiley, can you tell me what happened with Captain Vallan in New York City?"

Straight to the only point he was interested in with this cop. Wiley responded in a tone that suggested he had all he needed for that incident, and homicide.

"Yeah Lieutenant, we've worked that case through in the City and I think I got what I needed from the Captain. It's pretty buttoned-up. Case of mistaken identity an self-defense…nothin' more. Vallan was on the run and crazy lost in the City. Sat down on a bench in a park to rest and some really bad guys thought he was a narc. Would have been some tough acting for a guy like him, eh Lieutenant?"

Barry did not react.

"So he found himself with some dealers who were thinking he was talking to a stooge. Our guess is Captain wound up in the middle with the stooge about to be murdered and got sucked into the fight. Accidents happen in circumstances like that. You know? No chance Vallan was meant to be any part of that. Murder One here in Vermont will be the story for him, I guess."

Barry leaned forward and placed both hands on the table, possibly planning to stand up. He heard all he wanted to hear. Wiley got it and hurriedly spoke again.

"Lieutenant, Henry Vallan showed me something from the paper this morning about the death of a young woman this weekend. Did you know that woman was one of about ten people at the hospital interviewed by the Captain as part of a patient's case he was investigating for possible drug diversion in the hospital?"

Barry stayed in his ready to stand position and responded.

"Detective, the Captain told many people he was using a random patient's files to study and learn all about patient care in the hospital and the role of IT programs in the hospital. We hear he talked to a large number of people. No mention of any investigation from anyone."

Now he did stand up. Before Wiley could do likewise the Lieutenant had one more thing to say.

"Detective, those interviews you're talking about…did you know Kathy Conover, his daughter, also was in on the care of that patient but was never interviewed?"

As he ushered Wiley out of his office he wished him an uneventful return trip back to the City today.

* * *

A CRITICAL JUNCTURE?/   "You know Henry, maybe I should go back to the City."

Henry was unhappy but not surprised. They each agreed there was every indication Barry's investigation was biased but didn't know what they could do about it. And Wiley wasn't at all sure Vallan wasn't guilty anyway.

"James there's more to do. I bet my dad will come around and help himself soon. I know you're not happy we haven't talked to my mother…"

"Or your sister," he interjected.

"Yeah…" Henry looked off out the window. "But what about those emails? Can't we track down the info about them?"

"Maybe I can show them to our computer forensics people in the City and see if they can work that at all. Of course everyone might be watching that email account by now and any NYPD snooping might not be so good."

"James, there's this guy at the hospital who was helping my dad learn about computers. My mother told me. My father knew nothing about them when he started; a real Luddite. I wrote his name down. He's in charge of IT services. Must be a geek."

So, Wiley noted, Henry was talking about some of this with his mother.

"Maybe we can talk to him and see if he might be willing to help. My laptop is in the back and my dad gave me the info for getting into his account."

Wiley decided he could be patient for a while longer. He did want to leave today though. If this next effort fell flat he was going home.

* * *

The last few days Hiram Wouk felt like he was living in a cyclone. Everyone was asking him what he knew about Ted Vallan; State Troopers, local cops, a bunch of hospital administrators, and almost everyone he ran into. Some were long interviews and he had to show them what was on Ted's hospital computer. He was falling behind on his work so he tried to do some from home at night. He was getting worn out. He hoped it would all settle down with the new week. Wouk tried not to think one way or another about Ted Vallan, although he liked him. He sure knew nothing about what happened. All he could really tell anyone who asked was he suspected Captain Vallan was in over his head working with computers. But he admired his tenacity and he was improving.

Wouk listened patiently over the phone while Henry Vallan explained his needs and asked if he and the Detective could come to the hospital to meet with him. Hiram wouldn't have minded helping Ted out and was attracted to the idea of an interesting search but he was too busy.

"Listen Mr. Vallan, I'm so far behind I haven't even had lunch today. Maybe in a few days. And I can't do anything in the hospital. No, can't use this equipment. I…"

"Mr. Wouk, We're practically next door, at the Catamount. I can pick you up and bring you here and get you lunch while you use my laptop and the hotel's WiFi. Just to get a quick Idea about what you think and what, maybe, could be done. I don't mean to sound crazy but we may be getting down to my dad's last chances to prove his innocence."

There was a pause on the other end of the line.

"I can't do anything like this with any detective around. If you pick me up can't risk anything maybe could be illegal. Just willing to consider a favor for your family, Mr. Vallan. I may not be able to help anyway."

* * *

So they walked to the parking lot and Wiley listed his questions for Henry. They decided Wiley would take the unmarked to a place a short distance away to try to get the faulty lights fixed.

Wiley cracked, "maybe I can get this fucking car street legal anyway. Might make my next pull-over a little easier."

* * *

Walking into the room with lunch for Hiram Henry was disappointed to find out this relatively new thing called WiFi wasn't available at the hotel. But Hiram was intrigued by the problem presented to him. Henry had covered the body of the messages so Hiram only had access to the technical mail features of the paper copies he showed him. He had some immediate ideas. They came up with a plan. Hiram would take the laptop and all of Ted's account information and work on it in the evening.

Henry knew Wiley would be disappointed and probably try to plan to leave. He wondered how he could entice Wiley to stay at least another day? He was pleased with Wiley's initial response when he returned with his repaired his car.

"Well, getting something from him could be very big. If the dead man was doing it, from way back, who knows what that story was but it's over now and won't help your dad. Otherwise, if anyone else or others, all bets are off and would be good to track all that stuff down. But you know Henry, this guy will be able to read all those emails. And, I guess if he wanted to he could delete all of them. Guess we're at a point where you got to trust somebody."

It sent a chill down Henry's spine. No other option. He tried to move on to abort any plan Wiley might have about leaving today.

"James, you should come to my house for dinner and talk with my mother. I think I can get Kathy to come over sometime also."

Wiley said nothing, but he was pleased. With the unmarked now more cosmetically and electrically correct all he had to do was drive very carefully and he'd probably be okay. If he left on Tuesday he doubted the Commander would care. He'd call in later.

* * *

MONDAY'S PROFILE IN COURAGE?/   After an hour Detective Wiley was edgy. Pacing in his small hotel room was unpleasant. He thought of Ted Vallan, or any perp for that matter, locked in a small enclosed space. Not likely to breed relaxation. He still had a few hours to go before he was going to the Vallan home in Richmond…for dinner? Strange crew to break bread with, he thought. He was committed until the morning. He decided he would call Tessie and try to spin his time as more productive than it had been. No, first he'd call Idelia and hope she could cheer him up.

Two firm knocks on the door interrupted his plan. Stronger knocks than he figured for Henry or imagined from what he knew of that Hiram Wouk. He quickly scanned around the room for where the revolver he brought with him was. Located it but didn't get it.

Standing in uniform at the door was Trooper Donald Dark. 'Maybe his name tag really did say Duck.' There was another young man with him, wearing a cheap suit like Wiley's, carrying a six pack under his left arm. Dark and Wiley nodded and Wiley stepped back for the two men to enter and Dark closed the door after they were in. Wiley's brain took off for a few seconds. Was this going to be his equivalent of the last supper? Was he about to have a drink and then a police escort to the city limits, or state line?…Or worse? And it did say Dark on the guy's tag.

"Detective Wiley, this is Jack Hardy a detective with the BPD. He and I, mostly him, are investigating the death of a woman who worked at the hospital pharmacy. Don't know if you know much about it." Not really a question.

Detective Hardy and Wiley shook hands. Wiley motioned to the two chairs in the small room and he sat on the bed. So far Wiley had said nothing.

"Detective, your guy, Vallan, and maybe Vallan's daughter are in big trouble."

Wiley had not been so sure Kathy Conover was considered more than a big thorn in his side by the Lieutenant. 'Big trouble' could only mean involvement in the poisoning of that Becker or, no… not possible…the stabbing? Or somehow involved with her father in the death. 'Shit!'

"We're all cops, right Wiley?" Dark didn't wait for a response. "We should all be working for the same thing, right? Well I guess it's looking like there may be more going on with this case than we thought a few days ago."

'Who was we' Wiley wondered?

"Detective, Jack has looked into the life of that lady who died and it's looking more and more like she was tied in with the dead man, Becker." Dark turned his head toward Detective Hardy. "Jack."

Detective Jack Hardy was relatively new at the BPD and only recently promoted to detective. The three of them sitting there in that confined room were all beginners in a way. Wiley looked older but he probably wasn't. Hardy looked on the ball but with an easy smile which suggested he knew what a good time was also. As Hardy spoke Wiley mostly watched Dark and his reaction. As important facts flowed from Hardy Dark looked down at the floor, a grim expression on his face; maybe disappointed in himself.

"Detective Wiley I talked to a bunch of people. Dead woman's brother was very clear he had figured his sister was having some kind of relationship with that Dr. Becker for maybe a year. She wouldn't talk to him about it, that's one of the ways he was sure he was right. Had to press her parents hard but after a while they said they tried to ask dead lady, Harriet, once and she ran out of the house." Hardy stopped, pulled the six-pack apart and distributed a can to each of them and popped one for himself.

'Interesting way to do policing,' Wiley thought. He reminded himself to keep his guard up; but he was relaxing.

"I been talking to the people in the hospital pharmacy. Where she worked, you know. Really nothing obvious there on a quick check for a diversion but Director there admitted to me it's not always that easy to be sure. Told me they had an outfit come in about five years ago and they caught someone. So he said from what he understood from the Medical Examiner he's planning to get that group back in. The guy is suspicious but, on first look, something on nursing may be more likely he says. But that doesn't fit with the lady.

"As I was leaving his office I told the Director there might be some link between the technician and that dead Doctor. Director said it was a puzzle to hear that quiet lady could be connected to Dr. Becker. I guess this Becker had a rep of being as loud as she was quiet. And Director said he was a doc and she handled drugs and punched a clock, so this news worried him. Know?"

All interesting and maybe major findings in a case stacked so strongly against the Captain. But why were these guys coming to him? Not likely to want to share a beer in the middle of the day and shoot the shit with an out of state cop for the hell of it. For a minute or two they sat, quietly sipping their beers, staring at nothing. Wiley decided not to ask the obvious question yet about what this had to do with him. Then Trooper Dark spoke.

"Detective Wiley, this is a nasty case that's put a big strain on lots of people. Even in the force. My boss started out acting like he could handle all that was going on. But I've watched him get angrier and angrier. It's affecting how we're working this case. I don't see anyone in the brass challenging the way he's running it. I think everyone has convicted your boy, Vallan. And maybe he is guilty. Still looks like it." Dark's features on his face sharpened. He leaned in.

"But that doesn't mean we shouldn't be following leads; evidence. You know what I mean?"

Both detectives were watching Dark intently and nodded in the affirmative.

"Well the Lieutenant doesn't want to hear about the things Dave is finding. Told me to drop it and stop wasting my time and his time." Dark paused and looked at both men. "I don't think that's right."

The tone of his last sentence teetered between defensive and forthright. The guy was torn.

"Guys, I like my job. And I like the Lieutenant. But he's lost it over this one. Wiley I'm hoping you can find a way to get to the officers who run the force and get them to see this case is going off the rails. Innocent people could be getting hurt. If I go with Jack to his Chief my career in the force will be over…no matter what happens. You know what I mean." Dark took another long pull on his beer.

Wiley understood. He liked the way Dark presented it. Looked like Hardy did too. Dark was looking for some help and presented it like he'd do the best he could with Wiley. If Wiley couldn't help he figured Dark would do the right thing eventually, even if it meant the end of his career in the State Police. These were good guys.

Quiet again. Both the Vermont officers looked at Wiley for some kind of response. About an hour before he was marking time until he could politely excuse himself from the Vallans and return home. Then, only minutes before, he was jolted by a thought he might be packing right now, an escort standing by to ensure he left the state immediately.

But it wasn't that. He was being asked to take an active role in making sure everyone somehow involved in this case got a fair shake. Yeah, a search for the truth no matter where it led. Until this moment Wiley hadn't said a word. Now he spoke only one sentence.

"I have some ideas."

Hardy passed around the second round of beers. On duty, in an intense, covert moment, the three of them tried to relax…and shot the breeze for a while.

* * *

CHANCE ENCOUNTER/   Kathy Conover was set to meet in the afternoon with the same lawyer she and Liza spoke with late Sunday. The lawyer reviewed Liza's and Kathy's interactions with the State Police since the homicide and came away more concerned about Kathy than Liza. When Kathy recounted her last interview with Trooper Dark he seemed to take the implications of the trooper's words more seriously than Kathy. Kathy reacted the same way with him as when initially told by Trooper Dark Dr. Becker was not only stabbed but poisoned. She blew him off.

The lawyer asked why she wouldn't take the Trooper's words more seriously? Unless her defense was to be aggressively offensive it didn't make sense at such a dangerous time. Kathy repeatedly acted like any idea implying any involvement by her was outlandish; really, an insult; too ridiculous to be taken seriously. Finally she agreed to meet with him, privately, Monday afternoon.

Through the morning Kathy continued to stew over the whole business. Thinking about Dark and talking with the lawyer had made it all come alive to her again last night. She was not surprised the way Shawn was handling her father's case. Nor was she surprised he might react to any nuances or odd features that came up as an opportunity to go after any of them if he thought he could. Her hatred of him was chronic; her long simmering anger easily re-ignited. As this business ate at her she was also angry she had ever let herself, even for a moment, work through in her mind the potential impact of trying to help her struggling father after he was publicly attacked. And, of course, there was anger from, even fleetingly, wondering how she would feel if he was effectively gone from her life. Kathy cancelled the appointment.

Kathy had taken an open-ended leave from her work. With the hour or two she now had free in the afternoon she decided to run over to her office at the hospital to organize some materials for the other staff who were covering for her. Time was tight. She had to get one kid at daycare and the other came home by three-thirty. Before dinner she planned to go back to Richmond. Dave would take over with the kids then.

It really was a run. The Conover home was two miles from the hospital. She had no appetite but hydrated and took her usual route when she ran there. She hoped it would relax her. Heading to a rear entrance for the nursing school she had to cut through two parking lots. As she rounded a corner to a short, paved cul-de-sac between two buildings to get to her entrance Shawn Barry exited from an adjoining hospital exit. No one else was in that small space. The sun-shielded area was getting dark.

"Oh shit!...You hangin' out here looking for more Vallans to go after, Shawn?" She was a few steps from distraught and she was really pissed. Any relaxation generated by the run instantly vanished.

Shawn felt trapped. Arguing with Kathy would do nothing for him or the case. At first he considered ignoring her and continuing to walk to his cruiser. Then he decided he would stand there for a minute, let her vent, and go on his way. He reminded himself it wasn't his fault the Vallans had gone off the deep end. But Kathy stopped talking and just stood there, a few feet from him; glaring at him. He had to say something.

"You know, Kathy, I never started any of this. Your dad's done this to himself. And I'm sorry to see you in the middle of all this too." He looked away from her fiery gaze. "I'm gonna do my job. I can't cut any slack for anyone in this one Kathy." He kept his tone even. A shouting match wouldn't be good.

He disgusted her. Kathy's face projected her complete distain for him. She could not tell if he believed what he was saying.

"Well Shawn, this is not your finest hour. My dad didn't kill anybody. I took care of that fucker Becker for two shifts. Whether I hated him or not I'm a professional. I did what you're supposed to do: I gave him good nursing care… cause that's my job! Doesn't matter what he did. And you know what? Doesn't matter my dad got his ass in the wrong place with me ever since you and I hurt him. He's not your murderer and neither am I."

Kathy tightened the fierce look on her face.

"You ever think Shawn…what's gonna happen to you when this all blows up in your face?"

He heard what she said. He may not have liked what she was saying, but he understood what she meant. Shawn started to formulate a reply, then thought, 'fuck it,' turned from her, and went on his way. Kathy stood there and watched him go. She battled herself not to shout after him and didn't, but she wished she had.

* * *

MONDAY EVENING AT THE VALLANS/   Henry Vallan grew up, well, bookish. Liza mostly, and Ted to a lesser extent, thought he became noticeably distant after the terrible upset and lingering fallout for the family from his older sister's affair. He went to college in New York City and stayed there after he graduated, determined to be a writer. Henry remained an active member of the family, stayed in touch, and visited Vermont regularly. Still, Liza and Ted realized they actually knew little about Henry's life in the City. So much so that when he announced he was bringing someone home with him one weekend they decided it was fifty-fifty it would be a woman or a man.

Despite a few subtle signs otherwise Liza really believed all her family were truly in the dark about the most personal details of her life. In reality, her take on the way Henry used some relatively minor marital tension in his more recent book gave her the idea his brief narrative flirting with that actually protected her. He made it seem harmless. From time to time Kathy wondered about the possibility of her mother having an affair but, on reflection, thought there was likely nothing. But…well…yes…Henry was a very perceptive young man. His suspicions more than likely contributed to his writing.

* * *

Kathy Conover left shortly after the informal dinner she organized. Never said a word about her run-in with the Lieutenant. Liza started out the evening in a little better control. She wanted all of them to understand the huge impact of a major depression on a person. Everything she was hearing about Ted made it very likely.

Maybe he still wasn't going to get much from a Vallan but tonight Wiley's desire to make contact with Vermont State Police command leaders was much stronger now.

"Is that Cap'n Rondell Jewish?"

Henry was startled. Not many Jewish people in Vermont and Rondell was as un-Jewish sounding a name as he could think of. A little incredulous, he nodded no.

"Well, in the City I guess almost everybody would say somethin' going on up here that ain't kosher. Thought maybe you could say that to him and he'd get it… Just tell him this police investigation is biased."

Henry remained reluctant but nothing was really getting any better. Shawn scared him. Just the way he looked at the traffic stop. Like a man on a mission. Possessed.

Henry had mentioned Captain John Rondell to Wiley early on during the drive up. Until his retirement about six years before Ted's he had been Ted Vallan's immediate superior for most of Ted's investigative years. Not a man to get close to, the guy was notably more rigid than Ted. Endlessly disciplined, a requirement he demanded of others, he also was totally honest and fair. Rondell and Ted worked well together for years.

From the start Wiley suggested contacting him to bounce all this off him and get his input. Henry had no formal reason for why he held off. Maybe he considered Rondell too removed from the force and too old to likely offer anything. Probably a waste of their precious time. Always a hard guy for Henry to talk to as he remembered him. Tonight Wiley was really pressing him. He insisted.

Things were bad. His dad had fallen apart. Ted was right saying even if he eventually was cleared it might take forever and what would be left of him? Wiley seemed sure the investigation in Vermont was prejudiced and he was probably right. Monday evening Henry went ahead and tracked down Captain Rondell, a retired Chief of the Vermont State Police Major Crime Investigative Unit.

Rondell lived in Waitsfield, a beautiful small rural location made more sophisticated by its close proximity to several ski areas. At least the general store had wine and cheese selections that would be totally foreign in a majority of Vermont country stores.

For some reason Rondell asked to call Henry back in an hour. Wiley was disappointed and didn't want to be driving out late. He told Henry he was going to call Myron Smith, from NYPD Inter-State Agencies Liaison, about this in the morning since Mr. Smith had spoken with VSP officers on Saturday. Calling NY State Police Captain Regardi again on Tuesday was another option he was considering. None of them might be able to help, but he needed to try.

That evening Henry never queried, much less challenged, Kathy in any depth when she was there. And, just as the night before, he really gave Wiley no good opportunity to ask Liza any pointed questions that might relate to the emails. What there was no question about was Wiley's growing frustration with Henry. He motioned Henry to follow him to the hallway as he was leaving. His words were direct and Henry sensed his anger.

"Henry, we've been on this for twenty-four hours now and we got nothing, really. We know this Becker didn't do this to himself. We got no one else to even consider. Lieutenant Barry might want to bring your sister into this, and who knows, maybe even your mother. But you say that's bullshit. So Henry, there's someone else out there who wouldn't seem out of place in that hospital.

"Come on Henry, if those emails mean anything they go back years so it's not a stranger."

Henry looked down and shuffled his feet a bit, then looked up at Wiley. He looked like this was still a difficult subject for him to talk about. Henry also appeared to be worried they'd be overheard so he opened the front door and they took their discussion outside to the front porch.

"You know I wasn't around very much the last few years. My sister and I have noticed how my mom has been more and more committed to her work and I have wondered about some changes in her and in my parent's relationship together. But Jim, honestly, I haven't been around. if I pick out a name of someone I know of there's really no reason to think I know even half the people she knows or works with. How do I ask her such a question?

"My mom works with a lot of people on a regular basis, especially as a doctor but also in some of the community work she's always done. For many years her office in the ambulatory center has been right next to another internist and he's a really nice guy and I know they are both in the office and at hospital activities together all the time." Evidently considering that guy wasn't an entirely new thought for Henry. But he obviously had rejected that, believing he had no good reason to suspect any specific person he knew of who they needed to be looking at.

"Look, just like that fellow, I could probably think of eight or ten names of doctors or people who I know have worked with her or you might call friends of my mother; some married, some not. I mean it Jim, you want us to go after Samir, the ME? Or that Doc who's been in her clinic for years who's a really nice guy? You know, he's very smart and super educated. He actually was a major help and maybe a big part of me getting my first book published."

"So?"

Henry had no response. The man sounded like an obvious choice if you were considering people who might fit the picture they were looking for. They stared at each other for a few seconds and then Wiley turned and headed down the front steps.

Once again Wiley was struck that even in the midst of profound disaster all the Vallans, including Henry, might still be keeping secrets. Wiley was on his way down the few steps when Henry surprised him by suggesting he had yet to show any of the emails to his mother. After expressing that he said nothing more to Wiley but, in that stinging moment, resolved to definitely show the copies to his mother... now.

Wiley drove off, finding himself repeatedly shaking his head as he worked his way, slowly, back to Burlington in the dark.

* * *

Of course Rondell was following the case. When he spoke later with Henry the few things Wiley had written down for Henry to tell the Captain seemed to shake him. But Rondell really said nothing definite. He asked Henry how his dad was doing. Henry wasn't sure what he should say. He decided to tell him Ted was in a bad way; very depressed. Rondell thanked Henry for the call. That was it. No advice or plan offered. In the morning Henry told Wiley it was a waste.

* * *

After hanging up the phone Henry walked from the kitchen to the small den where his mother was curled up tightly on the overstuffed chair. Like his dad she was down. Her eyes were red and puffy and her cheeks reflected her off and on tears. Liza looked up at Henry and then her head drooped down again. What a disaster. Both his parents were doing terribly five days after it all began.

"Mom, we're all in bad trouble. In the two days I've been here with James Wiley nothing's any better. This may go on a long time before it gets better. You and Dad have to hang in; take care of yourselves, so we can all see this thing through. Do you know what I'm saying?"

Liza nodded her understanding. Earlier he thought he had talked himself out of bringing up anything more about the murder this evening. After Wiley's rebuke he felt had no option; nothing he could dream up to allow him to delay any longer. He didn't want to but he went ahead anyway.

"Mom, why did you say that knife was Dad's?"

She looked up at him and kept her head up. She was remembering the scene.

"It *is* his knife, Henry. With the yellow handle. I was shocked. I don't know how it got there."

"But Mom, Dad agrees, he never had a knife like that…"

Liza shook her head disagreeing. "No, you should remember… from the book, Henry."

The emails would have to wait.

* * *

HACK YOU BACK/   Hiram Wouk recalled once reading an article about anonymous emails. He told Henry he heard there were ways to send an anonymous message but tended to believe that nothing is untraceable. It was just a matter of how much effort you are willing to put into doing the tracing. As soon as he said that he regretted having Henry think he was committing himself to the task and raising his expectations.

Among the better known options out there for anonymity were a small group of re-mailers who were willing to facilitate non-respondable (DO NOT REPLY) emails using a valid, but otherwise actually forged, sending address. Working backwards to determine an initial source would likely involve finding IP data and other things. He didn't see why that couldn't be accomplished or, at least, be possible. What might be harder, maybe much harder, was figuring out if someone was sending true email with another person's email address. Difficult enough for an individual to come up with a way to accomplish sending it. Solving that person's effort sounded even more difficult.

Hiram decided to start with the potentially easier problem. Someone who paid for or in some other way was using a form of an alias based system for anonymity might not have adequate knowledge about what they were doing or have protections to thwart someone from looking back into what they were using and did with it. Hiram was a geek and he was pleased he was making a career of his passion. 'Wow!' This was like consulting; one of his goals.

Initially he worked with the laptop but also his much faster desktop. He cracked into window after window and converted to data and code and back again. Mostly, as the geeks called it, he used command line interface, following algorithms and a trail. If he was unable to trace to a unique email his efforts would be for naught.

Later in the evening he thought he was successful. An AOL account looked like that was it. Hiram took a break and put that email address aside. He couldn't miss seeing some of the content of the emails. He felt bad for Ted. Would Ted Vallan really kill someone over these emails?

Around ten o'clock he started on the more challenging task of trying to determine who sent Ted emails with *hbecker* listed as the sender. From the start he knew they could have been sent by Dr. Becker or the address he thought he already had. But maybe not and that was a big maybe he guessed in a murder case.

Right from the beginning everything was more difficult. He thought it should be easy enough to determine if the emails came from Becker's account, but even that was uncertain. He was bogged down. He also was getting more tired and had to be at work early in the morning.

About one a.m. he gave up for the night. He was exhausted but frustrated and disappointed also. He knew he was in a business where you could always think you were very close and then something else would show up and need to be figured out, so the process would drag on. Hiram went to the bathroom to clean-up. While he was brushing his teeth he walked over to the desk everything was set up on and stood over the gear. He considered if there was any back door way to test if the email from the DO NOT REPLY, really AOL, posts could be the origin of a fake hbecker address. Still brushing, Hiram set up the laptop and opened Ted's account. He opened *compose*, typed 'testing' and played with a few technical possibilities. Nothing looked good. He was too tired to think clearly anymore.

He would call Henry Vallan in the morning and tell him what he had. Hiram began to clean up his work area. He reached over to close the large, cumbersome laptop cover and choked slightly on what was in his mouth. That caused a small cough, spraying a little toothpaste and saliva. Reflexively his hand barely grazed over the keyboard, removing a spot.

"Oh shit." 'Something might have gone out,' he thought. Then he doubted he had correct information up anyway. For a moment he wondered if he should wait up to see if an undeliverable message might come from Ted's provider. Too tired. He would check in the morning. Hiram decided to close the program down and check it at work in the morning. He put the laptop in his backpack, rinsed his mouth in the bathroom, and went to bed.

****

PART III - REVELATIONS

TUESDAY MORNING AND THROUGH THE DAY

TIME'S UP?/   James Wiley didn't want his continuing time in Vermont to develop into any kind of a routine. From his waking moments very early in the morning to the time the coffee shop opened and he could get breakfast any thinking about the homicide was contaminated by his growing intention it was time to return home. He kept watching the clock, waiting for the hands to move to the hour when he could try to contact Myron Smith and Captain Regardi. He hoped it wouldn't take all day. Wiley felt he had made a commitment to Trooper Dark to speak with VSP superiors before he left for home. Not hearing any word later last night from Henry about his phone call with retired Captain Rondell suggested nothing came of it.

Wiley wasn't sure what more the Vallans might be expecting from him. He worked for the NYPD. He wasn't on assignment or on his own to do private dick work. It bothered him quite a bit that he figured Ted Vallan wasn't guilty and he was truly astounded to see a cop like that Lieutenant Barry getting away with a badly tainted investigation. Beyond finding a State Police superior to speak with what else could he do about it? If the Vallans were more square with themselves he thought the investigation might go better, but he wasn't sure. They were rudderless, reacting not surprisingly, like a family acutely under a great attack; actually quite a disaster, he thought. Without some big breakthroughs Wiley could foresee the investigation taking a long time. Too long for him. James Wiley still had mixed feelings about his trip but he definitely wanted to go home.

* * *

LATE FOR WORK/   Tired and cranky, Hiram Wouk worried his whole day was in jeopardy. He had overslept. He dived into his work. Sometime around ten he remembered he had to contact Henry Vallan. Before he called him he thought he should check Ted's account. Hiram pulled out the laptop, plugged it into the Ethernet, and pressed start. He left the office for a few minutes and almost forgot about it when he returned. Doing two things at once he logged in and again left it for a few minutes. When he finally looked at Ted's email he was shocked. There was a new *hbecker* message. He opened it.

All it said was 'fuck you'… Well, whoever wrote that wasn't dead.

Hiram called Henry's cell but there was no answer, not unusual with spotty service in rural Vermont, so he left a message. Liza wasn't at her office. Frantically, he ran around the hospital until he found someone who knew her home number and was willing to call her. Only a message there also. What should he do?

* * *

MEMORIES/   How often do two people, or even more than two, recollect an event or something shared in their past differently? How can that be? What really happened? Or did it happen? If the old adage our memory plays tricks on us is true how can you be sure of anything in the past?

Memory not a worry for you? Don't be so sure.

* * *

SHAWN AND LIZA SEEK THE TRUTH?/   An hour or so before Herman Wouk appeared to confirm a screen name Henry Vallan was looking for Liza Vallan stiffly got out of her car in

Waterbury. It was a fine early fall day with a pleasant, expected, mild chill in the air. No one at the Waterbury State Police Barracks made any attempt to stop or even query Liza Vallan as she walked in the front entrance and through the commonly unlocked side door near the public window. She made a bee-line to Lieutenant Shawn Barry's office. Everyone knew Liza and were aware Liza knew Ted's old office location well. She acknowledged none of the startled faces. Heads turned as she passed. The look of sadness and shock on her face was obvious to each of them.

Shawn was equally startled to look up and see Liza Vallan in his doorway. For a moment he just stared at her. She looked terrible; she had aged in days. The only Vallan he felt remotely comfortable with these last years was Ted. He felt even better about Ted now that he was behind bars. He tried to think what he should say to her. While he dithered Liza spoke.

"Shawn, I'm told this is your case and I think I have important information for you. There are some things you should know. I don't believe Ted stabbed Harvey Becker, and I'm pretty sure I know who did."

While she spoke Shawn stood up and walked to his door gently ushering Liza to a chair while he closed the door with his other hand. He couldn't believe what he was hearing. He was still confident he had his killer…maybe killers. There were a bunch of wrinkles outstanding but no one had sure evidence Ted didn't do it, much less anyone else who did. What was this lady talking about? What did she want from him?

Shawn felt some sympathy for the hard luck of some of the Vallans lately and he understood what all this meant to Liza. But what did she want from him? Liza had given key evidence very early when she remarked in a crowded room the knife impaled in the dead man was Ted's. What was she going to do now? Change her story? He was sure nothing useful was about to happen but he was stuck. She showed up at his door and he would have to let her talk. He imagined she was quite desperate. She looked like shit.

"Shawn I'm complicit in this murder."

"What!" He let it out as a howl. 'Holy shit. Did she know what she was saying?' Did she understand she was telling him she was part of the homicide? He was shocked and astounded. He wondered if he should get someone in with them to take a formal statement? He tried to calm down. He decided he wanted to know what she was talking about before he'd have her share anything for the record.

His words contained a hint of anger. For five days he had controlled the case and information about it. His theories about both Ted Vallan and Kathy Conover left them as the prime suspects, as far as he was concerned, which was fine with Barry.

"You know, Mrs. Vallan you just walk in here and start telling me this five days after the homicide. How can that make any sense? What do you mean?"

Liza had tears and dabbed at them with a tissue in her hand.

"It's complicated Shawn. I'll tell you everything I know and I'll answer all your questions. It wasn't until last night that I remembered what happened years ago that helped me realize I was mistaken in that room."

'Mistaken? What the hell does that mean? What is she talking about?' He thought she was wasting his time. Shawn always found Liza a serious and pleasant person. He had no idea she would do something like this. She looked and sounded desperate. He reminded himself to be patient even if she planned to try to bullshit him. He was reluctant to admit to himself some slight pleasure in seeing a Vallan acting like this. Shawn was also pissed anyone was trying to complicate his effort at establishing the case that made sense and, admittedly, satisfied him.

* * *

"Shawn, I haven't slept in days. Last night I lay in bed staring at the ceiling again. So I got up and for no good reason picked up the first book Henry wrote. A cold sweat came over me when I realized what I had done. It was about the book. I remembered everyone, I guess except Ted, was excited Henry was writing a book about us, even if it was a little confusing how much of it was true. Most of it never really happened, you know."

Well Shawn had no idea what did and what didn't. There was that book again. Did it matter? Liza took a breath and raised her head and looked straight at Shawn.

"Shawn, for almost fifteen years I have had a strong friendship with Harold Dobson, a doctor who works in my office…This is difficult for me to speak about with anyone because at one time we were briefly intimate. Years ago Harold Dobson and I sometimes talked about Henry's first book as he was working on it. Henry mailed chapters to me and Ted for our comments and suggestions. I would often show the pages to Harold. He was much better read than I or Ted and if he had some comments I thought might be helpful I think I passed some of them on as though they came from me."

Liza could tell Shawn was having difficulty with her last words. He was still stuck on her mention of an affair. Actually Shawn was speechless. 'What the fuck' was the best he could do in his mind. After what he had been through with the Vallan family this was unbelievable. The secrets individuals…and families lived with were 'fucking unbelievable' he thought. He was absolutely stunned.

Shawn wasn't sure he could contain his anger and a hundred other emotions he was feeling. But he understood Liza was going to tell her story whether he listened or not. Liza looked so pitiful. Didn't matter If she was or wasn't on to something big, now she was going to lose, either way. But nothing she said yet made her complicit in anything so far. After a pause for Shawn to absorb the words she knew would shock him and probably almost everyone who knew her, Liza continued.

"Harold often said the work was not descriptive enough. It was only last night I remembered he said that knife played an important dramatic role in the story and needed to be better described. I said 'so should he say it had something like a bright yellow handle?' He liked that but thought there should be even more distinguishing features. He made it get so complicated I told him I wasn't going to say anything about the knife to Henry. But, we laughed about it and agreed Harold and I would privately know that knife should have at least had a yellow handle. For months we regularly joked about that yellow handle off and on.

"Shawn, you can look in the book. There's nothing about the handle one way or the other. It wasn't ever described as yellow. After talking about a yellow handle for months Harold Dobson and I remembered it that way over the years. It was my mistake in that room. I knew Harvey Becker was fighting with Ted and it upset Ted greatly. When I saw that knife in Harvey I didn't know what to think. I can't believe I was a part of making Ted appear guilty… I'm the guilty person.

"Shawn, Henry told your investigator there never was a yellow knife. Why didn't that make a difference?"

It was good Liza was too upset to pursue that with Shawn. She had to finish so she was clear she told him everything. After feeling good through most of Liza's confession he recognized if her story was true his management of the investigation was bound to be challenged; by his superiors and others. Who was this Dobson? Mostly he was still stunned by her admission of an affair. Probably going on while he and Kathy were together…and after!

"You can believe me or not, Shawn. Harold Dobson and I have continued to work together but he never got over our very short affair; even years afterward. When Ted began to work at the hospital I noticed Harold got angry at Ted being there. Harold didn't like Ted but he never disparaged him so openly in front of me before.

"I heard he refused to do his on-call on Sunday and didn't go to work on Monday, or today. Shawn, he needs to be checked to see if he's all right and I need to confront him about what happened to Harvey Becker."

Barry was going to have to find out what this was all about; soon. He could send somebody else, with or without Liza. But then more people would become involved and his ability to tightly control the investigation might be compromised. It would have to be him. Shawn agreed to go to this guy's home in Colchester, another suburb of Burlington.

"Shawn, I can drive right behind you. I know how to drive fast and follow closely with my blinkers on. I did it behind Ted sometimes. After all this I want to go to the jail to see Ted."

Shawn still felt an aura of officiousness in this unusual interaction with Liza. He tried to push away other feelings that were poking at him. This lady, a model for all motherhood and womanhood to everybody, maybe considered some sort of saint, had wound up in the same spot as he and Kathy did at one time. He wanted to try to remember more completely how she had reacted and behaved when his time with Kathy came out. He was too jolted and confused to remember much at the moment.

He felt some anger, but looking at the tearful, desolate, heartbroken woman across his desk softened him.

"No, I'm sorry Mrs. Vallan you'll have to ride with me. To use your own words, you may be complicit in a crime. I can't let you be on your own until this all gets better figured out."

Liza was in no state to do much more than take orders. She insisted, though, on calling Henry and when he didn't answer left a message on his cell telling him only where she and Shawn were going.

* * *

RIDING WITH AN ENEMY?/   Later, Henry was angry about what happened next. Through all the days of this horror story Liza had heard surprisingly little from Ted's recent colleagues and other leaders on the force. They probably did not know much of the history the Vallan's had with Shawn Barry but it still seemed unusual and awkward to Henry how little the VSP's commanding officers reached out to Liza during such a traumatic time. Leaving virtually every detail of the investigation to Shawn made no sense, almost out of character for the way the force ran; certainly when his father was there. Shawn had been afraid to spend time with Liza, or Kathy, which had to have delayed the progress of the investigation.

Able to check his phone and hearing Liza was driving alone with Shawn, Henry, probably affected by some of Wiley's very negative views of Shawn Barry, worried Shawn might be planning for this case to be resolved the way he wanted, no matter what. Convictions for Ted and Kathy would clear Shawn's slate of perceived personal hurt. Would Shawn do anything to harm or allow his mother to be harmed if it suited the outcome he was after?

Where were his superiors? Could one of Henry's unspoken observations over the years about his parents and the force actually be true? Did the Vallan's come across as too perfect? Too good to be admired? If his family was now reaping the effects of that perception that was sad and unfortunate. Any of his superiors who sat down for an hour with Barry to quiz him and discuss the case would have realized his involvement with the Vallan's probably disqualified him from leading the investigation.

Early on Wiley picked up on Shawn's feelings about his perp. This was never an unbiased investigation. There was plenty of complexity to this case, nevertheless both Henry and Wiley thought Barry was constantly trying to blow off many details. He was only focused on the Vallan family.

Called immediately by Henry, Wiley shared Henry's concern about Liza traveling alone with Barry. They each questioned why she didn't come to them first instead? So far only Liza knew the answer to that: unbearable embarrassment and guilt.

Until Henry and Wiley were together Wiley was unaware the home they needed to get to was owned by the helpful close associate of Liza Vallan Henry had spoken about last evening. Henry had been to his house once or twice so he remembered where he lived.

When Henry arrived in Burlington Wiley was waiting for him in the unmarked. After finding out who Dobson was Wiley looked alarmed and wondered out loud if he could be a link to the emails. With some intensity he verbalized a worry that if Hiram Wouk's probing of the emails last night was successful that could have set off some sort of alarm or warning to the man Liza mentioned. They had to hurry.

* * *

SHAWN NEVER QUITS/   They each stared straight ahead as Shawn drove; fast. Lights flashing and siren on. He decided he should get an idea if Liza knew anything that might implicate Kathy.

"Did you know that they found a lethal amount of morphine in that Dr. Becker?"

His words barely registered with Liza. She gave no thought to her response.

"What? Well that's crazy, isn't it? I had no idea. Why did that happen?"

Fortunately she left it there. Either Shawn was going to risk disrupting this trip and possibly Liza's cooperation or he would let it go and not imply anything that might lead Liza to consider any possible involvement of Kathy in her role as a per diem nurse last week. He said no more about it and noted no further reaction by Liza.

* * *

WALK RIGHT IN/   Often a bad sign in police work when the front door is more than unlocked. Although it wasn't too many years before that many Vermonters rarely locked their doors or their cars, Dobson's door wasn't just unlocked it was actually open a few inches. It was still a pleasant fall morning but most were using heat for their homes by now and a flow of warm air was apparent at the slightly open door. Lights and siren had been turned off many blocks before they arrived at his house, located in a quiet and secluded, heavily treed subdivision of large, gracious appearing, wood frame homes.

Shawn was about to knock and announce the presence of the State Police but Liza motioned him to let her go in first and talk to him. Liza still looked drawn and upset but her face began to take on a slightly more resolute appearance. She walked in but there was no one in the immediate living area. Shawn quietly followed her in.

"Harold! Harold! Where are you?"

A long pause. Then, muffled, from behind a door.

"Oh you've come! You've come! Please come here…to the bedroom that has been waiting for you for forever…Please!"

Shawn thought this guy, a man he had never interviewed or heard about before this morning, sounded crazy. What was going on? Was Liza setting this man…or Shawn, up? What was going on? Did this guy know they were coming?

Shawn looked, sternly, at Liza with a questioning face. She clearly was also confused.

"Harold I need you to come out here. The State Police need to talk to both of us."

"No, no, no! Liza you need to come to me. Only you. Please! …Alone!"

That sounded ominous. Shawn grabbed her arm to indicate no. Liza looked almost like a zombie again, she was so drained. And now another new wrinkle. It was unlikely she was thinking completely rationally. She motioned it was okay and pulled her arm from Shawn. He never should have let her go in.

All her worst fears were realized the moment she opened the door and walked into his bedroom. She left the door open a few inches and he didn't seem to notice…or care. He was a mess. He was sitting on the unmade bed in sweat pants and a T-shirt. Always known for his sharp dressing and grooming, his hair was disheveled and a couple of days growth darkened his face. An odor in the room suggested he had been drinking.

"Goddammit, Lize. After all these fucking years you finally show up in my bedroom when it's too late." He paused. He moved his head around but he never looked at her. "I used to keep it…the whole place, clean and neat, always ready for you to walk in here one day, to me…and to stay. I based my whole life on you, Liza. And you knew that. You let me. You loved me. You know you did."

He sat up more completely now and looked right at her. He was crazy. But mostly he looked angry. She stayed closer to the door. She had never seen him remotely like this. Through all her upset and guilt and the numbness she was feeling now, this man, her shadow lover, her two nights in so many years sexual partner but daily work companion, frightened her for perhaps the first and only time. He was probably drunk but she knew it was more than that.

Shawn stood just outside the doorway. He could hear everything clearly. He had a fleeting personal reaction to this doctor's words, reflecting his own sense of what he thought the Vallans had done to him. He also suspected the man was crazy, maybe drunk, but he didn't know. He wasn't sure if he should go into the room.

Harold Dobson got up, unsteadily, and with his legs braced against the side of the bed for support stood about five feet from Liza.

"When Liza? How long?…A lifetime? How long was I supposed to wait for you to come back to me? How long?" He was always a talker and he wanted to keep talking. Liza started sobbing. To see him this way and also know her suspicions were probably correct was devastating. He knew she knew too. But she had no idea why he was falling apart just now. She would not respond and she assumed Shawn was listening.

"It never got good again, did it? I tried to find someone else but it never worked. You knew we were so special and perfect together. Why did you fight it?"

His face visibly tightened and his anger made him look ominous. If Barry had been in the room he probably would have acted. But he wasn't there.

"Fight it? Fight it? HAH! What did you do a few months ago? You brought that loser to the hospital. Our hospital! Our shelter and refuge for us, where we, you and I, are revered for what we do. You cheapened it all, didn't you? Everything!

"You made me finally realize I had one and only one last chance. That loud-mouth schmuck Becker was my opportunity. You know he was my patient once and I knew his story. I figured out why he was after your Ted and how mean he would get. Then you had given me the hint years and years ago when you told me about the yellow knife from that book…"

Shawn Barry pushed the door wide open and strode in rapidly. Had he heard enough? Probably…His eyes were practically popping out and his jaw was hanging from his open mouth. 'Holy shit! Liza was right.' Until just that moment he still hadn't seen this coming.

Dobson calmly gazed over and regarded the Lieutenant as he entered. Before Barry could say a word the now very old appearing Doctor began talking again.

"No, no Trooper, you needn't worry. Everything will be fine. The law understands all this." His face relaxed and resumed the kind and friendly appearance Liza knew so well. "You see, it's been this way since very ancient times. It will always be the same. It's about the Sirens."

Shawn was startled. So what if this nut heard them coming. What would that mean?

"You can't fight the song of the Sirens… Well Liza did, but I couldn't." He appeared despondent. "The Sirens challenge you ceaselessly. They can pull at you for a lifetime. I know. I tried to fight." He looked directly at Liza. "You don't know it but I tried. I couldn't succeed. I had to have you…us. We would be perfect together"

Dobson didn't have the gleam in his eye Sportin' Life had in the film. But he didn't look as unhappy anymore. Suddenly appearing like he had some work to do he altered his attention and reached into his baggy sweat pants pocket producing a snub nose .38 caliber revolver. Initially he stared at it sitting in his hand, puzzled, like it was some foreign object. Then he looked at Liza and he began to lift his arm with the pistol and point it at her.

Fortunately he had a little more to say.

"What's the use. I doubt we'll ever meet again."

With that, just as he pulled the trigger, Shawn Barry, for reasons forever known only to him, but maybe the reflex of a true law officer, yelled "Don't!" and jumped in front of Liza literally taking the bullet intended for her. As Barry crumpled to the ground Harold Dobson calmly put the pistol to his own head and blew his brains out. It was unclear if he even realized Liza was unharmed.

Sure Liza shrieked, but she also immediately tried to tend to Shawn. Among the reasons she hoped he was alive was her awareness he was the only other person who knew, for sure, Dobson had killed Becker.

Liza Vallan had fought the sirens and that fall morning she made her choice again. Either way one of her two loves wasn't going to be around any longer.

* * *

911...AGAIN/   When Henry Vallan and Detective James Wiley drove into the neighborhood they were looking for they had no difficulty locating the house they were after. A Vermont State Police cruiser sat in the driveway. Wiley pulled over and parked on the street. They sat in the car as Wiley advised Henry of their possible options depending on what was going on inside. Wiley was aware he probably had no business being there and might wind up the one in more trouble than anybody.

Suddenly they heard two 'pops.' Wiley was out of the car and on his way up the driveway before Henry was out his door. Wiley wasn't supposed to have a weapon, but he did. He slowed at the entrance and went through the door in a crouch. In seconds he yelled for Henry to call 911.

Henry was devastated. As he dialed his cell he yelled frantically to Wiley asking if his mother was okay.

"Need two ambulances…with EMTs…Mother okay!"

And that's what Henry called in: Two ambulances with EMTs and his mother was okay.

The quiet neighborhood, with spacious two acre lots, had slowly started to come alive earlier when a State Police cruiser was noticed. By the time Henry was shouting there was a small crowd flanking the Doctor's property. In another short time the usually sedate neighborhood was lit up like a light show with reflections of the many colors of lights from the myriad official vehicles quickly assembling for this emergency.

* * *

Shawn Barry was barely alive. With the arrival of the EMTs Liza and Wiley stopped working on him. Wiley quickly whisked Liza and Henry from the house and the three of them sat in the unmarked until a superior officer with enough courage to interview Liza would arrive on the scene.

"We don't have much time, at all, Dr. Vallan. I need to know absolutely everything that happened in that house, especially what that man said. Every word. Later we can talk about why you and the Lieutenant were there."

Wiley's intensity jolted Liza out of some of her shock after what she had witnessed. She couldn't shake her guilt but she concentrated on telling them what she just experienced. Yet she knew they'd have to know about the knife, so, despite his admonition, she very quickly brought them up to speed about that also. Henry was dumbfounded by her words and with a startled expression on his face pointedly turned to Wiley, who curtly acknowledged him.

Liza did well reporting on Dobson's soliloquy; even, painfully, what he said about her and their relationship. Struck by his words about Becker she told them she didn't understand everything he said. Wiley knew more but said nothing.

She got emotional again when she reviewed the sequence of events.

"Oh Henry, I think Shawn is going to die. He did it to save me! Why did he do that? I want to see Dad. I have to speak with him."

Liza wasn't the only one surprised. Wiley had carefully explained to Henry and Ted how Shawn, intentionally or not, had been obstructing the investigation. Their unplanned run-in at the jail with the ME made it plain to everyone. And yet he may have sacrificed his life for Liza. A puzzle. This time Wiley glanced at Henry, who thought he understood what Wiley was thinking.

"Henry, no more beating around the bush. Now the leaders of the force are going to come to us. We have to be ready. We're getting closer but this changes a lot, don't you think?" Liza understood none of this, but Henry did. Thoroughly emotional but with admiration and respect he said,

"Jim you're the cop. You're the person who should be running the show. You're a lifesaver."

Henry was wound up; almost euphoric. Wiley stayed deadly serious. He was well aware there were still problems to solve and answers to find.

"Henry, now you need to find that lawyer for your mother. At the very least she is a material witness to a probable suicide and maybe murder. At worst she could be accused of being the shooter. Good chance they will try to keep her locked up for now."

Henry and Liza were shocked. How could everything get bad again so quickly?

A fist tapped on the window of the rear door where Liza was sitting. It was Wendell Partin, the Chief of the Burlington PD. He knew Liza socially and his face showed great concern for her.

* * *

CAN YOU PROVE IT?/   Chief Partin was out of his jurisdiction in Colchester but he was the senior law enforcement officer on site for the first hour. Senior investigative troopers were on their way. Liza recounted the events at the Dobson house for Chief Partin and re-enacted the scene for the investigators who were there. It was unclear if Liza even mentioned anything about the knife to them. Wiley understood the need for the police procedures but he knew the details of this man Dobson's death weren't going to set Ted Vallan free just yet, whether the Lieutenant lived or died.

The BPD Chief was usually a calming voice in the midst of calamities and this day was no exception. He could see Liza was breaking down. He didn't ask, he told those in the car he was sending Liza home in a patrol car and she was going to have to stay there until everything was better sorted out. He had headquarters tracking Kathy down so she could go to Richmond and stay with Liza. He wouldn't allow Liza to be alone. Anyone who wanted to talk with her would have to go to her home. Wiley nodded to Henry they should be appreciative of the Chief's plan, which would keep his mother out of custody…for now. They stood beside the patrol car as it left, headed for the Vallan home. Standing at the curb Henry paused.

He was more than just catching his breathe. A strange feeling came over him as he stood there and surveyed the scene around him. After days of terrible tension and stress Henry sensed a sudden calm. Even as police and emergency responders continued to move around everything seemed muted now. And a notable slowing, as though a quiet ending of a day, had descended over them. Like a movie where the music would become slow and peaceful; soft minor chords reminding everyone it was over; the camera panning slowly across the remnants of the carnage. The disaster, the unbridled roaring of the ocean storm, had calmed and the terrible story was over. Henry described his feeling to Wiley.

Wiley wasn't at all sure he was right.

* * *

THE LAW IS THE LAW II/   Liza couldn't go see Ted but they could. Turning the corner a block from Dobson's house Trooper Dark's arriving cruiser slowed as he passed the unmarked. Dark looked devastated. Henry didn't catch it but Dark and Wiley, barely perceptibly, nodded a sign of recognition.

Henry directed Wiley as they drove on county roads weaving their way to the correctional facility just off Spear Street. Along the way Henry checked his cell messages and jumped as he listened to Hiram's message and then played it on speaker for Wiley. Yes, Wiley's suspicion something spooked Dobson, like receiving that email from Ted's account, now seemed likely. Wiley wondered if Liza hadn't shown up at his place whether Dobson might have just killed himself and that would have been the end of it.

WUP, WUP!

"Oh no! What the fuck? I'm legal! What is this?"

"No! You're not legal, Wiley! You're supposed to be out of the state by now."

They were beginning to sound like an old married couple. Spending too much time together. Bottom line was Traffic Patrol Officer Andy Smith's memory was quite intact.

"Shit!." Wiley slammed his hands onto the steering wheel. Then he pulled over and got out of the car. Henry also. Officer Smith understood their action but he did not like it.

"Proly don't know what it's like to do traffic patrol, Detective, but you're s'posed to stay in your vehicle till I tell you what to do." 'These assholes aren't teachable,' he thought.

"License and registration please."

Wiley looked straight at Smith. His eyes widened as he began to gather what Officer Smith might be planning for him. "You know I don't have a license."

"And your stay in Vermont free card is expired, isn't it?"

Henry was beside himself. His emotions were raw and brittle. He was at a breaking point. He couldn't believe this was happening… again. Maybe it would be worse this time. He and Wiley were flummoxed and Smith was major pissed. Henry stepped forward and looked as though he was about to speak.

"Sir, I'll let you know if and when I want to hear from you… Just stand there; both of you."

Smith walked back to his patrol car to call in to his Sergeant. He was fuming but realized he didn't know what he should do. He kept his eyes on the fucked up duo in front of him and reached inside his car for his radio mic. The sound of a vehicle pulling up behind him diverted Smith's attention and he turned to see a Vermont State Police cruiser with its lights on.

It was Smith's turn to say "Oh shit." Officer Smith placed the mic on his seat and turned to the cruiser. Smith didn't have time to begin to think what was going to happen this time but assumed he was going to be screwed again. Was this New York cop always tailed by troopers?

Both front doors of the cruiser opened and the Director of the Vermont State Police, Colonel Max Blair, known to enjoy driving his own cruiser, and, from the passenger side, retired Captain John Rondell exited the vehicle. The Colonel had a grim expression on his face. Officer Smith wasn't sure exactly who the man in uniform was but seeing 'COL.' on his name plate led him to assume he was high up, if not the top.

Contrary to what Officer Smith thought Wiley figured more trouble was now in the mix for them. Henry knew John Rondell and quickly alerted Wiley Rondell was the retired trooper he called last night. Colonel Blair extended his hand to the Officer.

"Officer, I'm Colonel Blair, the Director of the VSP. What have you got here? Captain Rondell here tells me he thinks the man on the right is Captain Vallan's boy." Henry nodded to the Colonel's glance.

"Unless these folks are in really big trouble here Officer we're gonna have to move along and have them follow us. Captain and I need to talk with them about an important police investigation. Is that okay? Just coming from the ICU, Smith."

Smith mumbled, mostly to himself: "They don't have licenses." Then he spoke louder, looking at the Colonel. "Yes sir. The gentleman on the left is driving without a license. And the other fellow doesn't have one either. Yesterday VSP Lieutenant Barry told him and me he'd let him drive in Vermont yesterday but not today."

Blair looked at Rondell. It was a 'what kind of shit are you getting me into' look. Everyone Rondell told him about was acting very strange.

"Well Officer, you did the right thing. We got a complicated homicide investigation here and I'm gonna ask you to let me take charge of these two so we can get on our way. Okay?"

Blair was worried and pissed about a lot of things and he wanted to get moving. Smith knew where this was going anyway and offered no resistance.

"Yes, Colonel …Oh Colonel, If I see this car tomorrow should I let it go?"

Now the Colonel was again pissed he had to play politics.

"Yes, I think so." He paused and looked at the couple. "If I change my mind I'll let your Chief know."

* * *

THE BEGINNING OF THE END?/   The four of them filed, silently, into the interrogation room with the two way mirror and sat down. Introductions walking from their cars to the facility had been brief. Colonel Blair was all business and his face continued to broadcast his great upset. His words were delivered formally, but as he spoke it was clear he was incredulous about what had been going on.

"Mr. Vallan, Captain Rondell has filled me in on what your father has been going through. This has been a faulty investigation. To put it kindly, the VSP have messed up. I apologize to you and I will expect to apologize to your mother and sister after a few things are cleared up. I'm here to apologize to Captain Vallan."

Some might have hoped for more than that, but neither Henry or Wiley expected anything else. Henry wanted it all to be over, nothing more. The Colonel's words about his mother and sister were confusing to him but not to Wiley. The Colonel continued.

"Mr. Vallan we have no record in VSP files relating to Captain Vallan or Lieutenant Barry of any mention of a personal indiscretion by the Lieutenant. I will have to ask the Captain and your mother and sister about that. Are you sure that happened?"

Henry lifted his head and said what he had to say.

"Yes, Colonel, not a lot, but plenty of people knew about it. It was long ago. But I guess that ill-conceived short affair left a lasting scar on everyone involved. The anger and hostility from that time has lingered and still exists for some of them."

The Colonel shook his head, accepting, but at the same time signaling how odd and almost unbelievable it all seemed.

"That affair began and ended years before and yet it had a major impact on the investigation of that Dr. Becker's homicide." He shifted in his chair. "Lemme go tell them to bring in Ted."

* * *

Any lingering skepticism the Colonel might have about the gravity of what was happening, even after his visit to the ICU, vanished when Ted Vallan shuffled in. Forty eight hours in Vermont hadn't done much, if anything, for his mental state. Physically he was clean but still looked ancient and enervated. Ted did not know the intent of the meeting and assumed it was to be another in the long series of law enforcement questioning his situation. For what?

Seeing the Colonel, and especially John Rondell, embarrassed him. He knew he looked awful and, from Ted's perspective, he was guilty. He had failed at so many of the things he was repeatedly castigating himself for. Over and over.

"Ted I'm here with John to tell you we think we know who committed the homicide and know it wasn't you. I need to apologize to you and your family for the way this investigation has been run. Lieutenant Barry did not do his job like he was supposed to. This was a bad VSP investigation. We did not know there were personal animosities between the Lieutenant and the Vallan family."

Ted had included this in his long list of his failings. He looked up and spoke.

"I really messed up. I was on the force before I had my baby, Kathy."

Ted started to break down. He was still beyond the ability to show tears but his face melted in sorrow.

"Those two hurt me so much. I let myself blame her as much as Shawn… My own daughter… I didn't want to blame the force and it felt like making Shawn get out would be doing that. So I let him stay… But it was awful for Kathy. How could I have done that to her…? I chose the force over my own daughter… Shawn and I disliked each other after that…and it was never the same with Kathy either… All my fault. I should have talked with John and worked it out then…but I didn't."

It was very sad. Henry had tears, more a release after days of utter tension and fear. But they weren't happy tears. That terrible scar.

Indeed, with Becker's death it opened and like a bullet slammed into all of them again, years later. The Colonel was no longer sure if he should tell Ted what just happened in Colchester and Shawn Barry's tenuous grip on life. Rondell spoke up next.

"Colonel I think this is enough for now. Ted you look pretty rocky. You're not ready to come see the barn I'm building in Waitsfield just yet. After they get you out of here very soon I'm gonna come see you every day until you're ready to make the trip. Okay?"

Ted looked over at him, making sure he knew who the man was. He may not have completely understood his point but he nodded.

"Colonel" Ted looked over at him. "What will happen to Shawn now?"

Eye contact bounced from one to another around the small room.

The Colonel cleared his throat and told Ted Shawn had been shot and was in very critical condition. Ted's eyebrows moved up but that was his only visible reaction.

Henry stayed with Ted and the other three walked out. They sat together quietly. Ted silently castigated himself one more time, for even briefly wondering if he wanted Shawn Barry to live or die.

* * *

In the hallway the Colonel asked Wiley a few questions, then thanked him.

"You're welcome to go home now Detective. Trooper Dark said you have been very helpful and the force appreciates your efforts. I will find out who your Commanding Officer is and let him know."

Again and again since arriving in Vermont Detective Wiley kept telling Henry he was going back to the City. Now Wiley wasn't ready to leave, just yet.

"Colonel, if you don't mind, I'd like to contact Trooper Dark and find out what he's got planned to try to complete the investigation.

There may not be much more to do."

Blair wanted to send the Detective back to New York City. This entire episode was embarrassing enough. But he knew Wiley was well informed about the case and especially the Vallans. He told Wiley a day or two was fine with him; up to his superiors in the NYPD.

* * *

'NUTS AND BOLTS' POLICE WORK/   Very late Tuesday afternoon Trooper Dark and Detective Jack Hardy invited Detective Wiley to join them for some back room investigation at the hospital. No beer this time, just soda and coffee. They sat in a small charting area with an attractive young clerk from the hospital medical records department. Both Dark and Wiley were annoyed that Hardy was distracted and maybe trying to make a move on her.

Dr. Harvey Becker was intentionally overdosed and substantial amounts of Oxycontin (same pills as used in the hospital pharmacy) were easily uncovered in his home Tuesday morning when his home was searched for the first time. There was no reason to assume his poisoning in the hospital was organized or implemented by anyone other than Harriet Summer. A major emergency audit of the hospital pharmacy was already underway.

Didn't matter to the police who killed Becker first.

Kathy Conover was in the hospital the night of the murder, working on a different ward, but the use of the yellow knife seemed to rule her out. Liza as a kind of black widow committing a crime damming to her husband was unlikely but had to be considered. The thought of Liza masterminding the stabbing and using Kathy or Dobson was rejected .

If Dobson or even Liza, or for that matter Ted Vallan, stabbed Becker the law enforcement officers knew they had to find some trace of the presence of one of them in the hospital very early the morning of the murder. None of the staff in the hospital recalled seeing any of them. What they decided to do was have all the charts of both of those Doctor's patients in the hospital every day that week, Monday through Friday, brought to them for review. They needed to see if there was anything different reflected in the charts the morning of the homicide. As they did their review they found there was a change in Dobson's charting for three days. But that didn't turn out to be the slam dunk.

The officers told the clerk any sign of those Docs in the hospital through the over-night would be suspicious. But she told the officers it was not nearly that simple. An attending physician in the hospital at something like five a.m. was not at all unheard of. The clerk explained it happened especially if a doc with a number of inpatients was beginning a day that was going to be very busy in the office or surgery. Or maybe when the attending was planning to be at meetings or away during the day and so couldn't come at the usual times.

Harold Dobson was guilty of murder and he probably was also guilty of over-thinking his plans.

For cover, in case he was seen during his dawn visit to kill Becker, Dobson didn't go see but reviewed the charts and wrote notes on two of his patients and also an order on one of them. One of those two patients was on the ward where Becker was. He signed and dated the notes and order and put the time of his visits at nine a.m.; around the time he would return to the hospital later and actually go into their rooms to see those patients. The officers noted Dobson only put the times of his progress notes on the charts for the last three days of the week but always put the time for all orders. That caught their attention.

As it happened, no one noticed Dobson in the hospital at that early hour. When he slipped into Becker's room and plunged the knife into his chest a little after five he had no idea the man was probably already dead.

After the murder was discovered Dobson conveniently ran into Liza who told him what she had just witnessed. He maintained a serious demeanor and encouraged her to try to hold herself together. He offered her whatever support she needed during the terrible days ahead. Over the remainder of the morning Dobson was seen by many people, including the two patients whose notes he had already written.

Through it all he overlooked what would happen after he wrote his one order of the day in the chart. He had signed it, dated it, and written '0900', just as he did with the progress notes. But he forgot the nurse would note the time she took the order off. As the eleven to seven night nurse completed her shift she did her charting and transcribed any new orders flagged on charts from the hours before. On that Dobson patient's chart, next to 'noted' and her initials, was the date and the time, '06:52'. Donald Dark found it.

Ted Vallan was a free man…and James Wiley could go home. Donald Dark and Wiley said they should keep in touch.

* * *

CASE OVER…LESS THAN ONE WEEK/   It was the first time they were completely alone. They sat across from each other on plain silver metal institutional chairs in the windowless room. Ted's appearance remained suggestive of a broken man. His head drooped as though his gaze was fixed on something on the floor. But he wasn't staring at anything. His continuing sense of exhaustion trumped all the myriad other feelings in his body. He was relieved, angry, and so much more. As he peeked up at Liza he realized he hadn't had his terrifying and vexing dream in two days. He still didn't know whose face that was but it didn't seem important anymore.

Seeing Ted for the first time in five days, and the condition he was in, greatly intensified Liza's heartbreak. She was stunned. Whatever nurturing hormones remained in her aging body were being furiously pumped out by appropriate glands. She was desperate to go to him but held herself back. She prepared to speak but, surprisingly, Ted spoke first. His head bobbed up for his words and then dropped again.

"You know Liza, I'm never going back to that hospital again unless it's on a stretcher."

Liza was overcome with love at his gracious attempt to ease the strain of their personal reunion.

"Ted, I have always loved you, since the day we accidentally bumped into each other folding blankets for our rigs at the Emergency Department doing volunteer rescue squad shifts. Who said a doctor and a trooper can't have a life together?" She flexed her head down slightly, hoping his gaze would catch hers.

"Years ago Ted, I chose and I chose you. I can't change what happened but, if you can believe it, it all helped me love you more." She cried again, but she wanted to say more so she let out a sniffle and went on.

"I'm leaving my practice. It's time. I can do some teaching and have free time. Time for us to be together, like you say, till health do us part. I think we should get on a plane as soon as we can and go to Tucson. Remember Henry's new book where he had us go there? He had us kind of recommitting there.

"Hiking in those mountains he described sounds awfully nice. We can hike and make love again."

Liza left it there. Ted lifted his head slowly and fixed his eyes on the only woman he ever loved. He thought of his great affection for the other women in his life; his mother and daughter. Not the same feelings. He was wounded by Liza's history. But Ted knew he was what he was. He shouldn't be and wasn't ashamed he was a practical man. Maybe more nuts and bolts than intellectual interests. Travel; even enlarging his own horizons in other ways sounded reasonable. Who could know what was ahead for Liza and Ted Vallan?

Ted shifted in his chair. Then he slowly stood up and put his arms out for Liza. She sprang to him, tears flowing, and squeezed him as tightly as possible. He reciprocated, but he could not yet cry. He whispered in her ear.

"Babe, Tucson sounds nice. But you've planned our activities in the wrong order."

****

THE END

Lightning Source UK Ltd.
Milton Keynes UK
UKHW010853210722
406179UK00002B/553